desert
shadows

JOSHUA DOWIDAT

Desert Shadows

Published by Wheatmark®
1760 East River Road, Suite 145
Tucson, Arizona 85718 USA
www.wheatmark.com

ISBN: 978-1-62787-374-1 (paperback)
ISBN: 978-1-62787-375-8 (ebook)
LCCN: 2015959468

To my mother, who has always supported me, and my brothers, Luke and Matt, who directly supported me through this book

Beware, lest you lose the substance by grasping at the shadow.

—Aesop

To Catherine,
One Author to Another!

Chapter 1

JUST AFTER STOWING ROCKS in our bags, Liam and I heard the chime of a bell, followed by our mother shouting that it was dinnertime. The bell, an inheritance from our grandpa, was mounted on a piece of four-by-four about twenty feet from our front door.

"We'd better get going, Liam, before we can't come out tomorrow."

"Yeah," he replied. With a grin, he added, "It's getting dark, and we'd better beat the coyotes, monsters, and goblins home!"

Sometimes the coyotes would watch us make our way home from the desert, but my imagination is what got the best of me. Monsters and goblins were something we'd been fascinated with for as long as I could remember. We'd often joked about it, but an eerie feeling would creep upon us when the sun faded. If a coyote came after us, we'd seek out one of the occasional taller trees. We had no idea what we'd do if the predator was something other than a coyote.

Living in the desert a long way from the nearest town was different from what most people would imagine. Southeast Arizona has a different kind of desert that includes trees and shrubs since it quite often rains and even snows occasionally.

My brother and I loved living there. We spent most of our free time hiking as we explored the area, becoming familiar with all the animals, like the rattlesnakes and other venomous creatures. We were only allowed to hike around the parts of the desert that kept us close enough to hear someone call from home, but we'd go out for hours at a time.

Every corner became a new mystery. What might be ahead, or what was down the next abandoned mine shaft? The shafts were mostly pits with large tailings of crushed rock lying outside the entrance, making them easy to spot from a distance.

We'd often rummage through the discarded rubble, looking for something the miners missed a century ago. We always thought we might find some gold or gems, but most of the time we ended up finding discolored blue-green rocks that we thought were turquoise. Mostly they were oxidized copper.

Picking through the leftover rocks was always a gamble because of creatures like scorpions and centipedes and the countless spiders that lived underneath rocks. We'd flip the rocks over with a finger or a foot, looking for possible threats before picking them up to search for our "treasure." Many kids would pay money for what we gathered!

We were supposed to stay away from the mines, sticking to the hillsides below and keeping out of trouble, but when we knew that no one was looking, we'd sometimes step as close as we dared to throw a rock down and judge the depth. Sometimes there was water in the bottom, but most of the time there was the all-too-familiar sound of rock hitting rock, followed by a high-speed rattling from rattle-snakes—an especially unwelcome surprise to anyone who accidently fell down.

"Max!" Liam yelled out as we headed up the driveway and toward our adopted dog. "How ya doing?"

Max had been left with us by a neighbor who never came back for him. We were the ones who fed and played with him, and he couldn't have been kinder. He had jet-black fur with a little white patch on his chest that made him look like he was wearing a suit. He was only average size, but he seemed big and tough to us.

"Hey, Max!" I said, attempting to get him to shake.

It was a nice feeling having a pet to come home to, and he was always happy to see us. He also filled a void created by the lack of kids around our age in the area. We lived far from the regular neighborhoods, so people were scarce and kids even scarcer.

Our house was newly built and a decent size, with three bedrooms and two bathrooms—but only one bathroom and two of the bedrooms were functional. Some rushed construction procedures had been made so we could move in when we returned from our summer trip visiting relatives, but somehow things didn't get finished.

As we neared the house, we'd pick up the aroma of my mother's cooking, and we'd try guessing what she was cooking for dinner.

"Hey, Liam," I said, my stomach already rumbling, "it smells like fried zucchini tonight."

"Yeah, I love it when she makes that with the breaded Italian chicken."

We headed inside and closed the door while our mother hollered from the kitchen for us to take off our shoes and wash our hands. These were her rules because there was so much dry dust around. Our mother liked the evenings to go smoothly, and we would usually eat early; this gave us ample time to enjoy some ice cream or occasionally some other delicious treat before bed.

"Are we eating right now?" I asked my mom.

"Yes, as soon as the zucchini cools."

Awesome, I thought. It was freshly cut and breaded with a tempura batter that always seemed too good to spoil with the ranch dressing. We didn't eat many fried foods, but we sure enjoyed them when we did.

We shared a room, which wasn't bad. Liam slept on the top of our old wooden bunk beds, and I slept on the bottom. Most nights, the shadows from the television bounced off clothes and other objects in the closet, giving them the appearance of coming to life.

Lying in bed that night, Liam said something that got my mind wandering. "Do you think when we're out in the desert that something's watching us?"

"What do you mean?" I thought maybe he was talking about a neighbor or our parents.

"I mean, what if an animal was just sitting there watching us? Deciding if it should eat one of us. Do you think we could fight it off or get home before it could reach us?"

Now my mind was racing, and my rising adrenaline would most likely prevent me from sleeping that night. If I did sleep, it wouldn't be very well.

"Why do you have to talk about stuff like that before bed?" I complained.

"Just thinking. I mean, what would you do? Would you try to fight back or run?"

"I guess it depends on what kind of animal it was. I mean, if it was hurting you, I'd try to kill it instead of running away. If it was something big or there was more than one, I'd try to run. Get to a tree, maybe."

"What if there wasn't a tree and you had to fight? What would you use as a weapon?"

Now I was thinking about weapons instead of what Liam originally asked me. Perhaps a rock or a large stick. This was a good question. It would be smart to carry something to defend ourselves against an animal. What if it wasn't just an animal, but a deranged person, like the ones who lived by our old house? They lived out in the desert and would come through the neighborhood, stealing stuff at the local truck stop. They even kidnapped kids.

4

As if Liam could read my mind, he asked, "What if a human came after us out there?"

A human could throw rocks or climb trees or even have a weapon, like a knife or gun. How could we defend ourselves so we weren't easy targets? I slowly began drifting to sleep as I pondered this and what we would explore tomorrow after school.

Chapter 2

I DIDN'T LIKE SCHOOL. I saw no need for it, and all the work seemed like something I could do on my own because it came easy to me. Recess was just time I spent in the corner trying to stay away from others who would find some way to point out my differences. I had a few friends, more like acquaintances, but no companions like my brother and I were to one another. The ones I hung around with would walk around with me as they waited for the recess monitors to blow the whistle and call everyone back in. I often waited for the crowd to disperse before walking in, to avoid others that much longer.

During class, I waited for the time to go by, sometimes watching the clock so much that I would lose track of what the teacher was saying. My teacher was a kind, older woman who had been teaching at the school for some time. I always wanted to ask about her hair because it reminded me of a golden beehive. She taught many of the kids at the school because the school was so small; there were only several hundred kids from kindergarten through high school.

"Read from Jason's point now, Caleb," I heard the teacher say.

I was so caught up in watching the clock and thinking about what type of weapon to make that I had no idea where to start reading. I wasn't a strong reader when it came to reading aloud, so this gave everyone a reason to laugh and stare as if I did something horribly wrong.

Later, on our way to the cafeteria, the teacher asked me to walk with her. She often seemed to take a particular interest in me, and sometimes I wondered if she could tell I was holding back and she wanted to help me break free.

"Caleb, are you okay today? Did something happen at morning recess?"

The other students were glancing back, trying to figure out what was going on.

"No."

"You keep losing your place in the group readings."

"I just get a little sleepy sometimes after being outside and then coming in and sitting right down."

"Well, if you get tired like that, maybe you need to take some vitamins or medicine or find something to keep you awake during class."

"No, it's no big deal. I'll work on paying more attention from now on," I said. She simply nodded before she left me to get in line for my food.

Out in the field, after lunch, I often liked to stay by a tree. For some reason, there was comfort in it. A few of us would gather there, never saying much, but we all knew why we were there. The kids would come and go. They would be friendly when they were part of the tree crowd, but once the normal or popular kids accepted them, they would turn their backs on us. Sometimes they would come back after a few weeks because something made them a tree kid again.

This recess always marked a milestone for me because I knew that the day was almost over, and I was counting down to the time to go home. That day the sky grew cloudy, but the rain never fell, so I was glad that I could go out in the desert with Liam.

We usually got rides home with a neighbor lady named Betty. She would take several kids in our neighborhood. We would sit in the far back of Betty's van, where there were no seatbelts, and the front seats were full of older kids. It didn't really occur to us that anything might happen to us in the far back without seatbelts. We arrived home to Max barking uncontrollably at the van, as he usually did, until it was too out of sight for him to be interested anymore.

In the valley area where we lived, the sun set much faster, the large mountains nearby took away thirty minutes or so of daylight, depending on what time of year it was. In the winter the sun set further south, and the mountains blocked it out sooner than in the summer. One of these mountains was scary to us, so we named it Spirit Mountain, like the one in an old Disney cartoon from *Disney's Halloween Treats*. We eventually found out it was actually considered a hill and was named something else, but we still called it Spirit Mountain.

We headed out into the desert after telling our mother about where we were going; this made her worry less. Up or down the desert wash, Black Rocks or Red Rocks—even a more vague direction, like toward one of the neighbors' houses, would work. Up the wash— the narrow, dry bed of an intermittent stream that usually only had water after a flash flood—was our favorite way to go on an afternoon's exploration, so we took that route. We could always find something interesting, and all the old mines were up that way.

"Hey, Caleb, did you think of a weapon to make today?" he whispered, in case we were still close enough for our mother to overhear. She seemed to grow exceptionally great hearing when we ventured out and was probably listening in case something went wrong or one of us screamed.

"Kind of. I've been thinking all day about what to use and how to make something."

"I got a couple good ideas, but until we can make something real good, I think we should just gather rocks and find some good sticks for now." I agreed that storing rocks at certain points between our fort and home and maybe in some of the trees would be helpful. "I want to make a stick into a spear on one end and a mace on the other." I could see that Liam was already keeping a watchful eye out for that perfect stick.

"Maybe we could use a big flat rock to sharpen them."

"I got a better idea. I'll show you when we get a little further down the wash."

We chose a quicker route into the wash and headed to an area by a small rocky cliff, which was far enough away that no one could see or hear us.

"Look what I got out of the cedar chest when Mom was down by the well." I brandished an engraved pocketknife with a metal Statue of Liberty medallion in the wood handle. It was small, but it was still a knife.

Liam looked a bit shaky but also excited.

"I'll put it back after we make our weapons. Just a few spears and some carved handles for future weapons."

"Okay. We can't let Mom see our spears because she'll be able to tell we used something to whittle them."

"I didn't think of that," I admitted, thankful for my brother's quick thinking.

An hour later, we had both found some good sticks for spears, spike traps, and our main weapons. We choose a spot near three large trees, old mesquite ones that appeared dead from the aged bark that covered their bases. One was easy enough to climb and stow some rocks for defense.

"We got a lot done today," Liam said as he climbed down. "We should call this place Three Trees. We should probably be heading back. It's getting dark, and we can't do any more today anyways. Besides, you need to feed and water Max and take care of the you-know-what without anyone seeing."

I gave him a look. "Don't worry, and we're certainly far enough away that you can call it a knife!"

"So this is your new hangout?"

I spun around to face our mother, petrified, thinking she had overheard.

"How'd you find us?" Liam looked at her and then back at me, trying to hide a fearful face.

"You told me which way you were heading, and I was done with my jobs, so I thought I'd come visit. I heard you talking from the wash, so I followed your voices. Cool tree."

"So you were spying on us," I joked, feeling annoyed.

"Yeah, it's cool isn't it? Come look. We got some really great ideas for what we're going to do. What do you think?" Liam already seemed to have forgotten about the knife.

The only thing she recommended was moving some larger rocks away from underneath the tree. When she was growing up, she knew someone who fell out of a tree onto some rocks and died. We had no problem doing this since it would keep her from asking too many questions about the area. I wondered if she'd noticed the sharp sticks or heard me talking about the knife. It seemed she hadn't.

Over the next few weeks, we built quite the defensive position and attached old planks on branches for us to sit on. We also built platforms on the other two trees nearby, hoping that we could build some type of bridge between them, or maybe just a rope swing.

We were working on the main platform one afternoon when we heard older people's voices coming up the wash—older people we didn't recognize.

"Do you think we should try to get home without them seeing?"

I asked Liam. My curiosity was turning into suspicion as we waited quietly. I was creating different scenarios in my mind for if the owners of the voices spotted us. "We could stay low in the wash, where they can't see us or mistake us for game."

We'd been told stories about hunters confusing people for game and accidently shooting them, but we also wondered if making ourselves known would be wise in case they were up to something else. "Coyotes," as some called them, used these back roads to do their business away from the eye of the law.

"It's just up ahead," I heard one of the voices shout, like he'd outpaced the people he was with.

I could see the brim of a hat rising above the desert broom in the wash. It was a raggedy straw cowboy-style hat, and as he moved, I saw a faded dark-gray shirt with a strange logo on it. I could also see his face and knew I didn't know him. Then we heard another voice.

"Gene, slow down, Dale had to piss one good," said a more heavyset man making his way around the bend.

"Well, Robert, if we slow down any more, we might as well head back, unless you want to be scurrying through the camps after dark. I'm not going to hang around to get bit up by rattlers and scorpions, so you two better hurry up."

A third person appeared, scruffily dressed like Robert. "Why can't we just drive? Why do we always have to walk?"

"You know that guy up the hill will chase us out again. Last time I was here by myself, I got back to the main road, and the sheriffs were waiting by my car. I guess this guy is just trying to hog it all for himself."

Just as Gene said that, the other two came to a stop and stared ahead. Liam and I exchanged uncomfortable glances as the hair on the back of my neck began rising. We knew we'd been spotted and both began looking around for Gene, who had disappeared.

"Hello, boys," drawled Gene from underneath the platform we were lying on. We were only about eight feet up in the tree and within easy reach. "What you doing up there? Just hanging out, spying on people, or have you got other intentions, like an ambush?"

"Nothing. Just playing. We live close by, and our parents are coming to see our fort in a little while. Do you want to meet them?" Liam said, quickly improvising.

Gene's smirk changed to a slightly nervous frown, and Liam seemed to have caught him off guard.

"I'm just teasing you boys. You have fun now, but don't be sneaking up on us. We might think you're after our buried treasure!" He'd tried to sound like a pirate with the last sentence. "Seriously though, don't come sneaking up on us. We carry guns. Make yourself noticeable so we don't confuse you for something or *someone* else."

"Got it!" I said loudly. I was glad they moved away, up the wash, disappearing under the growth of the desert broom. Once they were out of sight, we grabbed our spears and headed straight home.

We decided not to tell anyone about our encounter or to talk about it at home, but as night fell, we couldn't resist. "What camps were they talking about?"

"Maybe it's just an old campsite that they use to hunt from or hang out," replied Liam from the bunk above. "I heard that Scout troops used to come up here to camp and get badges. I even heard the area where we built the fort used to be an area they camped, and they had a big fire pit there."

"That would explain the pile of rocks by the wash. Maybe we should rebuild it. Who knows? Maybe they left something in there, like a time capsule."

"Yeah, that would be cool, but I'm still wondering about the camps. Maybe we should check it out or ask the neighbors what they meant."

"I don't think we should say anything to anyone. They'll ask us where we heard about them and maybe not let us go there."

It's strange how the forbidden could become an obsession—like the camps—and our conversation led into an argument about how to find the camps the next day. Eventually, we compromised on one of us heading up the wash a little while the other waited and listened in case our mother called for us.

"You know something, Caleb?"

"I know a lot of things," I said sarcastically.

"Even before those guys showed up, something was weird. I felt like we were already being watched. It felt close, like something was right there in the tree with us."

I thought about what he'd said and immediately agreed, remembering a weird sensation just before we had heard the voices. "Yeah, I think I know what you're talking about."

"Well, we'll figure it out tomorrow. I'm going to try to sleep now."

Every time we had a conversation before bedtime that really made me think, it was more difficult for me to fall asleep. Thoughts raced through my mind, keeping me awake, and I knew tonight would be harder to sleep. I was wondering about the camps and how we were going to sneak up the wash tomorrow. The only thought that kept popping into my mind was that Gene and the other two guys were trying to get to Liam and me to make sure their little secret didn't get out.

Every creaking noise from the house was them pushing sharp sticks toward my sleeping head. Every pop from the water pipes in the ceiling was one of them walking on the roof, trying to find a way in. I should have told my mom about Gene. At least she would know what happened to her precious children, when they were horribly speared to death and smashed by rocks dropped through the roof at night.

Pop! Creak! Snap! Pop!

My eyes remained closed, although I knew they were slowly sneaking up on me in the darkness. When I opened my eyes, Gene would be sitting on the edge of my bed. Somehow, what you don't see can't hurt you. Right?

Chapter 3

MY MOTHER CAME IN early to wake us. Well, at least to wake me. Liam was an early riser; I was the night owl. I looked out the window to see that the day was clear. No clouds. This meant the possibility of rain later.

I heard my mother holler, "Caleb, you need to get moving so we're not late again!"

"I know. Just looking outside."

"Well, you can look outside when we go to the car. You're going to make Liam mad if you make him late again. He doesn't want the teachers to be inside when we arrive."

Liam sometimes had the same problem with bullies, so being around an authority figure was always a good place to be.

"I know. I'll get going."

I grabbed my backpack and realized my papers were out of place, not stacked how I had left them. I liked to organize my books and homework for each period of the day.

"I thought you said you had everything ready," my mother said from outside the doorway.

"They're just stacked different than I remember. No big deal."

"Liam, did you do something to Caleb's homework?"

"No. Why?" He sounded believable.

"Never mind. You two just get in the car," my mom said, searching through her purse. "Have either one of you seen my keys?"

"I think I just saw them in the bathroom when I was brushing my teeth," I told her as she went to look in frustration.

"Hey, Liam, did you do something with my homework to mess with me?" I said when I saw him, knowing our mother had already posed the question.

"No. I was in bed before you. You probably got sidetracked doing something else and forgot to organize it."

"I don't think so. They were stacked really weird. Are you sure you're not just messing around?"

"I told you. Maybe you did it in your sleep again." It wasn't uncommon for me to sleepwalk or do other things in my sleep.

My mom came walking down the hallway with her keys. "Found them. They were on the kitchen counter."

I could have sworn I saw them in the bathroom.

I usually rode in the front seat on our way to school because sometimes a school bus would get in front of us, allowing the school kids to look at us. It bothered me some, but it really bothered Liam.

"I'll see you guys this afternoon. Have a good day, and Jesus bless you." This was my mom's normal good-bye for the day.

We walked in the school courtyard and parted ways early enough to slip into class before the other kids. I said hello to a couple of the tree kids and my teacher before sitting down at my desk.

"You still have ten minutes before class starts if you want to play outside," my teacher said, looking up from her desk.

"I know. Just making sure I got my homework done before class begins."

"What did you do after school yesterday?"

"Not much. Just played around at home and did some chores." I wouldn't dare tell her what I was really up to.

16

The bell rang, and the other students began coming in, replacing the smells of last night's cleaning products with those of cheap perfume and body odors. After everyone took their seats, the school day started and went by normally, but no matter what we did, I couldn't get my mind off the camps.

When we got home, the sky looked a little cloudy but not stormy, which meant we could still go out into the desert. We did our basic chores and said good-bye to our mother before heading out the door. We told her to ring the dinner bell in case we were hammering nails at the fort and couldn't hear her calling when really we would be somewhere we weren't supposed to be. Just as we were leaving, she stopped us to speak with us. It was like she was reading our minds.

Chapter 4

"HAVE YOU GUYS SEEN anyone out in the desert lately? The neighbor thought he saw a few people wandering by his property, and I wanted to check and make sure it wasn't you. You know he drinks and carries his gun around. I would hate for anything to happen, and I wouldn't know what I would do if he accidently shot one of you."

"No," Liam said quickly—almost too quickly. "We haven't been wandering around the neighbor's land." This was true, although we did see Gene and his friends going that way.

"Okay, but if anyone comes up to you out there, you head straight home or to the neighbor's house. There are a lot of crazies out there." She looked relieved yet still troubled. "Go have fun, and I'll ring the bell before dinner is ready."

"Alright, Mom. Love you," we both said as we began walking back down the driveway.

"What do you think Mom was getting at back there?" I asked Liam.

"Maybe there's more to Gene and his friends than we think."

"That'd make sense."

"Maybe we should try asking some of the neighbor kids about Gene to see what they know."

"Yeah, if we can without Betty hearing. Maybe we could write a note." I thought this was a really good idea, because it was mine.

We both agreed to write a note the next day and pass it around on the ride home. We also reconsidered heading further up the wash. We didn't want to take any chances, especially today when our mom might come around again, so we stayed around the fort.

We worked hard into the evening before hearing the bell. We managed to set up some good trip wires around the area but were careful to place them out of our usual path.

The next morning was a repeat, with my mother misplacing her car keys and frantically looking for them before shooting us a suspicious look and finding them on top of the microwave. Maybe she was multitasking too much and blindly put them there, not even thinking about it? Weird.

"Got them; let's go!" she told us, and we headed out to the car.

Just before we got to school, Liam said he was feeling sick—right before he puked all over the back seat.

"Caleb, go ahead to class. I'm taking him to your aunt's for the day." My mom looked pretty upset.

Walking toward the schoolyard, I had a strange feeling that someone was watching me. Once again, it felt like someone was right next to me, yet there was no one there. When I got closer to the schoolyard, I noticed that one of the older bullies who often messed with Liam was standing by the entry to the courtyard. Instead of chancing a confrontation, I decided to wait for the bell to ring before heading in, but at least I knew what was watching me. At least, I thought I did.

Around lunchtime, I was called into the office for a phone call from my mother. She was going to pick up Liam after work, and I would have to ask to stay with Betty until she got home. When the last bell rang, I headed toward Betty's van and explained the situation.

She was fine. Once we got going, I slipped the piece of paper out of my pocket.

Who is Gene? I heard about him the other day.

It was passed around and received slight shakes of heads before it reached an older teenager named Susan. She was nice to Liam and me. She read it and then looked around for the source of the note. I nodded to let her know it was from me. She turned around and began writing on the note before handing it back.

Bad guy! Tell u tomorrow.

I felt a shiver run down my spine as I shoved the paper back into my pocket. I would show Liam later.

Chapter 5

THE NEXT MORNING, I was anxious to see what Susan might reveal, but I didn't see her on my way to class. I hoped to see her during the day somehow, but if not I would see her on the ride home.

As I headed into the classroom, the teacher was writing sentences with errors on the board that we would write in the correct format. This was one of her "brain jump starts" to the day. The bell finally rang, and the students began finding their desks. Then a girl named Krystal slipped something onto my desk and signaled for me not to tell before sitting down herself. I felt awkward because it was the most interaction I'd ever had with her.

It was a note, and the whole first period I sat wondering what it said. Did she like me? Was she trying to let me know in secret because I was a tree kid? Too many questions were racing through my mind while I tried paying more attention in class. The bell finally rang for recess, and the anticipation to see what the note said was killing me. The note was written in cursive with the fine penmanship that I recognized as Susan's from the night before.

Hey, little bud. Sorry. I didn't want anyone hearing me talk about him. He used to teach my older half sister at the university. He still lives around here somewhere and got into some bad stuff. Ever since he got out of jail for breaking into a house a while back, he's been bouncing around. He's always looking to make a buck and has been known to beat up kids even your age. So I hear. My mom doesn't let me talk about him, so that's why I didn't say anything. She's just happy my sister isn't around him. If you see him, stay away and don't let him know about you. My dad gets really mad if I bring him up and gets really crazy sometimes.

He grows attached to people and doesn't leave them alone. He might try to figure out information about your house so he can break in or do something like that. If you see him, tell your mom. His friends are okay, I think. He's like their leader, but he's scary to me.

The information didn't bother me that much, since in my old neighborhood, this described most people who lived in the desert. The part that bothered me was her question.

P.S. Why do you want to know? Have you seen him or something?

I would have to answer her but wondered how well she could keep a secret. If I lied, she might get angry and tell. I wished I knew her better. I grew more anxious to leave until the final bell, and as I was packing my stuff in my bag, I found myself imagining an encounter with someone robbing a house. I wondered what people felt and what my reaction would be.

"Can I have a minute, Caleb?" said a voice from behind me.

I snapped out of my daydreaming to notice my teacher, who had a concerned look on her face, gesturing for me to come talk to her. I walked past the last few students heading out the door and toward my teacher.

"You seem to be staying on track more, Caleb, and I wanted to tell you I've noticed. However, I noticed I lost you during the last period. What keeps grabbing your attention away? Is something at home bothering you?"

She asked this in a persuasive voice, like I was hiding something, so I told my first lie that also had some truth in it.

"No, just a little bored. It's just too easy for me sometimes." Did I just ask for harder schoolwork?

"I had a feeling that's what it might be. I've noticed your answers are usually correct, and you're outpacing the class. I'll get some approvals to increase your level of difficulty in the class. If it's still not enough, they may want to evaluate you for accelerating to the next grade."

I didn't want this right now. Where did my lie (which was really the truth) get me? I asked if we could talk more tomorrow because of my ride situation and left.

Liam was better from the day before, and we found our usual seats at the back of the van.

"Liam, I found out some stuff about that guy," I whispered. He looked confused for a second before realizing what I was talking about and read the note.

"We'll talk about it later," was all he said.

We got close to Susan's, and she gathered her stuff and leaned toward me.

"Promise you'll tell someone if…" she whispered and left it at that.

A short while later, we were on our way to the tree fort. Liam had a small lighter in his pocket to burn the note. I thought it was a little overdramatic.

"What do you think?" I asked.

"I believe her. I'm pretty sure I've heard people speaking about him before. I also think he used to live in that old house on the hill."

The house he was talking about sat alone on the face of a hill and had been ripped apart by the weather and years of neglect. It seemed that the owners only made repairs that were absolutely necessary. Fragments lay scattered down the hillside where the wind had carried them over the last several years. Bad things happened to everyone who lived there.

"I don't think we should tell anyone," I said to Liam once we'd climbed into the tree fort.

He went up into his crow's nest perch before answering. "So what...we saw him one time. If he bothers us again, then maybe we should say something, but otherwise I think we should just leave it alone."

"Yeah, I think so too. You know, he might not be that bad a guy. People just mistake him somehow, and he uses it to keep going through life. You know what? We should ask him about the camps or maybe one of those other two guys if we see them again."

"I don't think so, Caleb. They seemed protective over it when they first saw us. What if they're really mean and think we heard too much? Maybe we should just keep our distance. You know, not dig too deep."

"So...you want to forget about the camps? I'm still curious. What if we tried to go up there tomorrow like we first planned? It's Saturday, so we've got all day."

"Sounds good to me. I was kind of thinking the same thing earlier. We should just forget Gene and his friends and focus on seeing what the camps are. I never saw them come back down yesterday so we should be on the lookout. I guess it would be hard to see them from our house. We were probably inside."

"Probably. They're grownups and don't have to check in. Heck, they probably stayed the night out here."

The walk home that night seemed lonely, even though I was with Liam. That eerie feeling of being watched came over me, and a chill went down my spine. I looked around, checking behind us, because I was bringing up the rear. Nothing was there. Just the desert plants swaying from the breeze in the diminishing light.

That night, we quietly discussed how we were going to go out the next day and explore the area we thought the camps might be. What if there were all kinds of cool stuff or actual hidden treasures?

noises also filled the valley and included radios playing, hammers banging, and motors revving. After absorbing this for a moment, I tuned them out to listen for my mom or Liam.

The next few moments dragged on, and I began drifting away, imagining what was going on at the neighbors' houses, at my house, with Liam, and with Gene. There was something I couldn't figure out about him, as if something was missing in him when he looked at me. This could be why people like Susan's parents didn't like him. He had a lost look in his eyes. While I stood there thinking, I stared toward my house and could hear the clothes dryer going in our metal shed; it was always loud. I was trying to keep Gene out of my mind by tuning into the other noises, but I couldn't. His lost eyes filled my thoughts.

Suddenly a sharp point swiped across by back, just grazing me. It was followed by a slight giggle that sounded like a little girl.

"Got you!"

I let out my breath when I realized it was just Liam seizing an opportunity to sneak up on me. I was usually the one doing the sneaking.

"You jerk!" I smacked his stick away. He just smiled, and we sat down in the sand. Although I was angry, I was excited to hear his news. Apparently, a smaller, hidden wash joined the main one a little further back. We could use that to sneak past the neighbor's house.

"Do you think anyone else knows about it?"

"Probably not. If I was taller, I probably wouldn't have seen it. There's a tree that spreads out real wide and low to the ground, covering the narrow wash."

This time, being short was an advantage.

We walked back to where the washes joined, and Liam drew a pattern in the sand explaining how he thought the washes flowed together. The shape resembled a peapod joining at both ends but flowing apart in the middle.

"You know, Caleb, I bet Gene doesn't know about this because it gets us clear of the neighbors' view. It runs deeper, with steeper sides, and has more overhanging trees too."

We spent the remaining morning covering the entrance to the small wash with more branches and brush before heading home, happy with what we accomplished. When we were ready to cross the road to our driveway, we had to wait for a truck flying down the road. The man waved out the window at us. It was the "crazy" neighbor.

"I thought you said he was out," Liam said with an irritable tone as we crossed the road.

"I said I thought I heard his truck go by. I didn't say I saw him leave for sure," I snapped back in frustration. As usual, our spats were short-lived.

"So, what do you wanna do after lunch?"

"Maybe we can do more at the Three Trees or something. I don't know, maybe hike down the wash a little further and see if anything's new down there."

"Yeah, maybe go to the cow-pond. We can see if there's any water in the back pond."

The cow-pond was usually empty except when the washes flowed and filled it up long enough to replenish some of the wildlife. It would be a good destination for the rest of the day now that the "crazy" neighbor saw us, but it would give us a chance to reach one of our other goals.

Chapter 7

AFTER WE ATE, WE headed back out and decided to stick to the outer wash to avoid any houses on our way toward the cow-pond, but we now had a different destination in mind. Once we saw the abandoned house on the hill, I felt exposed. The house overlooked the whole valley, providing a clear view of us if anyone happened to be looking. Our plan was to get to the cow-pond and wait for it to be clear before making our way up the north side of the hill toward the house.

When we reached the cow-pond, Betty passed by, honking her horn, and after her van was out of view, we began our ascent up the hill. It wasn't a steep climb. It was a little tough at the beginning and the terrain was almost barren of trees or bushes, so we took our time moving among the shadows.

The coast seemed clear as we made our way past a broken water tank and a demolished shed near the house. We still weren't sure if anyone was living there, but knowing how Gene and the others looked, it wouldn't have surprised us. As we came up on one side of the house, I started thinking about the guy who lived here before. Apparently, that thought crossed Liam's mind too.

"Hey, Caleb, remember that guy who lived up here before?"

"Yeah, barely. I think I only saw him once."

The guy he was talking about was once a keen hiker and out-doorsman. People said he was nice, and they had no idea what set him off. Some said booze and drugs, but there wasn't anything that anybody thought would be enough to push him over the edge like it did that one day a long time ago. He was never seen again.

I peered through the window and didn't see anything. I was aware that the loose skirting around the house was a good hiding spot for rattlesnakes; as I walked around, I was anxious to get inside.

I reached the back side of the house and looked in another open window. I listened one last time before pulling myself inside; Liam stayed outside to keep watch. A slight breeze blew through the house, delivering a foul, putrid odor that reminded me of vomit or a dead animal rotting for days in the desert sun. The wood floor supported me, but bent, rusty nails stuck out everywhere. The inside of the house was in a far worse state of repair than we'd imagined.

"No one seems to be living here," I said to Liam, and he climbed in.

"Can you smell that?" The scent grew more powerful.

"Yeah, what is that? Maybe the plumbing's messed up?"

"I don't know. Seems weird that there's any smell in here at all with the windows open."

There were holes in the floor, though, and the smell seemed to be coming from underneath. Every time the wind blew, it got nastier.

The wall farthest from the window had most of the paneling intact with some furniture and boxes next to it. A thin layer of undisturbed dust on the floor reassured me that no one had been inside recently except us. Before searching through anything, I wanted to make sure that we were alone. I could deal with a rat or a bird or the thousands of insects that called this home, but I wasn't ready to deal with a skunk or snake.

The door to the room was half attached and leaning into the

I watched Liam looking at the cobwebs as we walked toward the first room we came in. Aware of the kissing bugs, he probably didn't want a spider to fall on him. He hated spiders as much as I hated kissing bugs.

Back in the first room, I looked out the window and saw that the sky was beginning to fill with storm clouds. I was trying to recall if I heard about a storm coming in, but my attention was soon drawn toward a box on the floor labeled New Home.

I kneeled down and gave it a little push to warn any pests that I was about to open it. It was full of loose rags. One of the rags I pulled out unraveled, dropping a rusty nail about three inches long and fairly thick. I picked it up to see an engraving on the head. A stylish number was there: 53.

I had no idea what the number stood for, but I pocketed it anyways. It didn't feel like stealing because it was left behind. In a second rag was a small skeleton key that was missing some teeth and didn't look functional anymore, so I pocketed it also. I found nothing else in the box and placed the rags back in before moving on.

"Find anything cool yet?" Liam tapped the first box I looked through with his foot.

"A rusty skeleton key and a weird nail," I said as I began opening a second box.

This box had a bunch of paper, including some personal letters, bills, and old pictures. I could tell they were old from what the people wore and because they were black-and-white with little gloss. They reminded me of pictures I saw when we took a trip to Gettysburg.

"Hey, Liam, check these old pictures out."

"Where do you think that is?"

"I don't know. Looks like some old building or something."

"Yeah, kind of like those buildings out by that old west amusement park."

The pictures had buildings that resembled the structures in the amusement park that used to be an original part of the nearby city. I had a strange feeling I'd seen them before, but it wasn't from the amusement park. I decided to leave them.

Liam was looking through the dresser by the window. "Nothing but a bunch of candles, some matchbooks, and some old incense, it looks like. Wait, check this out."

From the top drawer, he pulled out a dirty knife. It had a rusty blade with no shine and a handle that looked like bone. In his other hand, he held a leather sheath so worn it was barely a sheath. He smiled and put it back in the sheath.

"What's with the creepy look, Liam?"

"We can leave this at the Three Trees, and no one will know we have it. We can make all kinds of stuff with it down there and carry it around."

"Yeah, cool. We can sharpen it on those flat rocks with some spit."

"We can't tell anyone."

"Yeah, somebody will probably think we're doing something bad."

He put the knife in the back of his pants while he closed the drawers and looked out the nearby window.

"Did you hear anything about it raining today?"

"That's what I was wondering."

"I know Mom didn't say anything, or she would've told us to be home earlier. Heck, she probably wouldn't have let us back out after lunch."

"We better go in case it starts raining. You know Mom will be mad." Liam took one last look around before climbing out the window.

I grabbed some loose papers to wrap the key and nail in and followed him out. I should have been watching what I was doing

35

instead of watching the sky, because when I jumped out the window, I almost landed on Liam.

"Watch it, Caleb. Just slow down a little bit."

Once we knew that we were clear, we made our way down the hill and back into the wash. We stayed in the shadows, but we weren't as cautious on our trip back. It occurred to me that when we were in the house, we didn't hear the wind outside, and there were no noises at all. Down in the wash, the wind was picking up and growing loud through the valley.

"Liam, we should probably get to the Three Trees as fast as we can. I don't think we would hear the bell or Mom from that house. She'd go there first if we didn't come home after she called."

"Don't worry. We would've heard her. The wind would carry her voice, and we were downwind."

He was right. The wind did carry noises more often than not in this valley. Sometimes distant noises were so clear that you could hear the neighbors talking almost a mile away.

When we reached the Three Trees, I felt like something was watching me, but I was probably paranoid from going into that house; I tried not to think about the tragedies that befell those who once lived there. Still, I looked around as I pulled the key and nail from my pocket to show Liam.

"So? I got a knife." Liam pulled it out cautiously from his pants.

"Yeah, that's a lot cooler. But they're all for the fort, right? I mean, we both can use the knife, and these are both of ours."

"Yeah, but this is a little more mine, and those are a little more yours. Of course I'll always let you use it if I'm not doing anything with it." He had to keep holding the knife and looking at it as if it was the world's greatest treasure.

I began folding my treasures away into the piece of paper I grabbed when I noticed some writing on it. It said something about someone

36

named Robert. I opened it to see what it said, and there was an age, a description—that sounded like Robert—and an address. Some of the other writing that was still readable mentioned assault, assault with a deadly weapon, breaking and entering, grand theft auto, and indecent exposure. This explained the sleeping bags. The house was most likely Gene's old house too or at least he had lived there with Robert. I imagined that the trio lived there together at one point but hadn't lived there for a while.

"Liam," I said, handing over the paper, "I think it was their house, or they had something to do with it."

"Well, at least we know where their place is; perhaps they were back there the other day for the night or something. It kind of makes us even. They know where we hang out, and now we know where they chill."

Liam handed the paper back to me and started climbing toward his crow's nest, where he wedged the knife in between two branches.

"Can you see it from down there?"

"No." I know he wanted to make sure that no one walking through, like our mother, could see his new knife.

I climbed up to the lower platform and found a hole in the main trunk to hide the paper, key, and nail. It seemed to be a good spot and not very obvious. Someone would probably find it and think nothing of it anyways.

After sitting there for a while, we decided it would be best to head home because of the storm. The wind was blowing a cool, creosote scent down through the valley. We reached the driveway and began walking toward our house. The weather was keeping Max huddled down in his house, and he didn't bother barking at our arrival.

Chapter 8

"WHERE WERE YOU TWO?" our mom asked as we walked in the living room.

Liam blurted out, "At the Three Trees. Why?"

"I called for you guys to come home a little while ago, when it started getting stormy. I don't want you getting caught in a flash flood or anything. I expected you to be back sooner. The storm is practically here."

"We just got caught up in what we were doing and didn't realize how close the storm was. When we did, we hurried home." Liam was good at setting stuff up so that it seemed like we tried redeeming ourselves by hastily getting back home.

"Okay, but you still should've been able to hear me. That tells me that maybe the tree fort is too far away."

"No, we can usually hear you fine," Liam replied quickly. "It was probably the wind."

"It's starting to rain outside. Is there anything we need to get covered up?" I asked her. With the lack of rainfall around here, people had a tendency to leave items out that they wouldn't want getting wet.

"No," said my mother. "I already took care of it after I yelled for you guys. What are you two going to do for the rest of the day inside?"

"Don't know. Probably play a game like *Battle Masters* or something. Maybe put on a movie. Is there anything you need us to do inside?"

"No. Go ahead and do what you were going to do. Just remember that tomorrow you have to get all your chores done before you go out. Did Max get food yet?"

"Yeah. Caleb checked his dish this morning."

From our bedroom window, I couldn't see much of the storm because a hill blocked the view. Liam was already getting the game out, and it took a while to set up. It was fun setting up because you could really look at the ogres, goblins, trolls, and the opposing knights. The game took up a lot of floor space, so the battles usually had to wrap up in one sitting.

The lights began flickering, which meant lightning was getting close. We would probably lose power, which lasted for some time out where we lived; my mother brought us some candles just in case. I liked the way the candles looked, making the room seem cozier, but at the same time, I knew that we could easily be plunged into darkness.

I looked out the window again and followed two ravens flying along the hillside, swooping up and down and dodging the opposing air currents with little effort. I always saw ravens in this weather, like they belonged in it. Perhaps that's why Edgar Allen Poe's "The Raven" was so eerie to me. I followed their flight as they flew across the path of something black in the distance by a small mesquite tree. It looked like a black trash bag had gotten stuck in the tree and was trying to break free with the wind.

I felt compelled to remove it because it didn't belong there. I imagined the two ravens removing it from the tree, but they disappeared. The whole desert was empty of any living thing. As I began to close the blinds, the bag started to break free, revealing a worn-out straw hat.

39

The blinds fell down in front of me, and I fumbled to reopen them. I scanned the hillside but saw nothing, not even the bag. It had to be my paranoia and imagination, but I decided not to rule out any possibilities.

Liam had gone for some cookies and milk, and after I lowered the blinds and pushed Play on the VCR, I sat down by the game board. The beginning credits of the movie always made me wish I was there, in that place, fighting off evil forces. When Liam came back in, I told him what I thought I had seen.

He just looked at me while he finished chewing his cookie and then whispered back: "What do you mean, you think you saw him?"

"I was looking out the window, and I thought I saw a trash bag stuck in the tree. But then the blind accidently closed, and I thought I saw his hat. It was like he was wearing a black trash bag around him against the rain, to not be seen."

"You're just nervous from earlier. Did you open the blinds back up and look?"

"Yeah, but nothing was there."

"See, then it was just a bag and your imagination. I think my goblin archers are going to attack your knights first," he said as the game began.

We played for a while, and it took scary things off my mind. But the storm worsened, and when the power flickered off, we left the game out for the night, determined to continue the following morning. However, if I listened to the thoughts in my head, I knew we wouldn't. I couldn't stop thinking about the creepy, smelly house and the black trash bag. Again, it seemed like my brother was reading my mind or perhaps it was obvious that he was thinking about the same things.

"Hey, Caleb." Liam leaned over from the top bunk. "Do you think Gene's out there right now?"

"Shut up. That's not funny."

I grabbed a book off the floor and turned on my battery-powered reading lamp. I needed to get my mind off things. The book was about mythical creatures and had pictures accompanying their descriptions.

Eventually, I could hear Liam snoring, and my eyes were getting tired, but then I suddenly heard a clinking noise coming from the window. The clinking turned into a whistle, and I realized a draft was coming through. I put my book down and went to close the window, and that's when I heard voices coming from outside. I eased it open a little more, and it sounded like an argument, but they were too faint to understand. I gently pushed a small part of the blinds aside to look out.

Not being able to see anything made me more nervous because I felt that they might be able to see me. I decided to close the window, but as I grabbed the handle, a gust of wind hit the window and me with an icy coldness that made me shiver uncontrollably. I shook the feeling off and managed to gently and quietly close it, hoping I hadn't alerted anyone. Maybe I did because I began to hear the voices again, and this time they sounded angrier.

I looked at Liam and whispered his name to wake him up, but he kept snoring. I pulled the blinds aside to have a better look out the window and found myself staring right at the pale silhouette of a human face pressing against the glass. I jerked away, leaving the blinds flapping enough for me to see the face smear the raindrops from the window as it moved out of sight.

I tried to wake Liam again by pulling the covers off him and shaking him. He was completely pale—his eyes were a grayish-blue reflecting a slimy look in the broken light. His face and neck were covered with scars that resembled bug bites that had been scratched until they bled and scabbed over.

I shook him again, but the only reaction I got was from the remaining air escaping his body. I jumped off the bed, twisting my ankle, and the floor suddenly felt like a magnet pulling me down onto my belly. I was wondering if maybe I was so tired and freaked out that I couldn't function, but I had to get help. My ankle began throbbing, and each yell for help only escaped my mouth with a whispered breath.

I dragged myself toward the door, hoping to bang on it if I couldn't reach the handle, and then everything was plunged into total darkness. My body shuddered before going numb. I jerked myself forward in my bed, and the book fell and hit me in the face. It was a bad dream.

"What's up, man? You alright?" Liam said, tossing around in the top bunk.

"Yeah, it was...just a twitch or something," I replied, but the dream had really freaked me out. I turned off my light and put the book away, hoping I would not dream again when I fell back to sleep.

Chapter 9

SUNDAY STARTED THE SAME as usual: do some chores before return-ing to the game. It was still raining steadily and showing no sign of letting up, but after about an hour of cat-and-mouse with the game pieces, we called it a draw.

As we were putting the game away, we heard a vehicle coming into the yard. Max usually took cover in the storms, but something got him barking. Our mother was already on her way to the front door when we joined her to see who was here.

"Who do we know with an orange station wagon looking vehicle?" she asked, looking out the window by the front door.

Liam was trying to peak through the window just in front of our mother. "I don't know. Can you see the driver?" The car stopped about halfway up the driveway before turning around and leaving.

"They must have been lost," my mother said, closing the blinds and walking away.

"Sshhh!"

"What you shushing me for, Liam?"

"What?"

"Did you just shush me?"

"No. It was probably the blinds."

"Oh really? So I'm hearing things now?"

Back in the room, we finished picking up the game before finding a book to sit down with. Liam couldn't decide which book he wanted so he brought several from the hall closet to his beanbag chair. The house became still with the faint sounds of the living room television and our mother humming while she baked.

Although it was fall, it was still warm enough that we had our ceiling fan going. It rocked just slightly off balance, making a light knocking sound as the pull-chain tapped on the glass. Sometimes a gust of wind came through the valley, making the rain hammer down harder against the house. Finally, I brought up the subject of the car.

"I've never seen that car before. Have you?"

"No. Why?"

"Just thinking about it, you know . . . it could be one of the neighbors that live around that house."

"Talk quieter when you talk about it. Don't you realize how quiet it is in here?"

"I know, but Mom would never know what we were talking about anyways. I was just thinking about it and wondering if maybe someone saw us and came to tell Mom."

"Don't you think they would've come yesterday?" Liam looked a little flustered with the conversation and shook his head as if to end it.

I sat back in my beanbag and continued reading, but then there was a knock at the door. I could hear my mother walking toward the door as I looked into the hallway, hoping to catch a glimpse.

"It's that same car again. Must be lost," my mother said before she opened the door, leaving the security door locked between her and the visitor. We still couldn't see and joined her as the door finished swinging open. I could now see who it was through the security door. Gene.

"Can I help you with something?" my mom asked with a confident tone, not giving any indication that she was nervous. "Honey, someone's here!" she said toward the living room, as if she was speaking to someone else in the house; our dad had left us a long time ago.

"No big concern. Wanted to ask you if you're perhaps the mother of those two nice boys I saw in the wash the other day?" Gene replied, trying to get a better look through the security door.

"Maybe. Liam, Caleb! Did you see this man in the wash?" She looked directly at me as if she already knew the answer.

"Just briefly, Mom. He said hi and went on up the wash," Liam said quickly, trying to gain control of the conversation.

Now she was upset. "Why didn't you tell me?"

"We didn't think it was a big deal. We were in the tree, and he was down below. He didn't say much. Right, Caleb?"

"Yeah, no big deal, Mom. Liam's right."

"Well, I will speak with you two later about this, but anyways"— speaking to Gene, she said—"was there something I can help you with?"

Gene hacked a couple times in a laughing cough while looking at the house on the hill before taking a deep breath and shaking some rainwater from his dirty straw hat.

"No, not really. I just wanted to see who they were and to let them know that I didn't mean to startle them or anything. People around here say things, and I wanted to speak with their parents to let them know who I was."

"Well, thank you for that. I assure you they weren't startled or they would have said something to me."

"That's good to hear ma'am. I pulled up earlier, but thought I was in the wrong driveway. The neighbors didn't seem to know anything about two boys so I thought I'd just knock on all the doors until I found out."

"I appreciate you letting me know. Is there anything else you need to tell me or was that it? They didn't do anything, did they?" My mother was already closing the door and seemed uncomfortable with the situation.

"No, no. They seem like good boys. I walk around here, and there's no need to be startled if they see me. Don't need anyone calling the cops for no reason or something like that," Gene said, looking at the house on the hill again.

"If that's all, then I really need to get back to my cleaning and baking. I hope you have a good day."

"You too, ma'am, and tell the boys I said hi. By the way, my name's Gene."

"Nice to meet you, Gene, but I must be getting back."

"Okay, ma'am. Sorry to take up your time. You have a good day yourself. Good boys you got there."

"I know, thank you," my mother said as she was closing the door. To her he was probably just a concerned neighbor, but to us he was something more.

"I wish you two would have told me so it wasn't so awkward."

I gave her my puppy-dog eyes. "We didn't think anything of it, Mom. That's all."

She stared worriedly at us and then walked toward the kitchen. Although Gene never entered the house a faint, sour smell of stale beer and cigarettes lingered in the hall from the brief conversation.

Liam headed back into our room as I watched Gene peel out in the muddy red clay before heading out of our driveway. I watched the fog from my breath disappear from the window as I let the blinds sway back into place, but then I noticed something else at the window. Not just something, someone.

I reached for the blinds, nervous to look out but pulling them aside regardless to see that the window was still fogged up from my breath. I held my breath to prevent any more fog and watched a silhouette on the outside move as the fog somehow increased. I quickly wiped it away with my hand and immediately looked out in case I startled anything that might try to run off. Unfortunately, the fog was coming from the outside. The fog centered on one area that kept getting larger and then smaller, just like it did when I was breathing on the glass inside.

Suddenly, a small hand cleared the fog, and two pale-blue eyes were staring at me. I began backing away from the window as the eyes followed me. They looked so alone and angry. Then, in a sudden movement, like flipping through pages of a book, the face looked to one side and then the other, and then back at me. The figure put a finger up to its mouth and pushed against its lips before the window instantly fogged back up. Then the figure was gone.

I didn't know how to react. Everyone would think I was imagining stuff, especially Liam, because we snuck around that house. I stood in shock until a hand landed on my shoulder, causing me to jump back.

"You coming back to read?"

"We have to talk, but later sometime. Outside. Okay, Liam?"

"Alright. You okay? You look sick or something."

"Yeah, just startled a little bit. Let's make sure the windows are closed and latched."

"Why?"

"Can we just do it? If Mom asks, it's because of the rain."

Liam looked at me as if he wanted to ask why again, but something in my expression must have told him to keep quiet. Finally, he just gave me a quick nod of his head.

"Okay. I'll get the back bedrooms, and you get the others."

While closing the windows I kept an eye out. Yes, it could have been a figment of my imagination, but I was certain I saw and heard something. The weather kept us inside for the rest of the day, and we relied on more books and a few movies to keep us occupied. I never took the chance of speaking with Liam because I feared our mother would overhear.

Despite the events of the day, I actually fell asleep quite quickly that night but was plagued by dreams. In the most vivid, a black fog rose out of rocks on a windy, cloud-covered day. The rocks were familiar, reminding me of the rock formation up the wash that we believed was old coral or lava, and the fog came out through cracks, rapidly swirling in the wash ahead of me and then at my feet. I began running away, but when I looked back, it was right behind me, and it felt like I was exhaling all the air in my lungs and then not breathing in again. But the feeling and the fog stopped when I crossed the road by my house.

Chapter 10

THE NEXT MORNING WAS just another school day. The rain stopped, but the clouds remained a threat. No keys were missing, no papers were reorganized, and I wondered why we'd had those problems to begin with. I could tell that it was bothering Liam that I still had something to tell him, but I was wondering if maybe I should let it bother him a little longer, just to mess with him.

When we arrived at school and were grabbing our bags from the car, my mother just sat there, staring through the window.

"Something wrong, Mom?" I asked her while grabbing the door to close it.

"I want to talk with both of you when you get home. It's about that guy Gene. I asked the neighbors about him, and there's some issues we need to discuss, later, about you two going out in the desert by yourselves." She sounded concerned and upset. "You're not in trouble or anything. I just want to go over some things, okay?"

"Alright, Mom. Don't worry. Okay," I said, starting to close my door.

"I love you guys. Jesus bless you and have a good day," she said as usual right before my door closed the rest of the way.

"So?" Liam asked anxiously as we walked off into school. "What did you want to talk about?"

I told him what happened, and it seemed like he didn't believe me because he didn't remember any of the windows fogging up. He looked disappointed, as if he had waited for nothing. He suggested it was a neighborhood kid, but I reminded him of how unlikely that would be. He still decided to drop it and changed the subject.

"Remember, it's a half day for teacher grading today and tomorrow, and then we have five days off."

"I totally forgot. How are we getting home? Did Mom say anything?"

"With Betty," Liam said before we parted ways in the courtyard.

By lunchtime, I was more than ready to go home, anxious to get to the Three Trees with so much time left in the day. On half days, the cafeteria staff usually served prepared sack lunches in the courtyard so they could avoid extra work. I found a comfortable spot under a false cherry tree where I could see the parking lot. This was a nice spot on the grass away from everyone else, but the fruits that fell from the tree often stained clothes, so I had to be careful when sitting down.

Two of the tree kids found a spot nearby, but we didn't talk. Then I saw Krystal and Susan eating their lunches and looking at me. When they noticed me looking, they shied away; I kind of liked that. I thought Krystal was pretty, and she was always nice to everyone, even me.

As I saw Betty's van pulling in, I started packing my stuff, but I didn't see Liam as I began to walk toward the parking lot. Krystal and Susan intercepted me, and I tensed a little; Susan could be somewhat rough around the edges, at least when it came to bullies at school. I didn't really expect any problems with them, but they both seemed to be scrutinizing me.

"Hi, Caleb. How're you doing?" Krystal said.

"Okay, I guess." I wasn't comfortable talking with most people, but especially girls.

"We were talking about that guy Gene and wondering why you wanted to know about him, He drove to Susan's house the other day and had a...confrontation with her dad. Do you know anything about that?"

Krystal usually excelled at school, like me, but probably even more, and had a tendency to incorporate new words she had learned into her conversation. But she also had a tic when she talked sometimes, like she was trying to think of more impressive words to use before giving up and deciding to talk like a kid our age would normally do.

"No, but he came to our house too. He wanted to talk with my mom. They didn't argue or anything."

Susan looked angry.

"Why'd you tell people that I told you about him, Caleb? I thought we were friends and that you'd keep this on the down low. You got me in a lot of trouble with my parents. That's not cool."

Because Susan was older than me and was known to throw a punch or two when she disagreed with people. I was beginning to worry.

"I didn't say anything. I swear. After he came over, we told my mom we saw him in the wash. I never mentioned you, Honest."

"Are you sure?" Susan looked like she was trying to read my mind or perhaps getting ready to punch me. "I'd hate to find out you showed anyone that note or said I told you something that I really didn't."

"No, I didn't. Liam and I talked about it but that's it—the note I mean. I'm sorry you're in trouble, but we didn't say anything. What's the big deal with this guy anyways? Why's everyone freaked out about him?"

"My parents said he was normal when they first met him a while ago," Susan said, finally calming down. "He said he was studying some archaeological stuff in the area for the university, but then he began to distance himself from everyone. He kept a few close friends, but they all started behaving like him, acting weird and not talking with their families or anyone. He lived in a house up by us, the one falling apart, and we heard he needed to get rid of something. That's all he would tell people. They thought he was into drugs; most people still do and that's why my dad got mad with him and then me."

"So he's a druggie and a thief?" I said, looking for a reaction.

"No," Krystal said. "Well, Susan and I don't, err...concur on that. He was into some weird stuff, and people say he's the reason some of the other people around him disappeared with no trace. Some say it was some plants in the area he was eating—at least that's what Susan's parents said. Like a drug or something."

I scratched the back of my head, a sign of insecurity I get before asking a question. "How do you think he found out? I mean, about us talking about him?"

"I don't know." Susan looked around and saw Betty beckoning us to get in the van. "But we better get in before she takes off without us."

"Yeah, we can talk about it later. I'm sorry you're in trouble, but I promise we didn't say anything."

"I believe you, Caleb. I have no idea how he found out, but I believe you." Susan said.

"Why's it such a big deal anyways?" I asked her as we began walking to the van.

"I guess it's like an omen or something. He makes people uneasy, so talking about him puts evil in the air or something."

Liam was already inside the van and working on his homework to get it out of the way; I must have missed him when Susan and Krystal were talking to me. Krystal was riding with us today because she was going to Susan's. I could tell that they didn't want to talk about it anymore, so I left it alone. However, I wondered how much trouble Susan had really gotten into because she could still have a friend over. Soon, most of the kids were dropped off, and our next stop was Susan's.

"What's going on here?" Betty said as we turned into Susan's driveway and saw the sheriff's car. The lights weren't flashing, which was perhaps good news, but it still gave me a bad feeling. Betty got out and went to talk with the sheriff and Susan's parents. We couldn't hear what they were saying with the engine still running and the radio on. Susan and Krystal went over to the adults but didn't seem to be part of the conversation.

"What are they talking about? Did something happen?" Betty's youngest boy asked. His older brother told him to mind his business.

Knowing not to eavesdrop, Liam and I went back to what we were doing until we got to our house and noticed that our mother wasn't home.

"Where's your mom?" Betty asked.

"I'm sure she'll be home in a minute. We have a key and will wait inside till she gets home," Liam answered.

As we began getting out, Betty kept asking us if it was okay with our mother for us to be home alone. Liam assured her that's why he had a key.

"Did Mom really say it was okay for us to stay here if she wasn't home?"

"Yes, but only for emergencies or if she's running late, like today. She probably had to work a little late, but she knew about the half day. She's the one who reminded me of it this morning."

"Okay, then. By the way, I know more about Gene."

"You heard more about him? I had a weird dream about him last night, like he was standing in some spiraling smoke or something. Just when I thought the smoke was going to touch me, I woke up. I was okay, but it was still a little creepy."

I didn't tell Liam that I also had a similar dream; he still wouldn't believe me about the window. While eating a snack, I filled Liam in about Gene, reminding him not to say anything to anyone.

"Don't you think it's strange that Gene freaks everyone out, but they don't do anything about it?" I asked.

"I guess he doesn't really do enough to do anything. Like call the sheriff."

"I think we should make sure everything's secure around here from now on. Do you think...?"

"Think what?" he replied, biting his cookie.

"Well, what about the stuff we took from the old house? Suppose he finds out and comes after us, you know, like revenge. He also knows where our fort is. What if he goes looking around down there?" I was getting myself worried now.

"The knife's way up in the tree," Liam said slowly, "and so are those little trinkets. He could find those pretty easily."

I began realizing where the conversation was leading. One of us needed to retrieve the items and hide them somewhere else before our mother came home. Problem was, we had no idea when that would be.

We decided that Liam would wait on the roof as a lookout, and we placed the rickety old ladder up on the back side of the house to be less obvious. I was pumped up and ready to run as quickly as I could down to the Three Trees. Once Liam was positioned on the roof and made sure that I was clear, I took off running. I barely looked for cars when I made my way across the road and then headed down the wash, running at full speed.

Chapter 11

REACHING THE THREE TREES was a relief. I was halfway done—well, almost—but could not stop thinking that someone was watching me and was there with me. I looked around, but no one was there, so I climbed the tree and retrieved the knife first before grabbing the other items. I waved to Liam from the top branches, letting him know I had made it, and he began pointing at something. Parked alongside the road about a quarter mile from me was Gene's car.

There was no sign of Gene, but I knew I had to move. My heart began racing as sweat dripped into my eyes, blurring my vision as I began climbing down. Before reaching the ground, I looked around to make sure there was no sign of Gene and missed a grip, snagging my finger on a nail holding a ladder rung to the tree. Blood began dripping onto the piece of wood as I checked to see how bad the cut was.

When I reached the ground, I took off running until I heard a cough come from behind me. I dropped to the ground and rolled into the wash, lying still and listening to the sound of footsteps getting closer. I raised my head slowly to see if it was Gene and if he was coming toward me. Sure enough, there he was, walking around the tree.

He seemed to have a twitch in his movement as he circled the tree and examined the fort. He grabbed the trunk of the tree, feeling for something, and his fingers flexed and stretched around the bark like he was trying to grasp a basketball by enlarging his hand. The minute he touched the ladder, he swiftly retracted his hand, like the feeling sickened or hurt him. He began licking his hand and groaning, like it pleased him, before he began licking one of the ladder rungs. That was enough for me.

I crouched low, making my way further up the wash until I knew I was clear, and when I finally stood up, I looked back but couldn't see Gene. Although I was desperate to put distance between us, I avoided running so I could remain as silent as possible. When I got to our driveway, Liam was already off the roof. I ran around the back of the house to help him get the ladder down.

"Did you see Gene?" Liam asked urgently from the lower rungs before he jumped to the ground.

"Yeah, but let's hide these first." I pulled the items out of my pocket and rolled the knife in the paper with the other pieces. We decided to hide them inside Max's doghouse because we were the only ones who went near it.

I showed Liam my finger, and we headed inside so I could tend to it. I told him about Gene licking his hands and the board, and as I told him, I realized that Gene was licking the same board that I cut my hand on. Was he licking my blood?

It wasn't long before we heard the familiar rattling of my mom's car trudging up the driveway. We waited for her by the door in case she needed help bringing anything in. She noticed my hand almost immediately, and I told her I cut it on Max's doghouse. She didn't ask any more about it and didn't mention Gene's car on the road. I was worried she would see it and wouldn't let us out to play. She obviously hadn't because she would have said something or seemed worried. We decided not to return to the Three Trees in case he happened to be around there. Today, our destination would be Black Rocks.

We knew it was possible that Gene was lurking around as we made our way over there. We looked everywhere, like hawks scanning the horizon for prey. Every rustle of a bush or a tree made us jump as we worked our way up the wash.

"You said you had a dream about some smokelike stuff?" I asked.

"Yeah, what about it?"

"Where were you? I forgot if you told me."

"At Black Rocks. Why?"

"I had similar dream." I felt nervous about the dream again, but Liam didn't seem to care.

"Whatever. Let's just try to have fun the rest of the day and forget about the crap with Gene and your voices."

I could tell that something was bothering Liam, so I didn't argue with him. He was usually more sympathetic when I was worried. I think he was worried, too.

We reached Black Rocks with no problems, and there were two good ways to climb. The first was around the bend in the wash, where some of the rocks had fallen in smaller sections and formed a path you could climb by jumping from rock to rock. That was the easier route, but we preferred the harder way to prove ourselves: straight up the face. The rocks had indentations that allowed us to get good holds while we climbed the almost vertical rock. Our usual destination was a small area halfway up the rocks that we could hang out on.

Liam climbed first, and I followed; it was an age thing again. We reached the spot and put our stuff down while looking out across the valley for any signs of Gene.

"Where are you going to check out today?" he asked as he rubbed at a slight graze on his elbow.

"I think I'm going to check out those crevices higher up to the left. I dropped down in one last time, and I think I can wiggle my way in a little further."

"Well, I'm going to go through those cat's claw bushes and see if there's another area to leave our stuff so it isn't so easy to see from the road. Maybe we could make a fort up here too. Like a watch post. Think about it. You can see the whole valley from up here."

"That'd be cool," I said as I began heading toward the cervices.

I looked around for snakes and other critters before jumping down. The air smelled damp and sulfurous, and water trickled from cracks in the rocks. I cautiously crawled in several feet, and the light became so dim I wasn't sure I could continue. I tried waiting for my eyes to adjust, but they wouldn't because of the light that still shined in at the entrance.

The crevice narrowed as I moved further in, but it wasn't tight on my body yet. I knew better than to get into a situation where I couldn't back up if needed. I listened carefully for any movement as I crawled; the shadows were already playing tricks on me. There was more water, and the trickling sound seemed to echo, drowning out any other noise. A few feet further in, my eyes weren't adjusting to the darkness, so I admitted defeat and started backing out. I only went a few feet before I heard it.

"Sshhh!"

I froze before my frantic reaction forced my body to contort around, and in a fast crawl on my knees, I scampered toward the opening. I tried to look behind me, but I couldn't see anything, so I hurried out of the crevice and almost dove into daylight in one movement. Funny what the human body can do when scared.

"Liam!" I yelled out, looking around for him.

"What?" he yelled back from over the ridge.

"We got to go! Now!"

I hurried over to pick up my stuff, dropping it several times in my haste before making my way down the easier side of the rocks. Liam was trying to follow but couldn't keep up.

"What are you doing, man?"

"Come on. I'll tell you later, but for now, let's just get home."

I got to the wash and waited impatiently for Liam, who was taking his time because he had no reason to rush. When he reached the wash, I was already walking toward home.

"What's the matter, Caleb? Got to go number two or something?"

"I don't know. Something. Again. A shush."

"You look sick again. Are you okay? You're not making any sense. Was there a snake or something?"

"Snakes don't shush people, Liam!"

"Okay, okay. Let's go home."

The walk home was more of a jog, with Liam trying to slow me down. About halfway home, I finally stopped to gather myself.

"Caleb, what happened?"

"You won't believe me. You haven't believed me lately, so why would you now?"

"Listen," he said, putting a hand on my arm to show he was genuine. "I was thinking when I was by myself up there that this is getting too weird. Similar dreams. Gene doing that weird stuff. Also, weird things have been happening at home lately."

"What weird things at home?"

"You know—the missing stuff. Things being unorganized. The other day, Max was barking at his doghouse, but nothing was in there. Then he backed away from me like he was being yelled at or scared."

"I heard the voice again, shushing me. Something's not right," I said quietly as we stood there, looking around. He seemed as lost as I was for any explanation.

As we made our way home, we didn't say anything else until we reached our driveway, and that was to decide what we would do the rest of the evening. We wanted something to distract us from the crazy stuff that seemed to be happening.

Chapter 12

THE FOLLOWING MORNING, WE arrived at school a little late because once again the keys were misplaced, and my homework wasn't only unorganized this time but missing. I found my papers under my bed, and Liam's were in my backpack. We both just dealt with it and never said anything to our mother.

When we got to school, I felt really nervous, like I shouldn't go to school that day, but another part of me felt that I needed to. I just sucked it up and got out of the car.

"I think I should try talking with Krystal," I told Liam, "and see if Susan said anything else to her. Maybe there's some connection to Gene and the weird stuff that's been going on. I mean, if you think about it, it all started around the same time."

"Good idea. If I run into Susan, I'll see if she wants to maybe hang out after school or something, and then we don't have to worry about talking about it. Maybe her parents will let her come to the Three Trees."

"I was also thinking about what would happen if we just left it alone and see if it goes away. I mean, what if we're putting ourselves into more of a mess by looking further into it?"

"I haven't thought about that, but I think it'd be a bad idea to not know."

I nodded my almost reluctant agreement and turned toward my classroom.

"Hey, Caleb."

"Yeah?" I asked, looking over my shoulder.

"Be careful today," he said. I nodded, appreciating my brother's concern.

"You too," I replied, and he gave me a quick wave of his hand.

I had a bad feeling as we went our separate ways but tried to shake it off before I quickly made it to my classroom door. I hoped to get inside to my safety net as usual, but the door was locked. Sometimes the teachers were in early meetings and didn't get to their classrooms until the bell rang. I decided I'd be better off waiting by one of the tables near the courtyard so the other kids wouldn't pile up around me by the locked door.

Just as I sat at the table, I saw the first few kids arrive and try the door.

"Hey, Caleb, where's the teacher?" one of them yelled out.

I just shrugged my shoulders, trying to look busy with some papers from my backpack. Three of them dropped their bags by the door and approached me, standing together at the side of the table and pushing their bodies against me to get a reaction.

"I don't know where she is," I said keeping my eyes on my papers. Eye contact meant two things: you either were ready to fight or would be the first to shy away. I wasn't scared of fighting. I just didn't want to fight, at least not three at one time.

"Then why couldn't you just say that? Are you deaf or something?" said the thinner one with spiked hair. He tried grabbing my papers. I jerked them back but not too fast, so I wouldn't provoke them.

"Do you mind? I'm trying to look through some stuff before class."

"Whatever, man. Why do you have to be so weird and stupid?" he sneered.

I then saw the teacher coming, and when they noticed her, they began walking away. As they did so, I noticed the talkative one had a stride to his step that he no doubt thought was cool. Actually, it made him look like he had hip problems.

I caught up with Liam at lunchtime when he joined me by the tree, and I found out that he had been pushed around pretty bad by some of the older bullies. They tore his backpack but hadn't made him bleed so I knew he wouldn't tell our mom. He did say that Susan and Krystal were already aware that he had been beaten up, and Susan was pretty mad about it. We looked out for them, and when they walked past, we called them over, and I asked if they wanted to eat with us.

"We're not eating until we get home. I like it better that way, and besides, I got some business to attend to with a few punks," Susan said. To me, she looked pretty scary. "Liam told us about those kids. They're just punks. I think I know who it was from what Liam told me."

"So what're you guys up to?" Liam asked, wanting to change the subject. I knew he was trying to find out more about Gene. Susan simply began picking at the grass, like she was frustrated.

"Would there be any way you two could hang out after school one day?" I asked, surprising myself that I had the courage to ask.

"Just *one* day Caleb? As in a solitary day?" Krystal said sarcastically, but she was grinning.

"You know what I mean. Can you two hang out *sometime, outside* of school?" I said, as if she was the one that was a bit stupid.

"I guess I could ask my parents. They would want to talk with your mom first. What about you, Susan?"

"Liam already asked me. I don't think I can until next week

because of the situation at home," she replied, looking fed up before she turned to me. "The sheriff was there, Caleb, because my parents saw people messing around that old house, and they just wanted to report it, but it was nothing serious. Liam told me you thought it had something to do with Gene."

I turned, looking at Liam and wondering what else he told her. "Well, that's good. I thought you were in serious trouble for something that you told me. I don't know. Just paranoid, I guess. Have you heard anything about Gene or seen him around?"

"I think my parents saw his car the other day. He still knows people around here, so it's hard to tell if he's up to anything. My dad says he's like a bad itch."

"A bad itch?" Liam asked, finally joining in the conversation.

"You know." Susan scratched her arm mimicking a bad itch. "The more you scratch it, the itchier it gets."

"That's not always true," Liam said.

"Anyways, you get the point." Susan suddenly stood up. "Come on, Krystal. Let's get our stuff. The bell's about to ring, and I wanna see if I can find at least one of those punks before it's time to go."

"See you guys by the van," said Krystal, standing up and wiping the grass from her legs.

The bell rang, and I stuffed my unfinished lunch in my backpack before we made our way to the parking lot.

"Is Mom going to be home late again?" I asked.

Liam nodded. "She's going to start staying another hour at work. Since nothing happened yesterday, she feels like she can trust us being alone."

"Well, nothing happened as far as she knows. Let's not worry her by doing anything like yesterday."

I noticed a chill in the air on the ride home. The clouds were blocking most of the sun and were resting on the mountains and covering the peaks giving them an eerie look. When we pulled into our driveway Max was doing his usual routine, and Betty noticed my mother wasn't home again.

"Are you guys staying alone again? You know you can come to my house anytime and play with the boys if you would like."

We didn't mind hanging out with her two boys, but sometimes they just wanted to do stuff that we didn't want to do.

"Thanks, but we're okay. I think my mom's going to call you later and let you know that it's okay," Liam said as we got out of the van.

When Betty left, we walked up to our house and carefully looked around for any intruders that might be waiting for us.

"That's funny," Liam said, reaching around in his pocket.

"What is?"

"I can't find the key."

"Did you put it somewhere else?"

"No. I swear I put it in my pocket. Maybe…maybe during the fight today, it fell out."

"Check your bag. Maybe you put it in there." We knew where the spare key was, but we didn't want to tell our mother we had already lost the key on our second day alone.

"Wait a minute. Here it is, but—"

"But what?"

"Isn't this the key you found up at the house?" Liam asked, holding it up.

"Looks like it, but I put that one in Max's house." This was getting really weird.

"Then how did it get on the key ring and in my bag?" he said, sounding like he was accusing me.

"I thought we went over this. I haven't been messing around, and neither have you. Right?"

"Right, but let's check it out after we put our stuff inside."

"You're probably right. We'll just make sure those things are still there . . ."

He looked at me.

"What?"

"What if mom found it somehow and put it on there to let us know that she knows."

"Why would she do that? Anyways, she wouldn't even know what the stuff is."

"That makes sense." I felt relieved. "Come on. Let's get rid of this school stuff and get changed and then check."

Liam opened the door and stepped in, dropping his bag in the hallway. I did the same. I reached behind to close the door, and then *bang!* The door suddenly slammed shut, and we both jumped backward, totally startled. Then the really crazy stuff started.

Chapter 13

THE WALLS IN THE house began fading to gray with black streaks, and a greenish fog flowed from the ceiling, as if the drywall were vaporizing into a gaseous cloud. The floor began cracking as the carpet receded to the walls, like a time-enhanced video of an object deteriorating on a nature show. The air grew sour and stale and cold, but I began sweating as I recognized the awful smell from the house we were in the other day.

The sound of wind and crackling came from everywhere. It was followed by glass breaking and objects falling. The windows fell down, and boards began splintering through them, blocking out the little light the cloudy day had provided. We had to get out.

We ran for the door and pulled on the handle together, but it was jammed shut from the ceiling above it moving down. I looked at the window in the hallway, but there was no way we could squeeze through the splintered boards and shattered glass.

"Let's get to the kitchen!" Liam yelled over the noise of crashing and slamming.

The smell intensified, and the gaseous clouds grew thicker and turned a darker green, almost black. There was a wetness in the air and on the walls, making the house seem like it was melting, but the temperature was freezing. We reached the kitchen and living room area to find that it was in the same condition. The kitchen sink was ripped from the cabinets and pressed against the ceiling, dirt came through the floor, raising the pipes and blocking that window. The cabinets were ripped out of place and smashed into the back door, blocking that path. One of the two windows was completely blocked by something on the outside, as if the whole porch had fallen down on it, but the other was only slightly shattered, leaving wicked pieces of jagged glass.

"What the heck is this? An earthquake?" I yelled out.

"Don't know and don't care. I just know we have to get out of here!"

"Yeah, I know. Let's get something to break out that glass, and then maybe we can crawl through," I said, already trying to dislodge a piece of wood from the couch.

I tried grabbing a fireplace prod from the rubble, but it wouldn't budge. I started seeing my breath in the cold air.

"Caleb, why's it so cold?"

"I don't know, but it's getting colder."

With a few more splintering noises and some final groans, the house came to a rest. The dripping fluids were now entirely black, and the gaseous cloud had stopped growing but was still hugging the ceiling. We looked at each other as the house went silent except for our breathing and the slight chattering of our teeth. We were cold, but the initial shock was wearing off. I began to feel petrified.

"Liam..."

He looked at me, and I could see he felt the same way. He shook his head as if to get rid of the feeling.

"We don't have time for that. We have to get out. Okay?"

I gulped as if trying to swallow a frog, and then I nodded.

We looked around. The ceiling looked like it might fall, and so we hurried over to the shattered window. Outside, there was a reddish darkness to the desert, and it looked like a sunset right before an evening storm, but it was only early afternoon.

"What was that all about?" I walked toward Liam. "Hey, wait a minute."

"What?"

"I don't hear Max barking. I hope he's okay."

We both listened but couldn't hear anything beyond a loud and intense dripping noise coming from the back rooms. Suddenly, we heard a shuffling noise, like someone was pushing rocky dirt around broken glass and concrete. It echoed down the hallway and seemed to separate itself from the rest of the house and the silence.

"Liam, what's that noise? It sounds like something moving—"

"Quiet!" he whispered harshly.

The noise kept coming. I wiped sweat from my forehead and then wiped the snot from my nose, caused by the burning sensation in my eyes and nostrils from the smell. Liam was doing the same as we listened.

Chink...chink...chink...shuff...shuff. Chink...chink...shuff. Chink...shuff...shuff...chink...chink...shuff.

Then it stopped. Everything went so completely silent, all I could hear was my heart pounding in my ears. Listening for what seemed like forever, we couldn't hear anything. We tried looking down the hallway to see if anything was there. Nothing.

"Sshhh!"

I'm sure I stopped breathing when we heard a crunching noise, followed by what we knew were footsteps in the rubble. I rushed toward Liam, helping him pull at the piece of wood he was trying to dislodge.

"We've got to get out of here, Liam!"

"I know! Pull!"

The crunching was getting louder as we tried to break the piece of wood free.

"I'll just jump through, Liam; I don't care. Let's go."

"What if you hit it wrong and it goes in your neck or something? Wait. If we have to, we will. Just pull."

We both jerked back and forth, trying to snap the board until it finally gave way. We both fell, rolling closer to the hallway. I wanted to look to see what it was, but my instincts told me not to. Liam jumped to his feet and started breaking the glass and moving it out of our way. We almost had enough room to jump through, so I got ready. Liam jumped first, landing outside as I positioned my hands around the remaining shards of glass so I could pull myself over. I looked outside, and Liam was gone.

"Liam!" I yelled, looking around. Where did he go? The sky looked like the most bizarre sunset I'd ever seen, and in the gloom, I looked down at the ground and readied myself. But there was one problem. There were three hands where my two should be.

Two were on the window frame, and the third was by my chest, barely making contact with my shirt as it moved around. I heard something just behind my left ear and felt damp breath on the back of my neck. Terrified, I didn't want to look because I was sure that if I did, it would get me. I kept my eyes forward.

"Sshhh!"

The hand went down my side, cutting me through my shirt. I felt blood trickle down. That was enough for me, and I flew out the window, literally, and hit the ground hard on the other side, landing on my cut. I saw Liam sitting against the wall of the house underneath the window we just came through. I stood up and turned around, forcing myself to see if the creature was in the window.

Chapter 14

ALL I SAW WAS my reflection in the glass. The whole house was normal, and the sky looked as it had when we got out of the van. I looked across at Liam, and he looked as confused and still as scared as I was, and then he grinned with relief.

"What the heck was that all about?" I managed to say, my voice squeaking like a cartoon character.

"I don't know, but there's no way we both imagined that!"

"Why's this happening?" I was still shaking but feeling relieved as I sat down beside him.

"How do I know, Caleb? But we need to find out, and soon. I heard the noise this time, and I believe you now that you were hearing something. Sorry I kind of didn't."

He paused and looked around as if still trying to be sure that everything was back to how it should be. "You think this has something to do with Gene?" he asked, echoing my thoughts.

"I'm not sure, but I bet he probably knows about it. Maybe that's the reason he's around all of a sudden."

"That makes sense, but why us? Maybe those things we took? Somehow that key got into my bag today."

"But why do you think he or it is trying to scare us? It didn't hurt us, but..."

I looked at my side, and there was no sign of a scratch or any blood. Liam didn't seem to notice my unfinished sentence.

"We should go around front and check things out," he said. I nodded, keen to be busy.

The front of the house looked normal, and the front door was still open, as it had been before all the crazy stuff started. I gingerly poked my head inside the house, and there was no lingering foul smell. We went to check on Max, relieved to find out that he was mostly okay, but he seemed to be cowering at the back of his doghouse. Either he'd sensed what we had experienced or maybe our treasures were bothering him. We decided to move them.

We coaxed him out and both made a big fuss about him until we got his tail wagging furiously again. Then I retrieved our bundle. Liam handed me the rusty key, and I wrapped it with the other things, placing them behind a large barrel cactus at the edge of our driveway. We could easily grab it on our way out.

I was carefully watching the clouds, hoping that it wouldn't start raining before we got to head out. If it even looked like it might rain, our mother probably wouldn't let us go out, even though it wasn't usually like this at this time of year. The clouds covered the mountains now and left only the lower hills visible.

I noticed Max was feeling better now, and even our house looked safe again, telling me that those things were part of what was happening. It wasn't long before our mom came pulling up the driveway, and I knew she'd be curious about why we didn't go inside.

"Hi, Mom!" we both said, perhaps a little too cheerily as she got out of the car. We headed toward her to see if she needed help unloading anything.

"How was your day?" Liam asked.

"Good. And you guys?"

"Okay. Nice and short; nothing interesting at all."

Why did I say that? That's what people say when something *did* happen. We followed our mother to the door, and I worried as we started heading inside. Why wouldn't we tell her about the possible danger? For some reason, I felt I shouldn't, but it still bothered me. Before she could make it to the door, I took a deep breath and went inside first. Nothing happened. Maybe *it* was waiting for all of us to get inside, and then *it* would flip out. I knew that when the door closed, everything would happen again. But it didn't.

"Why are you guys acting so strange? Is there something you want to tell me?"

We tried to act normal because it seemed like everything else was normal and was going to stay that way. I was just hoping that when we headed out for the afternoon nothing would happen when she was alone. My mother turned on the television and sat down. This was usually the only five minutes of the day she got to relax. I decided this would be a good time to ask her about Susan and Krystal. She was happy that we'd found some friends but wanted to talk to their parents first.

I headed outside to meet Liam. I grabbed the stuff by the barrel cactus and tucked it under my shirt until we reached the wash. I thought Liam was right with me as I began heading toward the Three Trees, but when I looked back, he was staring in the other direction.

"Something wrong, Liam? I wanna hurry and get rid of this stuff so we can forget about it."

"I was thinking. Maybe we should put it at Black Rocks instead. We went through the trouble getting it away from the Three Trees already. Besides, what if someone like Gene comes looking for us again and finds it? At least up there, we can deny it, because we almost never go there. The paperwork and the knife are what I'm nervous about."

"Okay, sure, but I told Mom we were going to the Three Trees."

"Even better," he replied with a grin. "She thinks we're going there, so no one will be looking for us at Black Rocks."

I knew the perfect spot for them: down in the crevice where even I could barely fit. No one would ever find those things there.

We reached Black Rocks undetected and climbed up to the ledge, making our way to the crevice. This time I wasn't going in. I would simply throw the stuff toward the back, where the sun didn't reach. When we reached the crevice, I leaned down and listened. No shush and no other noise except some drops of water.

I swayed my arm back and forth to build momentum and then hurled the paper-wrapped package as far as I could. I expected something to grab my arm, like in a horror film, but nothing did. And it was a good toss. We quickly began to make our way toward the Three Trees, and I was finally feeling better and more relaxed. But after a few steps, Liam stopped.

"What now, Liam? We got rid of the stuff. Let's go."

"Caleb...we need to find out what those camps are all about."

"Today?"

"Let's just go up there a little bit. We can take the hidden route, just to see, you know. I've been wondering why the crazy neighbor watches over it and stops anyone from going there."

"Okay, but just for a little bit, and then let's head back to the Three Trees. Actually, let's just head home and make sure Mom's okay."

"Alright. That'd make me feel better too."

As we made our way over to the camps, I was imagining that maybe the Scouts once used the area as campgrounds and that's why Gene called them the camps, and maybe the neighbor didn't want anyone trashing them. That would make sense and explain why he didn't want Gene up there.

When we reached the hidden path, we pushed aside some of

the debris we had piled and made our way through, pulling it back in place just in case someone happened to follow us. The path was narrow, with steep sides that in most places were too vertical to climb without equipment; I chose not to think about how that would limit our escape options.

The clouds resting on the mountains made the path dark, and all the trees and rocks along the way cast shadows, making my imagination run wild. The trees seemed to be mystical creatures that would snag my ankles at any minute. Every shadow was a hiding place for some wild animal or a horrific monster. Most of the trees seemed to be dead along the path, making it feel like nothing alive made it through there. A great place for the shush monster to live.

After a good hike, the hidden path joined the main wash again so we could use either pathway from this point and made another rock pile to mark it. We learned from the early years of hiking with our father that marking trailheads and other turnoffs could help you find your way. We decided to stay on the path we were on and soon reached a tight bend that required us to climb up an almost perfectly smooth rock formation about four feet tall. At the top, pools of water had gathered from previous rains or the natural springs that lay up ahead.

"Hey, Liam, you think we could drink that water?"

"Only if we had to. We don't know what's in it." I knew that; I was just trying to break the silence.

The wind was blowing harder now, meaning we were near the end of the path, where it would fan out across the hills, rolling with the ridges from one runoff to another. The clouds seemed low enough to touch, resting just above the wash and pushing through trees on the ridge and leaving sparkles of dew on the branches.

"Maybe we should call it a day, Caleb. We got pretty far up here, and there's no way we would hear Mom from here."

"I think we're already beyond that. Maybe a few more minutes, and then we'll make a rock pile and turn around."

"Okay, but only a few more minutes. It looks like it's going to rain, and we'll be in big trouble."

"I was thinking the same thing, and I know she'll be watching for it too."

We could now see the base of the larger mountain approaching as we climbed a short distance up the side and onto the ridgeline; we had traveled further than we thought. The hills rolled with wavelike patterns, dipping down into ravines and then back up several times until a range of higher hills broke the rhythm. There was little vegetation on the ridgelines in comparison to the thickness of trees and bushes in the ravines.

The clouds were making it difficult to see far, but we looked for any signs of the camps. I don't know who saw it first, but we both pointed at the same time. Near some white rocks, rising from a ravine, we could see a man-made structure. It looked to be intact and fairly tall, as if it was rising above the ridgeline. I knew it was the camps, but there was no way we could go there today.

"Look at that." I pointed ahead.

"Yeah, I see it. The camps," he answered grumpily, as if I thought he was stupid.

"No, not that. Over there."

He followed my hand. I was pointing toward the nearby hill quickly disappearing with the oncoming rainfall. The way it consumed the hill let us know it was heading our way, and fast. The steep ravines and wash ways would become dangerous places to be in case of flash floods, but they were our quickest route.

"Oh crap!" Liam yelled. "We gotta move, or we're busted."

"Well, come on!" I headed down the slope.

Once in the hidden pathway, we hurried along past our first rock pile, sliding down the smooth rock slope and toward our hidden entryway. Lightning flashed across the sky, and the trailing thunder followed quickly. I was thinking that we might not have time to place our covering back in place since the rain was right on top of us and the lightning was more intense. When we made it to the entry, we took our chances anyway and covered the pathway. Moving faster now, we barely made it to Black Rocks before feeling the first few raindrops.

I figured we had just run about a mile and a half, considering all the twists and bends in the wash, so we had to slow down. I looked to see how Liam was doing, and I noticed him looking back again—this time at something moving around from behind a tree.

Chapter 15

"I DIDN'T WANT TO SCARE ya kids, but I just need to talk to ya real quick," said Robert.

I reached down and grabbed a rock. I could see Liam was already armed with one.

"Don't come any closer, Robert, or we'll throw these rocks right in your face!" I meant to say "head," but it actually sounded worse. I would rather get hit in the back of the head than in the face, so I stood by my words.

Seemingly unperturbed, he stopped to look at the rain.

"You kids're running from the rain, are ya? I imagine your mommy would be worried, so I won't keep ya long."

"What do you want?" Liam yelled, maybe hoping a neighbor might hear.

"I want to tell ya something," he said as he pulled a handkerchief from his pocket and blew his nose.

"Keep your hands out of your pockets, or you won't have a nose to blow after this rock smashes it!" Liam yelled even louder than before, raising the rock higher. Both of us were probably more tense than usual, but then we'd had the experience in the house earlier.

"Sorry. Didn't mean to freak you out. Okay. Look, hands out." Robert held his hands up like he was being arrested and stepped back, which was comforting. I think he knew he had to explain himself and quick.

"So, what do you want to tell us? Hurry up because I'm not planning on getting stuck in the rain." I said.

"I just want to warn ya."

"About what? Is that a threat?" Liam said arching his arm back to throw the rock. Robert flinched and waved his hands in front of his face either to block the possible oncoming rock or to gesture that he meant no threat.

"No, no. Just about what's happening. I heard some stuff from my buddy. You know. Gene." Robert began lowering his arms.

"We've heard about Gene. He came to our house, and we don't want him around." I said, lowering my rock a little. I felt less threatened and more curious.

"Listen, you guys." Robert nervously looked around. "Gene's evil. Me, I'm stuck with 'im because my brother's pals with 'im. I don't like the stuff he makes Dale do, so I try to change that. People don't just be going and disappearing around Gene—he makes 'em. He does these things somehow. I bet ya since that first day we all saw you two is when Gene knew you'd be up to something. He knows things. I...I heard 'im talkin' 'bout ya."

"What did he say that makes you think he thinks we're up to something?" I asked, confusing myself with the way I asked the question.

"He thinks you two took something...said he could...taste it..."

"Taste it? Like, how?" Liam asked. But I shuddered.

"Don't know," Robert said, dropping his arms to his sides with a sudden helpless look on his face. "He just knows things. He was a really good professor and the like at one time. He did all kinds of weird research, and everyone reckons it ate 'im up. They say he found something, made 'im go all wacky. Next thing ya know, he gives this thing to some guy, and he goes crazy. Then another guy, and he goes nuts. Whatever it is, it ain't right. What he's doing and all, I had to warn ya. He'd probably hurt me or even kill me if he found out, but I took my chances waiting up here for ya."

"How'd you know we would be up here?" Liam asked. I was curious too.

"You mess with this stuff, and you get a type of sense about it. At least with others that have some of the stuff. That's how Gene finds others to help him."

We were confused, but the storm was getting closer, and raindrops were coming more frequently.

"Okay, look," Robert said, now pacing in the wash. "This stuff he fools around with has some bad 'n' good stuff to it. It makes 'im smarter, stronger, and younger, I guess, from what I can make of it. He looks like a skeleton most the time, but I've seen 'im throw Dale around, and he's bigger 'n me. Heck, I think Dale's about two sixty, and Gene can't weigh more than a buck forty. Thing is, it also makes him act like he's more out there. Lost."

"You're losing us, Robert, and the rain's coming too. So hurry up." I backed away, toward home. Liam was doing the same.

"Okay, okay. I don't know how else to say it. I guess I should've thought it better before tellin' some young kids."

"What's that supposed to mean?" Liam said angrily.

"Just let him say his bit, Liam. We don't have the time."

"Thanks. Appreciate your—"

"*Shut up!*" we both yelled, and he held up his hands again.

"Okay. Gene gets these things from places and uses 'em to do something. He's spent years gatherin' em. No idea how many or how long. Sometimes they're wrong, like the wrong pieces to a puzzle, and this makes him weirder, crazier, and even seems to make him sick. But, when he does have one, it doesn't always get to 'im right away. Sometimes it takes a while. He don't know which one's good or bad for 'im, so he uses other people to find out. When he finds out, well... people up and disappear. Then I reckon he knows how to use 'em."

"We have to go, Robert. I guess... thanks for telling us this, and tell Gene to leave us alone because we didn't do anything," I said, stepping back toward home. I didn't trust him and couldn't believe he only came to warn us.

"I'm sorry, but I won't tell 'im that since I can't say I been talkin' to ya. Thing is, I wish I could get away too because I'm scared to death of what he might do. Don't tell anyone you saw me because if Gene found out... well, something horrible would probably happen to me. I had to risk tellin' you two boys, though. Thinking about it and you two kids, I just couldn't live with myself if I didn't try. Hurry on and get home now, before the rain really hits."

As we ran toward home, I took a quick look back at Robert. I could see him coughing violently into his handkerchief before looking up toward the sky. Maybe he was hoping a bolt of lightning would come down and relieve him of his misery. I could hear the rain hitting the ground just behind us. We were going to get a heck of a storm.

"Hey!" I heard Robert yell. "Watch out for the kissing bugs! When they're around, he probably is too."

I shuddered as I remembered the kissing bugs in the old house. That just could've been natural infestations that occur in old buildings, but there were an awful lot of those miserable creatures.

Running as fast as we could, we barely made it home before the storm hit in full force. As we sprinted down the driveway, our mother was outside, getting ready to ring the bell. Seeing her out there was a relief because I knew she hadn't yet been trying to getting our attention to come home yet.

"Sure came in quick!" Mom yelled to us as the first drops of rain began pelting the roof of the house. We made it inside just as the heavens seemed to open and pour down rain. In the kitchen, she got us some milk and cookies and asked us what we were going to do the rest of the day. We were just telling her that we hoped the rain might not be around too long when she asked about the damage to Liam's bag.

"I guess I just grabbed it weird," Liam replied, tapping my leg under the table as a signal for me not to say anything. I thought it sounded like a really weak excuse, but she just gave him a look and went back to doing the ironing after telling us to put our bags away in the closet.

As I picked my bag up from the hallway floor and headed into our room, something compelled me to look inside. I reached in and felt something metal shifting around. I brought out my hand, holding the rusty key and nail. When I turned to show Liam, he already had the knife in his hand.

With a shake of his head to say to keep quiet, he quickly shoved it back into his bag, and I did the same before we pushed them as far back in our closet as we could. I know I threw them into that crevice. I suggested that we get more information, and that meant going back to the house to look through the boxes for possible clues. I was sure that was where the answer might lie.

"Yeah, I guess," Liam agreed. "And I think we should call them tokens, you know, to make it easier to talk about them."

"Sure, but how did they get back to us, though? I mean even if they are the tokens Gene is looking for, why did they appear back with us?"

"I don't know. Maybe it's a curse or something?"

"Maybe something from the camps, you know, something that happened a long time ago."

"You could be right, but we'll try to make our way to the house tomorrow unless it's still raining."

"Sounds good to me," I replied. But when I thought about going back there, I wasn't sure my suggestion had been a good one.

Chapter 16

THE NEXT DAY, THE rain had gone, and we made a quick stop at the Three Trees to figure out a plan for approaching the house. While we were there, we saw the crazy neighbor guy drive down the road and out toward town; this might help if we decided to head back toward the camps.

We decided to try a different route that ran closer to a neighbor's house to avoid being seen from Susan's in case her parents were watching. This would be risky because we knew the neighbor had dogs and horses, so we'd have to be extra careful not to startle the horses and hope the dogs were tied up.

"Looks clear from here on out," Liam said, climbing down the tree to our platform.

"Good. I think we should go, grab what we can, and take it to Black Rocks. Up there, we can take our time looking through it."

"What if we have the same problem with the new stuff we take? Like we do with the...tokens."

"I know, but we can't keep risking going into that house when we need information. One of these days, we're going to get caught."

"I just think that carrying all that stuff would be a lot of work. I mean, there was several boxes and even furniture with stuff in it. We can't take it all."

"Yeah, but we can skim through and take only what looks important."

"I like that better."

The neighbor's house looked like it was clear of any wandering eyes, but I was nervous that I couldn't see the dogs; maybe they had a pen for them in the back. When we reached the base of the hill, we made our ascent with just as much caution as we did the last time. There wasn't much vegetation on this side, and we walked fast but steady and followed the shadows from the clouds to help conceal us.

As we reached a large clearing on the side of the hill, we took a moment to make sure again that we couldn't see anyone watching us. Then we heard a dog bark. And then another. Then a third.

I could see the neighbor's dogs standing just behind their house. They were not in a pen. We started walking again. After several steps, the first dog started running toward us. A few seconds later, the other two decided to follow.

"Hurry up! Let's get to the house!" Liam yelled, starting to run.

No longer concerned about the neighbors, we ran straight across the clearing and toward the house. Most of the dogs out here were for protection and could be vicious if you weren't familiar to them. When I reached the other side of the clearing, I could see the first dog was already starting to cross it. I saw Liam jump through the window as I continued running toward the house, removing my bag to throw through the window first.

"Run, Caleb! It's right behind you!"

Just as I heard this, I felt a nip at my shoe and almost tripped. The dog yelped; my foot must have kicked its mouth when it tried to bite me. I tossed my bag in and jumped through the window as the first dog slammed against the skirting of the house, causing dust to fly up. The second dog jumped, landing halfway through the window. It was trying to pull itself in. It didn't snarl or growl because it was concentrating too hard to not fall back out the window. Fortunately for us, the dog lost this battle and fell.

Eventually things went quiet, and we went to the window and looked out. The dogs didn't seem to want us anymore, and they just sniffed around the house and took turns urinating on the walls and some of the debris and rubbish in the yard.

"Weird, huh? It's like they lost our trail or something." I waved my hands about to see if the dogs noticed.

I could tell that Liam was thinking about what I said before checking to see if anyone happened to be in the house this time. It was empty, just us two, but we kept in mind that the dogs were just outside so we tried being as quiet as possible.

The wire on the closed door across the hallway was still holding it shut, and I felt drawn to open it again. As I began walking toward it, the sounds of the world seemed to drift away. The smell of the house was becoming faint, and my head felt fuzzy and soft, like I was falling asleep.

"Caleb, stop! No one's here, so don't worry about that door."

This snapped me out of the trance, and we both headed back to the first room. Anything we needed to find was likely in there. The rest of the house was fairly empty. If something looked important, we stuffed it into our backpacks and then discarded the rest, managing to search through it all rather quickly.

While Liam worked on his last box, I made my way to look at the three chairs. I wondered again why the two ordinary-looking chairs seemed to face the third, more distinguished one. They seemed to be set up to make the one chair the focal point, so I decided to sit in it to see what it felt like.

The chair felt old, really old. I had trouble making out the engravings on the side. I wiped the dust off, revealing carvings of human faces and entire human bodies in different postures as if they symbolized something. Looking at the carved faces, I couldn't help but feel pity for the expressions they held.

I was so caught up in this latest discovery that I hadn't noticed the wire come loose from the door, allowing it to open a few inches. Only when I heard it creak did I look up. Several kissing bugs came out toward me, like they were waiting for me to be vulnerable, and I quickly stood up and began to go back to Liam. I had no idea how the wire came off the door and wasn't about to find out.

"Here," a child's voice said from the dark room.

I stomped a kissing bug in front of me and ran to the door, thinking someone might need help. I swung the door open and felt ready for anything except for the nothing that was there.

"Sshhh." This time it was behind me.

I quickly turned around after closing the door behind me, and there, in the middle of the three chairs sat a small boy. He appeared to be around my age, but smaller, like he had mild dwarfism. He was dressed out of style for the times, and I could tell he was looking at me, even though his black hair hid most of his face. I thought for a moment it might have been the face in the window, but it wasn't. The eyes were dark instead of blue.

He remained silent as he stared at me until the door began creaking open again. I looked at the door to make sure nothing else was there, and when I looked back, he was gone. I ran to the first room to tell Liam. He was just standing by the window and looking out at the sky.

"Hey, Liam, there's a small kid in here."

"What?" he asked, spinning around.

"I was looking at the chairs and in that dark room because I thought I heard something. When I turned around, there was this kid sitting on the floor by those chairs."

"As ridiculous as that sounds, I believe you. I thought I heard you tell me to run just a minute ago. I got to the window and realized you weren't here or even in the house at all. You were gone, just like the other day."

"I never left. I was in the other room the whole time. Do you think that has something to do with the dogs acting like we're not here anymore? I mean, that's how it seems."

"Maybe. But right now I think we should get the heck out of here and not come back," he said, looking as scared as I felt. "We pretty much went through everything, and I know you got a good pack of stuff."

"A little bit but not much. But I think you're right. We should leave this place to itself."

We stood by the window, looking out at the storm clouds twirling around. Because of the way they looked, I wondered if it was possible for tornadoes to reach us here. Most likely not in the mountain area, but it was not impossible.

We decided to use a door on the side of the house, hoping that the dogs were still busy around the back. When I couldn't hear them anymore, I hoped they'd given up and gone home. The front door was barely hanging on its hinges, and we were careful when we opened it. We didn't want it falling off and not allowing us to close it if the dogs came. Unfortunately, when Liam began pushing the door open, it crashed down to the ground.

We stepped slowly outside, looking for the dogs, and I could now hear them scuffling around the other side of the house. Then the scuffling stopped as a large golden chow chow rounded the corner and headed right toward us. It was growling and barking at the same time, while the other two dogs came running over, bumping into each other like they were in a race to get us.

We ran back inside and headed toward the first room. Once we got inside, we pulled the door shut as best we could, and I reached for a box to jam against it. The first dog hit the door, and we braced ourselves against it. One box wouldn't be enough weight to give us time to escape, and now the other two dogs hit the door, almost knocking it down. We would have to get the dresser over to the door to keep it shut while we made a break for it out the window.

I kept dragging boxes over to the door, hoping it would be enough to help Liam, and when the dogs stopped for a moment, I seized the opportunity to go for the dresser. Luckily, it was easier to push versus dragging the boxes, and once I had it in place, Liam and I stepped back from the now-silent door. Then came a yelp from one of the dogs.

Another yelp was followed by something banging around, and I could hear the dog's claws dragging against the wood floor as it fought back against whatever was pulling it.

Bang! Bang! More yelping followed the crashing noises.

I could hear one dog panting and whining just on the other side of the door and wondered if it was watching the other dogs while the others seemed to be fighting something. I stood on top of the dresser and tried to look through the crack at the top of the door to see what was going on. I caught a glimpse of one of the dogs being pulled backward from the door but couldn't see what was dragging it. The dog whined and scratched at the floor, trying to get traction to free itself before it was taken out of view. Then I heard a series of smashing noises accompanied by the dog yelping in pain.

The chow chow that remained began whining and then threw its heavy, muscled body against the door, throwing me off balance. I fell to the floor. It charged again, breaking through a wooden panel on the door and sticking its head through in a desperate effort to escape whatever was on the other side. It scratched frantically, trying to dig to make the opening bigger. Its face started stretching back as if something was pulling at it by its ears. The white of its eyes became fully exposed before receding into a squint because its skin was too tight to allow the eyes to remain open. Then it was gone.

Tentatively, I peered through the hole the dog had made and saw it slam up into the ceiling and then back down to the floor, yelping loudly each time it made impact; there was no sign of its attacker and then no sign or sound of the dog. A light breeze came twirling through the hole and into the room as silence ensued.

Bang! Crash! The dresser came flying across the room and what remained of the door followed it.

Chapter 17

THIS WAS OUR CUE to leave, and we jumped out the window before running down the hill with no concern that the neighbors might catch a glimpse of us. Thinking about the dogs, I cursed myself for not bringing our weapons. From now on, we would always be carrying them, even to home, but we would just have to hide them before getting too close to the house.

When we got to the Three Trees, we climbed up to the main platform and got our breath back before talking.

"So what happened?" I asked, still feeling like I was shaking.

"I've no idea, but it sure did something horrible to those dogs. Did you see anything from on top of the dresser?"

"Not really. I saw the other dogs getting dragged away but couldn't see anything else. I think the chow knew something was coming, but the first two were caught by surprise. Did you see the chow's face? It looked like its skin was going to rip right off its head. What do you think was in there?"

"Honestly, Caleb?"

"Yeah. Honestly."

"I think it was the same thing from our house. The voice or whatever you want to call it. And now you say you saw some kid?"

"Yeah, but I couldn't see much of him. I mean, it was like he was trying to hide his face with his hair. The weird thing is it seems like he doesn't belong here in our time, and he looked small for a kid his age."

"What? You know how old he is?" he asked, snapping his head toward me.

"No, just saying. Something about him looked a little different. His clothes were weird, too, all tattered and torn and worn out, like he'd been rolling in the dirt or something. He just looked...I don't know...dusty, I guess."

"It could have been from the house."

"The house didn't seem dusty except for the floor, and he was dusty all over."

"So what else?"

"It was kind of weird. Even when I was in the same room, right there with this kid or thing—"

"We should call him Dusty," Liam said, interrupting me as usual. "You know, because he's dusty."

"You want me to keep telling you?"

"Yeah."

"Okay, then don't interrupt."

"Sorry."

"Well, like I was saying, I was in the same room with him, and he didn't do anything to me. You know, he didn't hurt me or threaten me, like maybe he did with the dogs. I think maybe he was doing that to the dogs."

"Maybe, but he'd have to very strong, and you said he was only a small kid."

"Whatever. Dusty seems to be the only other thing that was there. Still, why? Why would he do that? There's another thing bothering me now."

"What's that?"

"The shushing. Is it him? And if it is, why's he doing it?"

Liam had no answer to that, and I got the chills just thinking about Dusty. Maybe the shushing was a warning because it usually accompanied something crazy happening. I began weaving a web of ideas in my head, concluding that perhaps Dusty was hiding from something. Maybe he shushed us trying to prevent these crazy things from happening.

I went over it with Liam, and he agreed it made more sense than the possibility of Dusty causing everything. He seemed too small. We only had a few more days before returning to school, and we still knew very little. We agreed that we needed serious help.

Liam was sitting there with a blank face, kicking his legs in the air and looking in the direction of the camps.

"Why do you think that guy tries so hard to keep people away from the camps?" he asked.

"I don't know, but it could be that it's his property. Maybe that's the only reason."

"I think we should try talking to him, even if he doesn't know anything. I forget his name."

"I hear Mom and Betty say it sometimes. I guess I never really pay attention when they're talking about adult stuff. It reminded me of a wrestler. The one with the snake."

"Jake." Liam suddenly smiled. "Let's go talk with Jake."

"Okay, but I saw him leaving earlier. Remember?"

"Well, let's just hang out until we see him go by again. We'll kill some time looking at the stuff we got."

"What if he gets mad and tells on us or tries to shoot us?"

"If he gets crazy, we'll just act like we didn't know. Play dumb and hopefully nothing will happen."

"If you say so." I wasn't convinced. "Anyways, let's look at the stuff."

I looked again at the picture I had grabbed the other day, the one that reminded me of the amusement park. Now I knew it was the camps, but parts of it looked different. There were fewer trees, and I knew from seeing other photos of the area that this lack of trees was common a hundred years ago. Most of the papers were just bills and useless information.

Liam opened an envelope that contained more pictures. That's when we saw him. Dusty.

There he was, clear as day, standing with several adults and children with the large mountain in our valley as the background.

"Does it say anything on the back?" I asked, desperate to snatch the photo from his hand.

"It looks like a date, but that's it. I think it says, October eleventh, 1896." Liam flipped the picture from front to back several times.

"Well, that finally explains Dusty."

"What does?"

"He's dead, but somehow here. He's right there next to that girl in 1896," I said, pressing my finger on Dusty's image in the picture.

As excited as I was, I was starting to feel really scared again, and I could tell Liam was feeling the same way. Dusty was a ghost or at least something like a ghost, and we now knew that he came from the camps and that Gene wanted something from the camps. I was pretty sure that Dusty was trying to warn us about something.

We'd certainly moved forward in our investigation, but not by that much. We both agreed that Dusty, the camps, the tokens, and Gene were all connected, but what was watching us before Dusty came around and before anything strange happened, like it had after school?

The next couple of hours went by without incident. No crazy encounters or visits from half-mutilated dogs or ghostly visitors. Then we saw Jake's truck flying down the road, so we headed straight up to his house, still not sure what to ask him or whether he would talk to us.

Chapter 18

I WAS TRYING TO IMAGINE what kind of person Jake was. Neither of us had really met him before and had only gone to his house once or twice over the years. Even then, we had waited in the car while my mother talked to him.

We came to an area in the wash by his house and decided to head directly up his driveway. It was barren on both sides, with only some small mesquites bordering the path of plowed dirt that designated the path with its contrasting colors. The sunlight that managed to break through the clouds seemed to reflect these colors, blinding us.

This began to agitate me. "Did he make his driveway like this just to piss people off?"

"I doubt it, Caleb, but it is awfully bright."

I tried to avoid looking down at the reflective surface as we made our way closer to his house. I could finally make out some features of Jake's house as we rounded the last turn in the driveway. Rattlesnake skins hung from the barbwire fencing strung throughout and piles of rocks were stacked everywhere. Cow bones and other decorations also littered the yard, making me wonder if he was once a rancher or something. Maybe this was just his way of decorating, like many suburban homes use gnome statues or twirling flamingos.

The house had a lonely, abandoned feel, but the yard decorations added life when the wind blew into them. It was hard to concentrate on any one object without becoming distracted by another twirling or reflecting elsewhere. Some people use this tactic to keep certain animals away, and maybe Jake used it for the same reason. It seemed to work on the two of us.

We stopped a short distance from the house to look around, and I had a bad feeling in my gut that we were being watched again. I started questioning if maybe he had a dog since I didn't want a repeat of the earlier incident. I couldn't see any sign of a dog, so I started moving again toward the house, and Liam did the same.

The house itself was a basic brown adobe with a porch wrapping around most of the front and sides. It looked clean, and there was no trash, no stink, and no noise. That bothered me. I couldn't hear a radio or television or anything letting us know that someone was possibly home. We froze again and listened. No noise except the trinkets and wind chimes hanging around, trying to find rhythm to a mysterious song. Still there was no sign of Jake.

"Should we just walk up there and knock? I don't see any dogs, and I haven't seen any sign of him either." I looked at Liam to see what he thought.

"Let's just hang out for a minute and see if we see anything. If nothing happens, we can head up there and knock. Besides, down here we aren't easy targets yet."

As we stood there waiting, the light sounds of the wind chimes began mesmerizing me. I was thinking that maybe Jake was inside, just waiting to see if we would make the first move. After about a minute, I decided I was done waiting and started making my way toward the house.

"Wait, Caleb. Get back here and wait a minute."

"No, we've been waiting long enough. If he's in there watching us, he's probably just getting suspicious or something. Come on."

As I turned back from Liam and continued toward the house, I noticed something move on the swing chair hanging from the porch rafters. I began stepping back. Liam must have also seen it because he was doing the same. I knew what we were both thinking. Dog.

"Ha, ha!" came a chuckle from the swing chair. "I wondered when one of you was going to make a move. To be honest, I didn't think it would be the younger one. Been watching you coming up the driveway; you two just stood there like deer in the headlights. Come on up here. You two are alright. I've been watching you walking around out here for a while. The last few days, I've heard you just down the wash. You know, noise travels." He scratched his head.

So this was Jake. He was an average-sized guy with a very tan complexion. He wasn't crazy-looking as we imagined from what people said about him and was actually clean-cut with just some mild facial stubble.

As we neared the porch, Jake was sheltering his eyes from the sun with one of his hands as he tried getting a better look at us. The clouds seemed to break in the sky right above his house, allowing a golden flow of sunlight to shine down on the yard. Jake's yard looked brighter than anywhere in the valley.

"I'm Caleb. This is my brother, Liam."

"I thought so. I know your mom," he said, walking across the porch and stepping down to where we stood. "Most people around here don't bother with me, so I tend to just keep to myself. Been living up here before anyone else, and no one wants to come hang out and talk to me for some reason."

"Maybe it's because they're jealous of all the cool stuff you got." I pointed around the yard. I liked the way it looked, and it reminded me of stuff I read about and studied besides mythical creatures and animals.

"You like it?" Jake asked, smiling.

"Yeah, I do," I replied, looking around again.

"I like it too. But tell me honestly, is it a little much?"

"No, it's not, and I like it too," said Liam, joining the conversation. "I wish I had some of it at our house. Can't say what it all is or what it means, but sometimes it's nice to keep people wondering. Most people don't like stuff they don't understand."

"Hit the nail on the head with that one. Liam, is it?"

"Yeah, it's nice to finally meet you and actually talk to you," Liam replied, removing his hand from shading his eyes as the clouds took the sun away.

"And you said your name is Kevin?"

"No. Caleb. But don't worry; everyone gets it wrong at first. You should see how some people spell it."

Jake laughed and then scratched at his head again.

"So what brings you two up this way? I've seen the two of you scouting around in the desert here and there but never thought that you would show up here."

"Well, we wanted to meet you, just to let you know we hike around in the desert so you know who we are when you see us."

"Well, I can appreciate that." Jake pulled out a lighter and fired up some bundled brush in a bowl that looked like it was made of clay. "I always like to know who's messing around up here. Can't seem to keep some people away, if you know what I mean."

"Not really. What do you mean, Jake?" I asked, trying to hide the fact that I knew about Gene. The smoking bundle had a strange, pungent smell to it, but for some reason I liked it.

"Salvia apiana," Jake said, noticing I was enjoying the smell as he fanned the smoke with a feather.

"What's that?" Liam asked, moving closer to try and get a better sense of the smell.

"White sage. It mostly grows in California, but it's cheaper and easier to get here compared to sages that come from other areas, like South Dakota."

"Is it like incense or something?" I asked, leaning in toward the smoke.

"Kind of, but it has other purposes."

"Does it keep the insects away, like citronella?" Liam asked.

"That's not really the other reason for it, but I'm sure it helps. I mainly use it for smudging."

He gestured for us to sit down on his porch, making me feel more at ease in our conversation.

"What's smudging?" I asked.

"Some Native Americans believe it helps against evil or with purification. I use it for the same reason a person might carry a rabbit's foot. You know, kind of a 'why not?' or 'just in case' type of thing. Sometimes I use it because, well...I believe in it."

The smoke seemed to dance around on the porch before dissipating out into the desert, and I was starting to feel lost in its patterns as the sunlight filtered through the clouds, making the smoke appear more clearly. A calm breeze blew through the porch, and a sudden gust of wind that muffled my hearing.

"Boo!" Jake shouted, breaking the silence. We both jumped, startled back into reality.

"What'd you do that for?" Liam said, shaking off his surprised look.

"Noticed I was losing you guys and wanted to get back to the conversation."

"Well, we're sorry to be a little edgy, but we got reason to be lately," I said apologetically.

"Yeah, I hear ya. Everyone should be a little that way with, you know, him around again." Jake had a weird look on his face.

"You mean Gene?" Liam answered as if he had just guessed a trivia question right.

"You said it, not me, champ." Jake began laughing; it almost sounded like a cough.

I looked at Liam while Jake had his laughing fit, wondering if my brother was thinking the same thing. This guy might actually be nuts after all.

"You guys look thirsty. You want a drink or something?" Jake said, heading inside his house. "You guys can have some water or some Coke."

"I'll take a Coke, please," I said as the screen door slammed shut behind him.

"Anything for you, Liam?" he yelled out.

"No, thanks." Liam gave me a questioning look, as if to ask if I thought this guy was okay. I answered with a shrug.

"In a couple years, you guys can have some of this or a beer," he said, a bottle and a glass of dark liquid in his hand, "but for now here's a Coke for the man Caleb."

I thanked him as I took the cold can from his hand, and we raised our drinks to each other.

"So, you two go to school right down the road some?"

"Yeah, since we were little."

"I hear it's got good teachers for the most part, but some of the kids are punks. You don't seem like punks. I can usually tell. I went to that school a long, long time ago. Some of the kids were punks back then too."

"You went to school there?" we asked simultaneously.

"Yup, been out here for a real long time. My family owned ranch property, but the corporations came in and bought most everyone out. Believe it or not, and don't be telling anyone"—he leaned in closer and whispered—"I'm actually pretty rich."

"Really?" I quickly stopped before saying anything rude, like why he lived like this if he was rich.

"How'd you get rich, Jake?" Liam asked, looking around and scanning the trees and bushes in the distance, drawing a curious look from Jake.

"You guys are naturally cautious, aren't ya? Heck, that's a good thing, though. Most people come out here and think it's a zoo where the animals can never get to you. Next thing you know, they're attacked or bitten, and they just can't understand why it happened to them."

He took a swig of his drink and fought back a bitter look as he turned his attention toward the mountains.

"I got rich from the corporations. They paid me for my land and then to shut up. At one time, they wanted to develop the land with homes like that huge neighborhood down the freeway."

I looked at the desert and absorbed its beauty, trying to imagine what it would look like with thousands of houses.

"I hate it when they do stuff like that," I said. "Where do people think all the animals go when that happens? I mean, out here, they can move around because the houses don't block them."

"You seem to have a good understanding for your age."

He took another drink and then set his glass down on an old green table. It kept wobbling, so he gave it a "whoa" gesture, like the table would listen and stop.

"So what really brings you here? I'm sure you didn't just stop by because you thought I was lonely."

He'd caught us on the spot when I was hoping to slowly work our concerns and questions into the conversation.

"Well, go ahead. I know you guys have been wandering around up this way. Even when I can't see you, I can hear you. I'm not going to tell on you, but I overheard you and was curious what you're looking for."

"So people have to be looking for something? They can't just be hiking around?" Liam responded defensively. I think he was upset because we were trying to be sneaky in the desert, and Jake knew we were there.

"Calm down!" he said with a smile, "I said I heard you guys talking. I didn't mean to intrude or nothing, but you were walking on my property when I heard you. I was just curious. Now tell me the truth. Is it the camps?"

"Can you tell us about them?" I asked nervously, unsure of what his reaction might be.

"I don't like people going over there because they might get hurt. That's my main concern. Not to say you two would get hurt and try to sue me, but some people do weird things for money when they know you got it."

Liam got up from the steps and walked over to sit closer to Jake.

"We heard about them and were curious. We also thought they might help answer some things. We couldn't ask anyone because we didn't want them knowing where we heard about them . . . for certain reasons."

"You mean you didn't want to ask that scoundrel Gene or his boys?" Jake said, smiling.

"Yeah," Liam answered, sounding embarrassed.

"Well, he's one messed up fella, and I've had problems with him forever," Jake said, standing up and pouring another drink. "That guy's got more problems than I got rocks in my yard."

"Can you tell us about him and the camps?" I asked.

"He used to live around here. Smart guy, I hear, but then he got wrapped up in some cult stuff or something and then kind of lost it. You know he's older than me, right?" Jake looked toward the camps.

"No. I thought he was probably about as old as the other two he's with." I rummaged through my backpack for the pictures to show Jake. As I reached around, the tokens fell out onto the porch.

"Uh-oh," Jake said looking at the tokens.

"What happened?" Liam asked, not realizing that I dropped the tokens.

"You two got yourself into it also. Didn't ya?"

"We think so. That's why we're looking for some answers," I answered.

"How deep?" Jake said, wiping sweat from his forehead.

"We don't know how deep, but we did...and got these...by accident." I said, picking up the tokens and putting them in my backpack.

"Accident's still not good, and I'm not trying to scare you two, but that's probably the only reason you're still alive."

"Why's that?" I felt scared but excited at learning some more.

"Because people who go looking for this stuff usually have one of two problems. First, they don't know what they're doing and mess around with it. Or second, they're working with someone who does know and that person's using them. They try to figure it all out for themselves, like Gene, and when that happens, the other guys get really mad. I think because...well...they probably feel like someone's stealing from them."

"What other guys?" Liam asked.

"What do you want to hear about first, the camps, Gene, or the others?"

"I guess the camps. That's the main thing we've been wondering about," I answered.

"Well, it doesn't begin there, but that's the best place for us to start."

Chapter 19

I HAD NO IDEA WHAT he meant by that; maybe this was a lot bigger than I originally thought. Either way, I wanted to hear about the camps and was happy to finally get some information.

"Can you tell us a little?" Liam asked.

"Well, I'll tell you a lot. It seems you boys could use it. I don't usually talk about it to anyone. Try to keep that in mind before you tell anyone what crazy old Jake said."

We both nodded to show that we understood. And as I drank my Coke, he explained things to Liam and me.

"The story of the camps goes something like this. A little while before my granddaddy owned this land, it was full of mining claims. People would pay little for land, hoping to get rich. If they found enough gold or silver or copper, the larger mining companies would offer to buy them out. Then they would come in and finish off the job with a bigger labor force. It was kind of an scouting project.

"Before this area was mining claims, the ancient Hohokam people lived around these parts. For hundreds of years, they benefited from the land, and in return, the land took care of them. After the Hohokam sort of vanished, maybe a thousand years ago, other tribes would pass through from time to time before the miners arrived.

"The area that you two keep calling the camps is an old mining settlement that grew to be a little bigger than a camp. There was a water tower, a few small buildings, and a makeshift church-like building up there. Anyways, they got a little bigger than the larger companies planned.

"The little mining settlement had three families who were all partial owners of the original claim, all trying to make a better life. The large mining companies tried to break their spirits by hiring muscle to harass them. The problem was the miners couldn't leave."

"They couldn't leave because they had nowhere else to go," I said.

"Slow down. I'm getting there." Jake laughed a little. "Anyways, they couldn't leave. Some say sickness prevented them, but the truth came out in a journal entry someone found a while back. It said that the hired muscle kidnapped some of the children to persuade the minors to burn down the buildings and leave. That was the ransom. The journal also mentioned they did not intend to give the children back. They would simply do away with them to keep everything a secret—well, as much as possible.

"A few of the children were taken one afternoon when they wandered too far from the mining site. The muscle then left the kids in their hideout, but when they got back, all they found was jimson weed and piles of crushed rocks. The next day, they went out scouting, and through a telescope saw the same children back at the camps. The hired muscle was too far away to be seen with the naked eye, but somehow the children knew they were there. They stood with their hands held out, like they wanted to be taken away.

"Some old records me and my family found at the camps state that the children began acting strange. Holding onto certain possessions like it was life or death. That key and nail I saw fall out of your backpack reminded me of something."

"We just thought they were something we found. No big deal,

you know. Then all this weird stuff happened," I said, showing him the tokens.

"Well, that was mining claim fifty-three, so I doubt it's a coincidence that it's stamped on the head of that nail. I don't think that stuff was supposed to leave there."

When Jake said this, he seemed to be nervous about accidently saying the wrong thing, and I wasn't sure I wanted to hear more of the bad news.

"There was a young girl up there," Jake continued. "When she was a baby, her parents let her play with key rings to make her stop crying. When she got older and lived at the mines, she wanted to be in charge of carrying the keys—a childhood obsession or something. Of course, this wasn't allowed, and so she wouldn't simply take them, the keys had to be hidden.

"She had a brother who was described as having dwarfism and the mind of a young child. He loved drawing, and his father would nail paper down to pieces of wood so he could draw on them without the wind taking it away. That boy always had a few of these nails in his pocket. I believe I also saw a knife fall out of your backpack?"

"Yeah, with a bone handle. Is there something going on with that too?" Liam asked.

"I have no idea. I don't remember anything from the old papers my dad and me looked through, but I could be wrong. Seemed like everything on the paperwork or in the tales is about the kids, and it mentioned some brief information about the keys and nails. It doesn't even mean that I'm right."

"So you think this doesn't have anything to do with the camps?" I said, showing the knife to Jake. As I tried to hand it to him, he retracted.

"Don't touch me with it. I don't want the curse."

"So there's a curse?" I asked, putting it away.

"Well, there's something, but it gets all messed up in the last documents. Whatever was happening to the children didn't seem to affect the parents. They could leave and come back, but the children seemed to be stuck by some invisible barrier. Even when the muscle had kidnapped them, somehow they appeared back in the mining settlement.

"The muscle went back another time, thinking they could harass them or take the kids again; however, when they spied on the area, they couldn't see anyone. They went down to the area to investigate and couldn't find anyone... at first. Everything the people owned was still around, showing no signs that they left, and at first, they thought it was a setup, with someone trying to catch them in the act with a county sheriff or something.

"I say at first because that night, according to a few of the journals, they found the body of one of the kids in their hideout with his eyes and ears pounded through and his lips shut together with nails. Another entry states they found the body of a young girl with most her skin removed from her body. It wasn't sliced off neatly but torn or ripped off."

"This is some messed up stuff. You aren't just fooling with us, are you?" I had to ask to make sure he wasn't just trying to get a rise out of us.

"Just as I read it, I'm saying it. Besides, has anything happened lately that'd make you not believe me?" Jake stared off again toward the camps.

"Sorry," I replied. "Just had to ask."

"The next day, the bodies were gone, and they all thought they drank too much the night before but figured they'd better head to the camps just to be certain. When they arrived, the adults at the camp were standing outside in a circle, surrounding a smaller circle of the children. After a moment of stillness, they all took turns climbing down the mineshaft. The last child to go down turned and looked in the direction of the paid muscle and extended his arms...one last time before heading down in the darkness."

Jake went silent for a moment, like he was building the anticipation.

"Rest of the journal entries say it stormed like hell afterward, and the miners were never seen or heard from again. When the big companies went to claim the abandoned mine, they searched the pit only to find some of the miner's belongings. Nothing more. They could never get anyone to mine there again after the stories got out. They abandoned it and made it all into ranch land, which my granddaddy used for cattle. He fenced off the camp and pulled the water tower into the shaft to help prevent any curious cows from slipping in. Unfortunately, it just got lodged sideways in the top of the pit."

"So that's the camps, huh?" Liam asked.

"Pretty much," Jake said, taking another drink. "Thing is, if it's haunted by those people, now that's one thing, but something worse made the whole thing happen to begin with."

This was a lot to take in. What did this have to do with us? We never went into the camps.

"So that all happened a long time ago," Liam said. "But where does Gene come into play with it all?"

"Well, those boys have been up to no good for as long as I remember." Jake said to Liam. "Seems you two got something that Gene believes is his; otherwise he probably wouldn't be messing with you."

"So if Gene thinks we have something of his, we'll just give it back." I knew it wasn't that easy.

"Have you tried getting rid of the stuff yet?" Jake asked, looking like he already knew our answer.

"Yes," Liam said.

"And what happened?"

"Somehow it came back," Liam answered.

"There you have it. For some reason, your tokens, as you call them, prefer certain people over others." Jake walked off the porch and looked up at the clouds. "You see, Gene knows he can't simply ask for them. In his mind, he has to take them. He has to make sure they have nowhere to return to. Get my drift?"

"You mean he'll make sure they can't return to us because we won't be around. He has to make sure there's no one for the magic, or curse, to return them to," I answered.

"Hit the nail on the head, Caleb, and in this situation that may be literal."

I shuddered at the thought, but my desire for knowledge and explanations still outweighed my fear.

"Why does he act so strange? He was licking some of my blood off the tree the other day. Like he could sense who I was by doing it."

"Well, maybe he's just finally lost it. Or something finally got to him…something to do with his obsession with this place. Maybe he saw something that made him lose it or that he can't let go of."

I didn't understand what Jake was trying to say. It seemed like he was trying hard not to say the wrong thing but confusing us while doing so. Finally, he came up with an explanation about people who die and then return to life. Many of them make statements about something they saw while they were dead. Some say it was so great they didn't want to come back to this world. Some see horrible things, but you never hear too much about that.

He believed that Gene saw this place, although not through a near-death experience. He knew how to control getting there and wanted it more than anything. Maybe he was shown a paradise where he would be powerful. Somehow, he wanted to control the passing between these zones. Some type of gray zone between this world and another.

For the next hour, we talked about Gene and the two guys he had helping him. Jake had more information that he wanted to look through to see if it might help. He didn't seem to want to talk anymore about this gray zone. He said he was protected because of the decorations he used around his yard. We both wished we had some, considering what had already happened at our house, and Jake had never heard of anything like that before. We talked about the tokens and how we thought they were bad. Jake didn't seem to think so, but he gave us something to hopefully help protect us.

"You two keep these to help protect you from evil spirits. It won't do you any good with Gene or his people, but it will help you against the darker powers, if you trust in it and believe." Jake handed me a necklace with some sort of tooth and gave Liam a black arrowhead that was made of what looked like obsidian.

We wanted to stay with Jake and find out more, but the day was already growing late. He said he would stop by and let our mom know it was okay for us to come up to his place anytime. As we headed out, I began realizing what Jake was saying about his decorations keeping him safe. I felt safe there, and I didn't feel paranoid when I was in his yard. Maybe they did form some type of protective veil over the house that the evil couldn't break through.

When we reached the wash, we headed toward the Three Trees. That's when we heard the voices.

Chapter 20

I T WAS THE SOUND of girls. We got out of the wash and hid behind some decaying prickly pear as the voices were getting closer. We didn't think they would try to harm us, but we decided not to take any chances.

"What if it's the little girl from the photo?" Liam asked. "You know, the one Jake was talking about that always was hiding the keys, the one with the ripped-off skin."

"Don't say that. It's probably just hikers or something."

"I'm just throwing out the possibilities of what we might encounter."

He was partially right. Given the circumstances lately, it would be stupid not to consider that something really weird might happen.

The voices grew louder and seemed to stop on the other side of the cactus from where we were hiding. Had they already seen us and were waiting for us to come out? One of them mentioned going to school on Monday, and then I realized who it was.

"Hey, Susan. Hey, Krystal," I said as I stood up from behind the cactus, not realizing how close they were.

Krystal screamed and jumped back while Susan froze in fear but seemed to recover quicker.

"You idiot! Jerk!" Susan tried to hit me, and I moved back just in time. "Why'd you have to startle us like that?"

"I'm sorry; I really didn't mean to startle you. We just didn't know who it was when we first heard you, so we hid."

"What're you two doing up here?" Liam asked changing the subject and defusing the tension "Susan, weren't you grounded or something?"

"No. I'm just on restriction because of the people my parents saw up at that abandoned house. Who knows? They don't make sense anymore, especially my stupid dad. Krystal, being such a smart sweetheart, convinced them that we should be able to go out because we would be around you two. That made my mom feel better."

"Makes sense to me," I said hoping that my agreement would avoid any more attempts to punch me.

"And *anyways*," Susan said, emphasizing that she wasn't done talking, "we wanted to see what you were up to. We know you've been up to something and wanted to hang out. Krystal has been really bothering me about it all week."

I found this strange because I barely knew Krystal, and Liam knew her even less. We were friendly at school, but she was somewhat popular, whereas I was the opposite. Then Liam started the conversation back up.

"You want to see our fort we've been working on? It's just down the way."

They nodded, and we all headed down toward the Three Trees. On our way there, I kept feeling like something or someone was going to be right behind me when I turned around. Because we were still a good distance from the fort, I separated from the others and waited in the bushes to see if anyone was following. It wasn't long before I heard Liam yell out to me, and the girls joined in and kept yelling my name. Did they ever stop and think that when they kept yelling, they couldn't hear anyone calling back?

I only waited a minute and didn't see anyone before running to join them. I could tell that Susan was flustered with me, and she seemed to worry a lot about people, although she was quick to try to hit someone who crossed her. The look on her face seemed to say she must have imagined that the most terrible things were happening to me during that short time.

"I just wanted to see if anyone was following us."

"Well, you can't just do that," Susan said, turning swiftly on her heels and heading down the wash, like she already knew where we were going.

"Sorry. Thought I was helping out," I replied as we all began walking again. I still couldn't shake the feeling of being followed, and it was getting stronger.

As I began wondering if I should bring this to their attention, something landed on my shoulder. I could tell it was wet from the saturation through my shirt and heavy, like it was pushing down. When I reached for it, it clenched down on my shoulder. I looked to see fingers pressing deep into my shirt under my own hand. Before I screamed, I decided to swing around, and when I did, I came face to face with Robert.

His complexion was a mixture of a sunburn and clammy paleness, with beads of sweat trickling down. His bloodshot eyes seemed to pulsate, like they were about to pop, and when he opened his mouth a horrible stench filled the air.

"Gene, spirit, slaves, no way away," he said in one breath, hardly moving his lips.

I jerked away, and he began picking at his face, his fingers popping small boils that I now realized riddled his skin. While he picked and popped, kissing bugs began crawling out of his clothing. They sought his uncovered skin and fought to absorb more of his nutrients by sticking their suckers into his flesh and draining their meals before Robert collapsed. In a panic, I turned to the others only to find that they were no longer with me.

Turning back to Robert's body, I found that he was not lying in the wash with hundreds of kissing bugs feeding on him but was now standing further away and appeared different. He had a mushy texture to his skin, like the kissing bugs put everything back into him, making his skin separate from his body and sag off him like loose clothing.

His eyes carried a blackened emptiness as he gazed up at the sun breaking through the clouds and then back at me. Only the two of us were in the wash, exchanging stares, not sure what the other might do. He never once blinked but would shift his head from side to side, like he was trying to make a decision based on the different perception this gave him.

More and more anxious, I decided to make a hasty retreat. Keeping my eyes on him, I took a step back, and he reached his arm up, pointing at me like he was accusing me of something.

"Hey, it was him!" he said as his mouth lurched open with a slackness that made me think there was no elasticity left in his face. I'd watched too many movies to know what happens when someone sticks around, so I made a run for it.

When I looked back, Robert was gone. Instead, several javelinas decided to join me in my run. Of course, they weren't running with me but after me, and I knew I would have to find a tree. They were quicker than most people thought, and it was no use hiding because they have a good sense of smell.

I could hear their legs kicking up the wash sand as they gained on me. I was frantically looking for a tree to climb—any tree to get me off the ground. In the distance, I saw one that would support my weight and knew if I could just get high enough, they wouldn't be able to see me. I was once told that javelinas have difficulty looking up, and I just hoped this was true. I wanted to turn and see how close they were but feared this would only slow me down.

The panting and grunts of the boar-like creatures grew louder as I made my way over some small bushes. I could hear them right behind me, trampling through the bushes that I was trying to hurdle. They didn't care about the thorns or anything else as long as they got their target. I was approaching the tree fast and had to decide how to get up without slowing down. I could swing around the side and then climb quickly or try to jump.

No time to swing. Just jump.

I began timing my pace as if getting ready to kick a soccer ball. When trying to do this, I accidently crossed my legs and tripped when the tree was only five feet away. Rolling on the ground, I felt slobber splash against my neck. Sand flew in the air as patches of charcoal-brown fur crossed my vision. Once I regained my footing, I found myself back in the wash, and the javelinas were gone.

"Caleb, were you trying to hide from us or something?" Krystal said as she patted dirt and pollen particles off my shoulder.

I was still trying to catch my breath. "Liam, is she kidding around?"

"No, man. We turned around, and you were gone. We waited for a minute and then came looking for you, thinking maybe you were getting sand out of your boot or something, but you were gone again. I thought you might be messing around, trying to sneak up on us."

Krystal came over by me and wiped something off my neck. "Gross, Caleb, what the heck is this?" She shook her hand to get the slime off.

"Don't know. Must have been in the bush or something."

"Looks like dog slobber." I had to admit she was smart, but it wasn't dog slobber.

"Sure does, but how would it get there? It's just some plant dew or sap or something like that," I said as she rubbed her hand in the sand to clean it off.

I saw a look of suspicion in Krystal's eyes and realized that she wasn't buying my explanation. I then looked at Susan, and she was standing with her hands on her hips as if waiting for us to tell what the heck was going on.

"Something weird is going with you two, and we know it started with that Gene guy. There have been people up at the old house, and we think it was you. Liam's acting like he keeps seeing ghosts and now"—she stepped forward and ran a finger disgustedly across my shoulder—"he's got some disgusting slime on him when we're in the middle of a dry desert!"

I started to think we all might be safer if they knew.

"Tell her, Liam," I said and felt a huge sense of relief.

We sat down on some rocks, and Liam recounted all the recent events to them; they seemed to take it pretty well. Of course, their constant joking and initial disbelief at many things made it easier. I wondered if it was right to tell them. What if it put them in danger instead of keeping them safer?

I think Krystal seemed to take it the best as we finished our journey to the fort and the discussion continued. We showed them around and pointed out the areas with booby traps. We tried avoiding any further conversations about the situation and focused on the fort, but we kept finding ourselves talking about it.

The hours passed by quickly at the Three Trees as we talked away, catching up on more everyday things and getting to know each other better. It was nice having two more people around, girls at that. They seemed to really balance out the whole situation. I noticed that

Liam was talking more with Susan, and I was hanging out more with Krystal, but this was no doubt due to the age differences.

Talking to Krystal, I sensed our conversation was leading in a particular direction, and I think that although she felt bad about it, she was nervous that hanging out with Liam and me would make her an outcast too. Then I thought that maybe the tokens came to Liam and me in the first place because we were outcasts.

When it was time to go home, we walked them halfway to Susan's house, feeling protective over them; it was a good feeling. I was also excited to tell our mom we made some friends.

Chapter 21

As I was trying to fall to sleep that night, I had a sudden urge to talk with someone about our situation and wished I could have spoken to Krystal. She seemed to share a more thoughtful approach to resolving things, while Liam and Susan were more inclined to only think of fighting their way to the resolution. I was hoping that we could get back up to Jake's. Maybe he would have some more answers. I couldn't help but feel we got Susan and Krystal involved in this mess, whether or not they wanted to be.

As I tossed and turned, I could hear Liam snoring and knew he wouldn't be happy if I woke him. I was just drifting off when something suddenly made sense, something that would unfortunately keep me up the rest of the night. The tokens were controlling the passing between worlds. That explained things, like why we'd been—well, had almost been—in contact with Dusty.

A little after the morning sun crept into the room through the cracks in the blinds, I heard the sound of birds on the roof, and this woke Liam up. I was so excited that I barely gave him time to open his eyes fully before leaping up onto his bunk and telling him what I thought. He was skeptical at first when I mentioned Dusty, but then I talked about Robert in the wash and how I was the only one there with the javelinas because I was the one carrying the tokens. I also pointed out the fact that stuff could cross from one world to the other, like the javelina slobber.

Liam finally sat up and stretched and then looked pleased with himself. "I think we should call it the shadow zone," he announced, looking proud. "You know … because of the darkness and the blurriness to everything. It reminds me of what Jake was saying about the gray zone, but a little different. It's not so much one way or the other; like black-and-white or gray. Also, it's not just a place but like another world or time, somehow. So, yeah, shadow zone."

"Okay, that works. So the shadow zone can allow things to come back and forth, but I'm starting to wonder how much can come through. Do you think that's how Dusty makes his way around? Do you think he's part of shadow zone, but the tokens allow him to come over to our world?"

"Could be, but before we get way into it, I need some breakfast." Liam crawled out of his bed and then down the rickety ladder from the top bunk.

After breakfast and after doing our chores, we persuaded our mother to let us make it a long day out by taking a packed lunch and taking some extra water. We planned to leave it at the Three Trees and head up to Jake's, hoping he could help us piece it all together. We wondered if he already knew what was going on and was just slow to tell us for some reason.

"Did you notice the clouds changing around again?" I asked Liam, pointing toward the tops of the mountains. "They seem to do it every time we come out in the desert these days."

"I was just thinking the same thing. It's weird how they don't really come from any direction but appear directly over us. You know, it's like in a cartoon when the sad person is followed by the rain cloud. Maybe we're that person, but we're not sad, just in a really bad situation."

"It seems to come around a lot, that's for sure, considering it's usually so hot and sunny here. I was thinking that since we're going to Jake's today, maybe we should talk to him about bringing the girls up next time. I think we should ask him first. I wouldn't want to be rude."

"Probably should. Also, when we get to the Three Trees, I want to check the tokens. I think it would be best if we don't get rid of them right away. But we shouldn't keep them on us all the time. Jake sure didn't seem to like them, so maybe we shouldn't bring them up there."

"I think so too. But I don't think we should hide them in the tree."

"Where can we put them, then? We have to find somewhere that we can get to them and quick, if we need to."

As we continued toward the Three Trees, it clicked. We could hide them in the old fire pit. Nobody would look there, and it would be hard for someone else to tell if the area was recently disturbed. I told Liam, and he agreed.

Once we reached the Three Trees, we began digging a hole in the fire pit. We left the tokens back up in the holes of the tree the day before when the girls weren't paying attention. Reaching a depth that we both felt comfortable with, we decided it was time to retrieve the tokens. Liam, being the faster climber, headed up the tree while I stood guard.

There was hardly any wind, and the air felt stale, like everything was beginning to settle down to Earth again. It was one of those calms that you feel before the storm, and I was hoping that we would have enough time to do what we wanted today. I was just starting to think about Dusty and if he knew how to control these things when I noticed something move out of the corner of my eye.

I motioned for Liam to stop climbing down by waving my hand

and holding out a fist. I was preparing to climb up the tree myself if needed. Nothing moved so I took a few steps to the side, trying to get a glimpse around the tree where I saw the movement... nothing. That is, nothing but a bad feeling.

"What is it?" Liam asked straining to keep hold on the side of the tree.

"Don't know. Just caught a glimpse of something. Can't see anything now, but it doesn't feel right to me. How about you? Can you see anything from up there?"

"No, don't see anything, but I do feel a little strange though. Probably because I'm sick of this stuff."

"Me too." I knew that, in a way, despite it being scary, we both loved it. "But we can't be too hasty, you know."

Liam finished climbing down to the main platform and looked out across the desert. "Why don't you come up here with me until we know the coast is clear?"

"Sounds like a good idea. Watch my back."

I started making my way toward our tree when suddenly I heard a snarling growl coming from behind me. I'm sure I made it up onto that first platform in about two steps and a short, quick crawl.

"The dog! It's a horrible, bloody dog!" Liam screamed out.

I found myself looking down at a partially mutilated dog, the chow from the old house. Its mouth was ripped at the corners, oozing yellow puss, and one ear had almost been ripped off. It hung on the side of its head, like coagulation started healing the ripped ear to open wounds on the side of the dog's head. Its nostrils were ripped back exposing, nothing but two cavernous openings where a normal nose used to be, and its eyes were filled with fury. The dog was full of mange, with dirt and brush stuck to the congealing blood. The dog whimpered in pain but was also growling with agitation because once again it hadn't gotten its prey.

"It almost got you, Caleb. How could you not hear it or see it coming from across the path there?" Liam said pointing to a clear area of knee high grass. I should have seen it. I might not have heard it, but I should have seen it.

We armed ourselves with the rocks and sticks we stored up in the tree as the dog moved erratically around the bottom. I needed to land a good-sized rock on the dog to scare it away, but it kept shifting from side to side and going under branches, making it hard to get a clear shot. Neither one of us really wanted to hurt an animal, but we had to protect ourselves.

Watching it move around, I realized that the dog was no longer just a dog. It was something else, like the javelinas in the shadow zone. These were vessels carrying some sort of evil to get us, and I didn't think the dog had anything to do with Gene; someone else sent it. The amount of evil and horror, like what happened to our house as well as in the old house, seemed to be growing, and my worry was whether this was just the beginning.

I finally thought I had a clear shot of the dog through some branches and took it but missed; looking over at Liam, I could see that he wasn't having any more luck. I was worrying that we might be up in the tree for a long time but was also concerned about the girls. What if they came up and the dog was still here? They wouldn't be safe on the ground.

"I don't think it's the same dog anymore, if you know what I mean," said Liam.

"Yeah, I kind of feel that way too. Just look at it. It was the neighbor's dog and was never nice to begin with, but it sure seems a lot nastier now. What if the thing in the house ripped it away from us that day because it wanted the dog, not to save us? You know, the thing captured it so it could use it to get to us? Hurt it to make it angry and attack us."

"Well, we've no idea what that thing is since stuff doesn't seem to just cross over, except us and maybe Dusty," Liam replied as he tried to line up a shot at the dog.

"Makes sense. We haven't seen it in the shadow zone so maybe it's just easier for the dog to come get us in this world. Each time we crossed over, we haven't seen it, but that doesn't mean it can't go there."

About ten minutes had gone by and the dog hadn't lost any interest or energy in its random attempts to charge up the tree trunk, so we had to come up with a plan. We decided that we had to get the dog to stand still somehow, and to do that one of us would have to be bait.

Liam pointed down to a clear area beneath the platform. "I'll distract it around this side, and I might still be able to make it back up in case it gets too close. Besides, I'm faster than you."

"I still don't think this is a good idea. Let's just wait a little longer. See if it goes away."

"Okay, but just a little longer. You realize that being stuck in this tree doesn't help any bit with our situation. If we don't find anything out soon, we'll probably go crazy. You first, of course!"

"Shut up," I said with a chuckle. It was kind of funny, but I was still really nervous.

The sky was steadily moving toward a solid overcast, and the thick storm clouds would probably follow. The locusts played their musical number in the bushes as the wind came and went. I wondered if perhaps the odd weather had something to do with the evil.

"Caleb, did you see that?" Liam pointed toward the grass line surrounding the Three Trees.

"What was it? I didn't see anything. I was looking at the dog."

"Over by the tree, on the right, I thought I saw something move."

I focused on an object moving around by the tree again. It was probably what I saw earlier, but failed to identify before the dog came. I noticed something because the trunk wasn't thick enough to conceal the entire object.

It finally popped out enough that I recognized it. "It's Dusty. Why do you think he's hiding from us? Do you think he has something to do with the dog? Think about it. Last time we saw the dog was just after I saw Dusty."

"Don't know," said Liam. "Maybe he's hiding from whatever dragged the dog away or maybe whatever's controlling it now."

I wondered if he knew we had seen him because just seconds later, he stepped into full view. The gray clouds were letting little light through, shading us with an ominous feeling as the breeze began to pick up. Dusty remained statue-still about halfway between the other two trees, watching the dog make its passes underneath us but with no concern toward him. Just as the dog circled around to the back of the tree, Dusty began moving toward us, and his expression was one of puzzlement and curiosity, like he was trying to figure out what the dog was doing. He must have seen enough because after only a few steps he stopped again.

I could feel the fall coolness blowing through the trees with the familiar smell of a desert autumn. Small mesquite leaves were blowing around though the wind, sounding like gravel when they bounced and glided along until being lifted up and away again. Dusty stood still, just staring at the dog that was now staring at us. There was no more whining or growling.

I think the dog realized it wasn't alone as Dusty approached the dog with a sad look on his face. He looked detached from the reality of this world. Without saying anything, he pressed his pointer finger to his lips.

"Sshhh."

The shush seemed as loud as much as it was a whisper, with the noise coming from all around us, not just from Dusty. The dog now noticed something was going on just as a big gust of wind twirled up behind it and encircled it. The vortex of wind became stronger and spun more violently around the dog, finally drawing its attention away from us.

Suddenly, it spun on its hind legs and stared directly at Dusty before it started to move, but not toward him, away from him. Its feet began to claw at the dirt and its legs moved from side to side, like it couldn't steady itself because the wind was pushing it around and was losing the battle.

As if realizing that something was about to happen, it charged at Dusty, jumping into a swell of wind and right toward the boy's face with its mouth wide open. Blood and slobber fell out, whisked away by the swirling wind, and then, right before I thought its teeth would sink into Dusty's face, a burst of pressure came between them in a twirling fury. My eyes shut as the pressure from the wind hit them, and when I opened them, they were gone. Dusty had helped us or possibly even saved us, and then I realized it probably wasn't the first time he did so.

"Caleb, did you just see that? That was nuts! Where did they…" A lot of questions came in my direction, but I didn't have an answer except perhaps one. We knew we had some help now in the shape of a person or spirit from the other side: Dusty.

We both climbed down, feeling safe again. Gene was no longer my main concern; I was more worried about whatever this other force was. Then I considered that maybe they worked together and "it" was trying to distract us so we wouldn't be prepared when Gene came back.

"We need to hide the tokens and get up to Jake's," said Liam, tapping me on the shoulder and breaking my reverie. "I feel safe there and would like to get there before anything else crazy happens."

"Yeah. I also think it would be a good idea to set times with Susan and Krystal from now on, just in case something like this happens again."

"You're right, and they might show up when we're up at Jake's, for all we know. I like having them around. We could use all the help we can get, but we need to talk to Jake first." He paused and then added with a grin: "I think you're just saying that because you like Krystal."

"Oh, stop it! I like her but not like a girlfriend." The truth was I did like her like a girlfriend but truly felt that she was out of my league.

"I'm just messing with you. But I think you do, and I think she might know it. Susan thinks so too."

"Oh really. What does she have to say?" I tried to hide my embarrassment by being grumpy.

"Not much," he added and then grinned again. "She just said you're sweet and that you two make a cute couple!"

Unable to answer that and trying not to think that Krystal might actually like me, I just told myself that relationships were just something kids did at this age from time to time and that they had no real significance.

We hurried and buried the tokens, marking the spot with a large rock. And after a sneezing fit from the ashes and dust, we decided it looked good enough and headed out.

Chapter 22

THE TRIP TO JAKE'S went faster than last time since we didn't have to sneak around anymore and, for some reason, neither of us felt scared that something might jump out at us. Maybe this was because we felt Dusty was watching out for us, or maybe we were just getting used to the situation. Either way we were at ease and moving swiftly in our trip.

Suddenly the air began moving in from different directions and blowing up dust. I didn't have time to think about what was happening before I heard it.

"Sshhh."

As quick as it happened, it was gone, and there, walking beside me like nothing happened, was Dusty. His eyes stayed focused on the path ahead, and he didn't make a single noise. This was the closest I'd been to him and in the calmest of situations so far. Nothing strange happened except for the fact that Dusty was walking with us.

I noticed he wore the same outfit I saw him in at the house, but this time he seemed to be less of an apparition. I knew if I touched him, I could feel him. His eyes were sad, but somehow they reflected joy when they glistened in the fading sun. I felt like he was trying to hide his feelings, or maybe just his fear.

I felt like Dusty had a lot to say to us, but maybe he couldn't speak in our world. It seemed that he was there to warn us about trouble, and he was there to help us. I wondered why the shushing noise never seemed to come from him directly, but from the wind around us. I felt that we'd have answers today if we got to Jake's before he was too deep into his bottle to give us answers that weren't so scattered.

As we rounded a bend, Dusty began pointing ahead and stopped walking; we immediately did the same, fearing that something horrible was going to happen. We waited for a moment but didn't hear or see anything except for the wash and Jake's house up ahead.

"What're you pointing at?" I asked him as I tried zeroing in on what he might be bringing to our attention. I wanted to call him Dusty but was sure he wouldn't understand because this was a nickname we gave him. He simply tilted his head from side to side, looking like a confused dog trying to hear a high-pitched noise.

"What do you think it is, Caleb?" Liam asked quietly.

"I don't know. Might have something to do with Jake's."

Dusty's head still moved from side to side, but he was as quiet as ever; even his footsteps were silent, like he floated along the sand but still left footprints.

"I don't think he can go any further," I said to Liam as we kept trying to figure out what Dusty was pointing at.

I thought it had something to do with Jake's house, and this made me nervous because I felt like Dusty was on our side. We also knew that he'd suffered a tragedy nearby and might be affected by that. I was pretty sure that Jake knew more than what he'd told us before, but why would he hold out on us like that? I then started to wonder if Jake was up to more than we thought in all this. Maybe he was like Gene?

"What if Jake hasn't been telling the truth, Caleb?" asked Liam. Again we were on the same wavelength.

"I was kind of thinking the same thing. We have no reason not to trust Dusty after he helped us out, and for some reason, he doesn't seem to want to go to Jake's. I think we should still go and try to sneak some information out of him. You know, catch him in a lie or something."

"Okay, we'll try, but it's a lot harder to do when you don't know how people think. I'm not sure how Jake thinks, and he might be on his guard for stuff like that, especially if he's hiding something."

Having decided to make our way to Jake's, we left Dusty behind. It was if he had read our minds, and when I turned back to him, he had vanished. When I looked back at Jake's, I began questioning if we were doing the right thing.

"I really don't think Jake's against us or anything like that," I suggested as we set off walking again. "But I think we need to play it safe. Dusty seems wary of him, but otherwise Jake has helped us so far."

"But it seems like he's holding something back," replied Liam. In a quieter voice, he added, "We should stop talking about him now because we're getting close to his house."

"Okay. So what about that dog? Where do you think it went?" I asked, moving brush out of our way as we entered a more narrow part of the wash.

"I have no idea. It was just there and then gone again, like the other stuff in this shadow zone. There seems to be no way of telling how long things will last, when they'll come around, or what will be on the other side. I'm pretty sure that whatever's causing it to happen, when it does, is trying to get us. It seems that something bad is always right there, waiting for us. I don't think whatever or whoever is bringing the shadow zone around has complete control. It seems like they can only control it for a while, and then they lose it."

From right behind us came laughter.

"That's about as right as hitting the nail on the head, Liam."

We both turned around to see Jake carrying kindling in his arms.

"I'm surprised you two are back up here so quick. After all that's going on, I would be working on protecting your house."

"Like your decorations?" I asked, walking toward him with Liam following behind.

"Is it that serious, Jake? If it is, why didn't you tell us yesterday? We would've been doing that instead of running around the desert trying to stop it...if we even can."

As Liam said this to Jake, they kind of stared at each other. I could tell Jake felt uncomfortable, like he was being accused. Eventually Jake dropped his stare, and we began making our way toward his house.

"Well, I think you two have some idea of what you're up against now, but I don't think—in fact, I know—you haven't seen how bad it can get. And I know that you have no idea how far it goes back..."

He stopped talking for a moment as his brow furrowed and his eyes narrowed, before shaking his head as if trying to rid himself of a memory. Then he gave us a half smile and continued. "Come on up to the house and we'll talk. I wasn't sure how much I wanted to tell you two yesterday, but from what happened to me last night...huh. Well, I really don't think there's any reason to hide anything, and I wouldn't be helping you any if I did."

I was relieved to hear this but still a little angry with him for holding out on us the day before.

When we got to his house, he set the wood down on an old wooden bench by a cooking grill. I noticed that his wind chimes and dream catchers were no longer hanging around the yard, and that the sunlight didn't pierce through the sky to add that feeling of comfort and refuge from the evil at work. This time, his house was enveloped in a gloom of eeriness.

"What happened to all your wind chimes and stuff in the trees, Jake?" I asked.

"Well, it has a lot to do with what I'm going to tell you about. I guess we can start our conversation there. You happen to notice how all of a sudden it gets windy out here for no reason whatsoever?"

"Yeah, kind of a lot lately," Liam replied.

"What really made you take them down, Jake? You said they're for protection against the evil spirits, and now you take them down right when this stuff's going on." I found a comfortable ledge to sit on around his grill. "I mean, it sounds weird to me that you take them down when you probably need them more than ever."

"I wouldn't have needed them if I never seen those tokens of yours yesterday. Now they don't do me any good. The other stuff is too strong around here, and the wind that comes with...well...it just drives me nuts hearing it bang my chimes around all night."

He clenched the grill scrubber in one hand and placed his other palm down next to the grill like his temper was about to get the best of him. He began taking deep breaths and clenched his teeth before nodding his head, letting me know he was calming down.

"I'm not mad at you two. I should have known something like this would happen one day, but I didn't think it would happen in my time. For crying out loud, it pretty much skipped over my father's time and my granddaddy's. Now me, when everything's so quiet. Kind of like the calm—"

"Before the storm?" Liam interrupted.

"Yeah, exactly. I should've been more prepared, or at least more ready in my mind for it. I'm constantly doing just enough to get by. And now...now it nips me in the butt at full force."

He shook his head and waved the scrubber around as if he could swat away what was happening like some pesky fly; then he shook his head again as if to tell himself not to be so crazy.

"The evil, this thing, goes way back throughout time, and you've only seen a glimpse of it. None of us thought—us watchers, so to speak—that Gene would go as far as he did. In some ways, he was just a vessel, yet he eliminated those who might actually have been strong enough to let the full evil come out."

Now I was really confused. I gathered that Gene was a vessel of some sort for the evil, but Jake and whoever else he was talking about—these watchers—knew this but let him carry on. It was clear that Gene scared a lot of people, but now Jake was suggesting that Gene was responsible for disappearances of other bad people.

"So how did he eliminate the people who might be able to let the full force out?" I watched Jake as he broke burned bristles off the grill scrubber.

"You heard enough about him to know that he was a real prominent professor at the local university, right?" Jake asked, looking at both of us.

"Yeah," we both answered.

"Well, some of those people who disappeared around Gene might have been more knowledgeable than he was about the tokens and the gray zone or what you two recognize as the place or whatever it is..."

"We're calling it the shadow zone now," Liam proudly interrupted.

"Well, that's a good name. So, many followers know your shadow zone. It's an occult type of practice meant to disarm others and making oneself more powerful. The more people a person on this side delivers to the other side, the more power the other side gives in return, but it comes at a great cost."

Jake stopped to pour himself a drink and offered us something. We were both content with our canteens.

"The cost from which a person can't turn back. They have to keep giving to stay alive and ahead of the game. In fact...Gene's so old that my father knew him when the two of them went to the university together."

"But why does the evil keep Gene around? I mean, why doesn't it just scoop him up when he leaves the other people in the shadow zone? Why does it keep rewarding him? You know, instead of just ending the trade out altogether or let him grow old and die?" Liam asked.

"Well, you see, that's the thing. The tradeoff works because it has to. The longer Gene sends people's bodies and souls over there, the more powerful the place gets. It's started to leave a permanent opening from this world to its world, with the help of those tokens and souls and whatnot. A while back, it had to be opened with special ceremonies, certain star alignments, and certain times of the year, but Gene has managed to keep it open longer. Now I wonder how many people he really is responsible for making disappear."

"So the more people he takes to this shadow zone, the longer it stays open and the more powerful it gets?" I asked taking a long drink of water.

"Pretty much there, Caleb. But it chooses who it wants. Regular people won't do if they don't have a certain mind-set. I assume that's how Gene chooses the people he takes over there. He knows they're evil people inside, and they believe in the forces of the other side, so that makes the place more powerful. It uses these bad people's fears and thoughts to leak out into this world, and soon it might be powerful enough to physically send its demons into our world."

Now this was getting really scary.

"These demons are just concentrated evil that take on the forms of things we fear, usually ancient things. They'll resemble things that those in the past feared because the evil has had time to absorb their thoughts in that place. The ancient crusaders and knights knew about it. People knew about it, all the way back before the time of Moses, Noah, the Mayans, the ancient Egyptians, the Shang Dynasty, and the rest of those ancient people. They tried keeping it hidden, forever, hopefully, but never fully succeeded.

"You never directly hear about it in the Christian Bible, the Torah, the Quran, or any of the ancient books, religious or otherwise, although signature traits of it come up from time to time. This evil was better thought of as forgotten so people would stop looking for it.

"In ancient times, when this thing was unleashed, armies from all different tribes, nations, religions, and whatever would unite to fight it off. The most they could do was push it back to where it came from, what you've called the shadow zone. Afterward, everyone would be aware of the power, and centuries would pass before it was forgotten, or it only existed in myths and legends.

"Some stories were told to cover it up. Some about religious battles, some about land disputes, but some of the stories are true and were, or are, told exactly how they happened. Think about the Arthurian legends—dragons, goblins, and enemies, like invading forces that just killed for no reason. This evil takes these forms in this world and in its own."

"The Hohokam people knew about it when the first Europeans crossed into these parts, many years before the history books say they came here. The Europeans hid them in the caves around this desert, thinking the area wasn't habitable for humans. However, they were proven wrong when they came across the Native Americans here. The Hohokam understood the evil the Europeans described to them and left the region, leaving no evidence of why they did. That's for the modern-day historians to try to figure out. They just upped and left, leaving behind much of their belongings so that their past would hopefully be forgotten.

"The people who made it here first weren't just settlers. They had secrets to hide. What better place than a far-off land where they thought no one else would be living? Obviously, as it turned out, they were wrong. The Native Americans must have seen a glimpse of the evil to believe it so well.

"The tokens or talismans were buried in the earth's crevices, caves, and makeshift funeral sites, and the people scattered afterwards. It wasn't until several hundred years later that Spanish expeditions stumbled across something hidden in a cave and reflecting the sunlight. The conquistadors thought it was buried treasure, the lost city of gold, or a sign for the fountain of youth. It turned out to be just a silver goblet, but more precious than they could ever imagine...and extremely evil.

"Over time, more stuff around these parts was found, bringing the evil out again and making it more powerful. People who found out might try to destroy an object, thinking it's a cursed relic, but even if they were successful, the evil just found another vessel when the original was destroyed. Even animals became possessed by the evil spirits. Why do you think we have those javelinas around here now?"

"Because the evil spirits got them?" I answered quietly, not sure if he was looking for an answer.

"Yes, because the evil needed something that could dig and smell real good. Something that couldn't see well, because the sight of the evil spirits might frighten a well-seeing animal. So these javelinas followed the Europeans up from further south. Not all of them were possessed, but those that were would dig around, rooting in the soil for signs of the talismans. The evil's little detectives, so to say."

"Is that why I saw them in the shadow zone when I saw Robert there covered with kissing bugs?" I asked, making Jake choke on his drink.

"If you've already been going into the shadow zone this much, then I fear we're deeper in this than I thought. If you saw Robert there...well, my friends, I believe Gene already traded him in. His brother, Dale, was walking around my barrier last night, and evil was with him, making the wind howl like a beast through here. That's why I took everything down; I didn't want it getting broken. He's probably looking for Robert, and they know your scent and your blood, so they'll use that to track you in this world and the other. Dale might think you two can bring Robert back, or worse, he may have some trade aligned with the evil spirits because you two are marked by the tokens now."

"Great. So we got a psychopath and his crazy friend, who blames us for his missing brother, and a sideshow of evil spirits tracking us down in this world," Liam muttered, as if to himself. "And then, if we happen to cross over, we have the other crazy brother, along with the forces of the evil spirit after us in that world."

"You have some control over the crossing," Jake said, leaning back in his chair. "That's probably why Gene's after you. You two have good, working tokens. One is the nail that came from the boy you call Dusty, and there's also the key that was given to the girl."

"But how...we haven't seen the girl. At least I don't think we have," I replied. I was about to ask how he knew all about Dusty, and then I remembered what he'd said about being able to hear us when he couldn't see us. It still felt weird.

"She might have messed up your house one of those times you two went into the shadow zone. You see, she's probably mad at everyone: the evil spirits, clowns like Gene, and the good people in this world who haven't helped her or her brother out of that place. They were tragically taken away, but like you, they also dealt with the evil in this world. Therefore, they know how to live between the two worlds, at least I reckon. I bet that's why Dusty has taken such a liking to you. He thinks you can let him out, but the girl might take some convincing. All the horribleness of her two worlds is a lot to overcome."

"When you put it all together like that, it does sound really nasty and horrible. I guess I would be pissed at everyone around me too.

Heck, even if they didn't personally do anything to me." Liam looked at us for reassurance.

I felt the same way, but neither of us said anything, and I was worried about how Jake knew so much about the girl and Dusty.

Jake still looked serious for a moment or two, and then he smiled. "Well, I know that you two have also treated all this like some fun adventure, and that's a very important thing to do in times like this. If you ever start worrying too much, then you might be in trouble. This thing feeds on that. Hopelessness and despair are some of its weapons. Even on the brightest days, it can make you feel down. Next thing you know, others don't wanna be around you either. Then I guess the best thing to do is crawl down one of those mineshafts and wait for the evil to come take you away."

"Is this something you think about, Jake?" I looked out into the desert, unsure I'd be able to see it all as a good game anymore.

"Well, when you're alone and keep to yourself, it becomes easy to feel either way, happy or sad. I've had my downs but figured, why? I got nothing to be upset about. There's so much beauty and good out there in the world that anyone with a good eye and spirit can find it. I think that's why you two fit in so well out here. Just like right now, when you turned toward the desert. Your instincts tell you to keep an eye out, Caleb. And you too, Liam. You never really took your eyes off the desert since you got here. You watch out for each other and notice that the little things are some of the greatest things in life. You shouldn't be concerned with what others say. You can think for yourselves out here without society's pressures."

"Yeah, that's the truth," Liam said, shaking his head.

"Well, Krystal and Susan seem to be on the same wavelength as us. They seem pretty cool." I looked at Liam to see if he agreed and saw Jake smile again.

We watched the desert shadows growing and fading across the landscape as if they themselves were possessed. Although I knew they weren't, it was the way my mind was working the last few days. Everything was an evil spirit. Jake broke the silence.

"You two should probably get going. I got some stuff to do and some things to think about. Sometimes I think a little better when I'm alone with no distractions. No offense."

"Nah, it's okay. We gotta meet up with Susan and Krystal too." I said, finally standing up and stretching my legs, only to find that one leg had a mild case of pins and needles.

"Yeah. Maybe we can stop by with the girls sometime, and perhaps you can tell us a little more?" Liam asked as he stood up.

"That should be okay. The more eyes you got watching each other's backs, the better. More minds sometimes work better also. Kind of like the enemies uniting and fighting the evil throughout history, but nowadays it's boys and girls uniting to fight evil." Jake said this with such an intense passion it sounded like something you might hear in a movie advertisement.

"You never know. Strange things can happen." I tried to mimic his intense voice.

Jake laughed and looked pleased that I had noted what he'd said about having fun. We started saying good-bye before heading out and were just on our way when Jake told us that we should start calling our tokens *talismans* instead. I guess that's what people recognized them as.

Walking down Jake's driveway, I had a feeling that Dusty would appear, but I didn't see him. As we entered the wash, I pulled out my wolf tooth necklace and began rubbing it between two fingers.

Chapter 23

ENOUGH SUNLIGHT WAS PEEKING through the overcast clouds to give my forehead an unwelcome redness. In Southern Arizona, the nights start to cool down in October, but the days can still get rather warm. The overcast sky helped seal in the heat, making me feel trapped as we made our way to the Three Trees.

I started thinking about going back to school and how it might actually be a nice break from all the worry, but I wasn't sure how far the evil reached. Jake mentioned it leaking out and that people would be unaware of it. It seemed that when we came home from school each day, the evil wasn't as powerful and had to return to its full force, and I thought this had something to do with how long we were back. Somehow, I felt this was how those miners got sucked into the evil. They never left the area, and it became stronger until they vanished down the mineshaft.

As we kept walking along, crunching in the sand with every swish-swash footstep, I was trying to pinpoint the locations of the remaining summer bugs making music in the trees. I was usually pretty good at this and could home in on their hiding spots. Then I heard another noise.

I stopped and heard Liam's footsteps fading forward...and

another sound of footsteps gaining on me. I looked down to see a pair of footprints appearing behind me, making just the slightest impression in the sand. I moved forward, hastening my pace to catch up with Liam and draw his attention to our invisible follower.

When we got closer to the Three Trees, we came to an abrupt stop, like we had already forgotten about our invisible companion. We heard voices. Then we realized it was just the girls waiting for us at the Three Trees. They sounded loud, but then again the valley was known for messing with sounds.

Eventually I could see Krystal and Susan sitting up on the main platform, chatting away. Just as I noticed something peculiar about them, the invisible footprint-maker went scuffling away in a hurry, kicking sand into the air. Liam noticed it too, but now we were both drawn to the girls in the tree... the *three* girls.

There was Susan and Krystal and another girl we'd never seen before, and she turned around, looking at us as we approached. This alerted Susan and Krystal that we were coming, right before they shot a glance in our direction. I was still far away, but I could see a glowing sparkle in the new girl's eyes that seemed to steal all the sunlight from the fading day and reflect it back at me.

"Hi, Susan. Hi, Krystal," I said, reaching the base of the tree and setting my bag down.

"Hey, Caleb." Krystal said, smiling. She turned and whispered something to the unknown girl. "Hey, Liam."

Susan climbed down to come and talk with us at the base of the tree.

"Hey, guys. Where've you been? We've been here like an hour and were getting ready to leave before your friend showed up. I thought you two stood us up, and I was getting a little angry until she told us you would be here soon."

"Well…here we are. Sorry it took us a while," Liam said setting his bag down next to mine and giving me a "what the heck is going on?" look.

We both looked up into the tree, and the unknown girl was giving us an intense and scrutinizing look.

"Hello, you two. What kept you so long up there? Also why did your buddy run off when all of us could have a good time today?" The unknown girl pointed in the direction we came from.

"Who?" I said, acting confused. But I realized that somehow she saw Dusty when we didn't.

She jumped down from the platform and walked up toward me, like she was trying to prove something. Then she pointed over my shoulder. "Him!"

I turned to look where she was pointing. "I don't see anyone."

"Oh stop, Jasmine. You're such a hoot," said Susan sarcastically. "How long have you three known each other, and why didn't you tell us?" she asked as she crossed her arms, letting us know she was irritated.

"Oh, just a couple weeks. I'm sure you know them way better than me from school and stuff. I don't go to school here. But yeah, why didn't you boys tell them about me?" Jasmine replied.

I was confused. I'd never seen this girl before, and I knew Liam never had. And why was she acting as if she knew us?

"Well, we just weren't sure that—"

"Sshhh."

Liam grew pale as Krystal and Susan still giggled at the "hoot" comment. I turned all my attention in Jasmine's direction only to see her pressing one finger tight up against her lips. She was pressing so hard that her lips turned a lighter shade, making them match her face's fair skin. Then, I realized that I was talking with Dusty's sister. That's why she saw him even when we couldn't. It seemed she liked to shush people here and in the shadow zone.

She began making eye contact with me, like she was trying hard not to blink. I felt like I was in some kind of staring contest, so I kept staring back as I heard Susan and Liam climbing up to the platform.

"You two freaks coming up?" Susan shouted.

Jasmine lowered her finger but continued her powerful stare as she whispered to me. "I'm not a freak. Do *you* think I'm a freak?"

"I don't know you," I whispered, unsure what she was capable of or what her intentions were. Dusty seemed to be a friend, but we'd heard that she might be angry. I wondered why Dusty had taken off in a hurry when he noticed her here.

She loosened her tense face muscles and took a deep breath before looking around and then back at me. Again whispering, but this time in a sad tone, she said, "I don't think anyone ever can or will. Even if you did, you still wouldn't understand me." Then she smiled and went up to the platform to join the others.

As I climbed up after her, I thought about what Jake told us about her and how the evil can consume you with its promises and rewards. Maybe she was just so upset that she went deeper into that evil than the others. Perhaps she didn't always have control over her powers, like a chameleon that couldn't control its colors. However, unlike Dusty, who was still dressed as he was all those years ago, Jasmine had appeared in jeans and a T-shirt, and she had no trouble talking.

They were talking about Gene and his two hoods. Apparently, Susan and Krystal had been on their way over that morning when they noticed Gene watching them from a distance.

"I don't like them either," Jasmine said, and the intensity of her tone made me shudder. "Gene or his buddies."

I had momentarily forgotten that she was something other than just a kid our age. I thought she looked pretty, even with those scary eyes reflecting the sunlight. Up close, I could tell that her eyes were such a dark shade of blue that they almost looked purple.

As our conversation carried on, I found myself uncomfortable when she stared at me, like she could see into my thoughts or soul with those piercing eyes. Maybe it was because I didn't trust her yet, or maybe, thanks to Jake, it was because I suspected her of being the one who transformed our house several days ago.

Lost in thought, I suddenly realized that the whereabouts of Dale had come up in the conversation.

"I think I saw him the other night. He was driving down the road. Actually it was last night, after we got back to Susan's," Krystal said, looking at me.

"Really?" I made sure I was looking at Krystal instead of letting my eyes wander back to Jasmine.

"Yeah, he was just driving down the road with some music on. Susan and I could see him from her place. We recognized his truck but didn't...err...actually see him in person."

"Jake saw him too. Last night at his place." Liam turned toward Jasmine perhaps finally noticing her staring at me with the intensity of a predator calculating its prey. "Did you see him, Jasmine? You said you don't like them. Why?"

Jasmine didn't once break her stare. "Because I don't like most people, but people like them cause problems. They come around and mess everything up. Just when you think you're in a good place, they go and screw it all up for ya!"

She finally dropped her gaze and seemed to be angry from just saying this. Her gentle-looking hands turned to clenched fists, and she breathed heavily. "I always see them up here. I see what everyone is up to. Just because you don't see me doesn't mean I'm not out somewhere, doing my own thing. I can do my own thing, you know? I don't always need people around. I can do stuff by myself."

Susan seemed to be concerned with Jasmine's rant. Perhaps because they both shared such a fighting, self-determined type of attitude. Susan nonchalantly intervened to change the subject. "Of course you can. You're a strong, clever girl."

"Clever." Jasmine giggled. "Yes."

"I was thinking," Susan continued, "since we're all going to be hanging out here more often, we should make this place more accommodating and do things like, you know, work out a designated spot for the girls and boys to use as…you know…a restroom."

Krystal seemed keen at the idea, and Liam and I just shrugged. Jasmine looked even less concerned.

"We'll take the trees over there," Liam said pointing in one direction and then another. "And there's some higher grass over there we call the willows. Well, Caleb and I do. That'd probably be a good spot for you girls, but we just have to move the booby traps a little further out in both places. No big deal."

"Best if we move the traps with the girls so they know where they are," I said, heading toward the ladder. Susan went with me to one side, and the others went with Liam. Jasmine added a whole new ratio to the group that we would have to work it out so she didn't feel like an outsider or turn everything upside down.

The wind was picking up and making the small yellow leaves drop from the mesquite trees around the fort. The three big trees only showed slight signs of the yellow coloration and thinning, but under the canopies of the smaller trees in the area, it was hard to walk around without getting small flakes of leaves all over your shoulders and in your hair. I didn't mind because they brushed easily out of my short hair, but with Susan's longer, thicker hair, it was another cause of annoyance.

Susan and I reached the first trap in a clearing about fifty feet from the main platform. It was the second in a series of traps to tangle the feet and break loose branches from the trees, alerting us. The other traps, about another hundred feet out, consisted of a few boards with long nails. They were camouflaged to look like natural dirt after the nails where driven through. I know how good they worked because I was once a victim of one of our own traps, and it hurt.

After repositioning the trap, I noticed the others were doing the same thing, except Jasmine didn't seem to be helping much. As Susan started retying the fishing lines around some new branches to pull loose if the snare was set off, I noticed Jasmine suddenly turn and look in the opposite direction of Liam and Krystal. Slowly, she lifted her finger to her lips, and with a wild smirk on her face, she stared at me. Then, somehow, I heard her.

"Sshhh." Then she ducked out of sight.

I walked past Susan under the tree and began making my way toward Liam and Krystal.

"Susan."

"Yeah...what?" She climbed down from the tree.

"I think we need to go check on Liam and Krystal. Right now!"

Just as I started running, I heard Susan say something, but before I realized what it was, I saw for myself. Not fifty feet from Liam and Krystal, Gene and Dale were watching them work.

Chapter 24

I DROPPED TO THE GROUND when I noticed they hadn't seen us yet, and Susan did the same, quickly crawling up to me but making sure she didn't disturb any of the high grass.

"What do you think they're doing?" she hissed.

"Don't know. I don't think they saw us though," I whispered back as I clawed around in the grass for a good-sized rock.

"How'd you even see them? I didn't see them from up in the tree, so how'd you notice them?"

"I think they just came out of the shadow zone. I think they used it to hide from us. Try and find some rocks."

"The shadow zone? That's the place you told us about?" she asked, feeling around in the dry earth.

"Yeah. I think Gene has better control over it than we thought. Jasmine's the one who noticed them first."

"Where did she go?"

"She warned me. Don't ask me how, but she did, and then she ducked out of view."

"Why didn't she warn them? She said she didn't like Gene or Dale either."

"I think she thought warning me was better."

"That doesn't make any sense. They're standing right there by Liam and Krystal."

"I know it doesn't, but maybe we can help them instead. Also, we need to have a little talk about Jasmine."

"Do you think they're going to hurt us?"

"I think Dale blames us for Robert's disappearance, and I think Gene's using that. I also think they're playing for keeps now. We're in too deep."

"What should we do?"

"We'll take some rocks and sneak up on them. We might be able to give Liam and Krystal a chance to get away if we have the element of surprise. Hopefully Liam will lead them through the traps so we can meet up at the fort and climb up to where we have more ammo and some weapons."

"I have a few rocks right here. Do you have any?"

"Yeah, one or two, and I'm pulling one out of the ground right now. I think we really need to throw them to hurt someone. Hopefully they won't move around before we can get a few good hits."

"Duh. I'm not going to throw it like a girl, if that's what you're getting at. Keep thinking that way, and maybe I'll save one for you later."

"Well, I like the way you think," I said with a grin, I enjoyed her fiery side and enthusiasm as well.

Gene had been giving us a lot of trouble lately and was obviously crazy. With pent-up anger and silent swiftness, I rose to a crouching position and worked my way toward him and Dale with Susan just behind me. She was being careful not to step into any of the traps and watched where I placed my feet as we worked our way closer.

About thirty feet from them, we stopped and took a kneeling position that we could easily throw from. I looked one last time at Susan, who had her arm arched back and was ready to throw. One little nod from each other was all we needed, and we hurled the rocks at our unsuspecting targets.

Of course, the rocks didn't fly at the same speed or angle, but the initial launch was still impressive. A gust of wind caused Dale to turn toward us, and he spotted us; he must have thought the wind was something else, and he was halfway right. However, the attack was already in motion, and it was too late for him to react. The rock Susan threw crossed paths with mine, striking Dale in the right temple, just next to his eye.

He screamed and staggered backward, falling to the ground as he held his face. This alerted Liam and Krystal to the intruders, and Liam looked at me before grabbing Krystal's hand. They took off the way I hoped they would.

My first rock never hit a target, so I launched another as hard as I could at Gene, who remained unharmed. This time I aimed for his body instead of his head, just hoping to hit something to render him a little weaker. As the rock took flight, I noticed Susan hurling rocks at him as well. Gene must have barely realized what was going on because he was already in pursuit.

My second rock was airborne and going to miss its target. It was the heavier of the two, and as he advanced toward Liam and Krystal, the rock bounced off a barrel cactus and sounded like a Congo drum. But it was just enough of a bounce to hit Gene in the knee and made him stumble badly.

"Come on. We've got to get back." I grabbed Susan's hand and took off running to the fort. Suddenly, there was a scream behind us.

"Was that Liam?" Susan asked, starting to turn round.

"No. I think Gene just found one of the traps," I replied, yanking her arm to get her to keep up with me.

From the corner of my eye, I glimpsed something moving through the brush. Dale was staggering toward us, blood pouring from his wounded head. When we got around the area that we called the willows, I saw that Liam and Krystal were already making their way up the tree.

We ran to the tree, and Susan climbed up first. I followed, kicking the makeshift steps loose from the ladder so no one could use it to follow us up. Climbing the tree seemed difficult as my fear began to grow. Although we had talked about fighting off an enemy from the tree, it never occurred to me that we would actually have to. In the tree, we got the girls onto the highest platforms we could and then began to look around.

Finally, we saw both of them, injured and standing about forty feet away. Dale had a rag wrapped around his forehead to stop the bleeding, and Gene was hopping around on one leg. We could hear him moaning at Dale, who had found a rock to sit on. He kept putting one hand over his injured eye and then taking it back off as if this would somehow reduce the pain and bleeding.

Gene limped around Dale, looking through the desert and then back at Dale. Gene cocked his head in one direction, like he was a doctor examining a patient or an artist trying to adjust his perspective in a way that would make sense to the portrait. In a few short strides, he approached Dale and gently cupped Dale's face in his hands. He tilted Dale's head back and forth in his hands and mimicked the motion with his own head. Dale reached up and pointed at his injured eye before placing his hands back in his lap and clenching his fists.

All the gentle cupping ended as Gene jerked Dale's head back by his hair, but Dale just sat there, clenching his fists together. From the distance, I could tell that Dale was breathing rapidly, and his breaths were getting shorter. Gene reached up to the injured side of Dale's face like he was picking something from it, like a small stick from one of the traps, and then I realized what he was doing.

Susan let out a small scream, and Krystal spun around to puke as Dale's right eyeball came out of the socket, glistening from the clear, lubricating fluids. Blood trickled down Dale's face as I saw him clench his fists even tighter and hold his breath to fight off the pain.

After the eyeball was removed from the socket, Gene gave it a sudden jerk, snapping loose any remaining muscles and tendons. As Dale fell to the ground, holding his face and shrieking in pain, Gene held the eyeball out toward us like he was using it to stare at us before pocketing it while he pointed at us. Then he abruptly turned and walked away...without any trace of a limp. After Gene was gone, I focused my attention on the injured and bleeding Dale, who was lying on the ground. I wondered if he was going to get up or simply give up.

I looked toward the others, and Susan's body rocked back and forth, like she was either ready to fight someone or was going to get sick. Krystal just seemed to stare into space, her face as white as a sheet. I decided that Liam looked how I felt, a combination of horror and relief that Gene had gone again.

"You think he's going to get up?" Susan asked. I had never heard her voice so quiet, and no one answered for a moment.

"I don't know. I don't know what to do either," Liam finally answered.

"I don't know either. What if this keeps getting more and more out of hand? What if one of us gets hurt or killed?" Now her voice was trembling, and I couldn't blame her. We had just seen someone's eyeball get ripped out.

"I don't think we should do anything, just...just observe him...from up here," said Krystal, a little color returning to her skin.

"Well, I'm going to go check him out. I need to know." I said this to the group in general but looked toward Liam for support.

"I'll go with you, but we'll check from a safe distance," Liam said as he grabbed our spears.

"That's good. That's good. From a distance," Susan said, still trembling and looking pale; Krystal said nothing and seemed to have gone back inside herself.

I climbed down the tree and had to jump the last four or five feet because of the removed steps. When I reached the ground and stood there waiting for Liam, I wondered what had happened to Jasmine.

As Liam and I gingerly stepped away from the tree, the wind was sweeping the wash sand into different patterns as it removed one fine layer of sand after another. These layers of sand would sometimes turn into spirals where the cool autumn air was forcing itself down on the hot wash sand, making the little cyclones we called dust devils.

"Liam, what happened to Jasmine?"

"I don't know. When all that just happened, I turned around, and she was gone."

"I don't think she's against us. She's the one who warned me about Gene and Dale sneaking up on you."

"How'd she do that from over there? You know, warn you." Liam waved his stick back and forth, pointing to where we were standing before the incident.

"Actually it was kind of weird. I could feel her watching me, and when I looked up, she held her finger up to her lips. Even though I was too far away to hear her, I heard her shush me. And speaking of our disappearing friends, what happened to Dusty? He sure took off in a hurry when he noticed Jasmine. She seems a little weird to me."

"I feel the same way, and I don't think Krystal's fond of her either."

"Does she have any idea of who or what Jasmine is yet?"

"No. I'm pretty sure she just thinks she's a neighbor."

"Maybe we should keep it that way for a while."

"Good idea. We're getting close to Dale. Maybe we should concentrate on what's going on."

"I can see him moving a little," I said as we moved closer. I was having a hard time focusing on Dale because I was also watching for Gene.

Liam moved closer, accidently stepping on a small pile of sticks, making several of them snap, alerting Dale that someone was near.

I could see blood oozing between his fingers as he held the make-shift bandage in place. He was whimpering, but it sounded like whimpers of fear and not pain. He opened his one good eye and looked at us before clambering to his feet and slowly walking away. I imagined the desert would be quite an obstacle for anyone who just lost an eye.

Regardless of what Gene just did to him, Dale was scared enough to keep following him. I guess that's the path he chose and the side he would be on. We watched the brush for a while after Dale disappeared and until our nerves settled, and then we returned to the Three Trees to find Krystal and Susan waiting for us on the ground. They both looked a little better but not great.

"Where's Jasmine?" Krystal asked.

"We were thinking the same thing. Maybe she got scared and ran off," Liam said as he walked past them.

He grabbed his canteen and took a nice long chug from it, like he hadn't had water all day, and I did the same before we offered them to the girls. As everyone took some time to calm themselves, Krystal wandered over to kick a load of sand over where she'd puked. I wondered how long this would go on before one of us would get hurt. Before one of us might not walk away.

Chapter 25

THE GIRLS SAID THEY were okay to hang around but turned down our offer to share lunch; in the end, Liam and I only ate about half. When we'd finished, the watery sun said it must have been about two in the afternoon, and I was thankful the temperature would soon start cooling down. The wind blowing through the trees was already cooler and not just dry and hot against our skin.

We'd all more or less calmed down after the ordeal of the chase and witnessing what happened to Dale, but easily got a bit twitchy. Susan was skeptical about pursuing this any further without telling an adult, but after some convincing, mainly from Krystal, surprisingly, she decided it was right to keep things to ourselves.

Liam and I explained everything else that we learned from Jake except the part about Jasmine. Without understanding the situation properly, Susan, being back to her old self, suggested that Jasmine had bailed out on us instead of warning us.

I kind of turned on her, which I guess wasn't quite like me. "If she yelled, it might have given away our position too," I said, somewhat defensively. "Then we wouldn't have had a chance to sneak up on them." I think I was sticking up for Jasmine because I didn't want to make her angry, and we needed allies.

"I was just saying..." Susan actually looked a little embarrassed.

"It's okay, Susan. We're all a little on edge, and Caleb didn't mean it like that," said Krystal, giving me a bit of a look. I simply turned away, wrapped up in my own thoughts.

If Jake was right and the evil could affect the whole world, as it had several times in the past, would school even be safe? It was all too much to think about, so I suggested we got back to what we were planning before and make the fort more accommodating.

"I want to work on that top platform first, you guys," Krystal said, looking up at the top branches with her hands on her hips in a posture of determination to correct the situation. "I have to be honest. That was the safest place I felt in a long time. Well, until the wind blew the tree around. Maybe we could...err...remedy that?"

Now she was really thinking along the same lines as Liam and me. We needed to keep in mind the possibilities, and I envisioned a spear trap that we could cut loose at a moment's notice, swinging down and making it harder for anyone to climb up.

We still had quite a few of the old planks we'd originally brought from home from when we'd demolished an old shed, and Krystal and Liam got to work securing the top branches and attaching a larger platform to the existing one. Susan worked on the second highest platform, making it a little bigger and adding a cover made from woven branches on the top and sides. She told me the learned how to do that in Girl Scouts and said it added strength. I was glad to see that Susan was feeling better but felt she might have been hiding her true feelings from the rest of us.

My spear guard worked out well, with several layers of sharpened sticks tied together around the trunk of the tree. By cutting a rope that bound them, they would swing down toward any intruders coming up.

Time passed quickly, and as were finishing things off, shadows began to emerge from the bottoms of trees, like arms stretching out toward the darkening eastern sky. The sun would set soon, and we would have to call it quits for the day. In the evening, the wash areas cooled first and sometimes made you question if something else was causing the rush of coldness.

Because we couldn't see which way Gene or Dale had fled earlier, we decided to walk Susan and Krystal all the way to Susan's house; Krystal was staying there for the night. The longer we were in a group, the safer we felt, at least until Liam and I had to make the trip home. We made plans to meet up at school the next day and then said our good-byes. Although I was still worried about our situation, I felt better knowing that tomorrow at school I was actually going to have friends.

The last of the sunlight diminished from the valley floor and only shone on the tops of the hills to the east. Coyotes began howling in the distance as we made it to the halfway point. We called it Red Rocks, because of the red clay slopes bordering the wash. The sunlight was now barely touching the peaks of the hills so we hastened our pace. It was a good thing we decided to go faster.

"Sshhh."

It came from my left side, and I looked to the trees for its source as we started running. Suddenly, I heard a slight giggling noise coming from the right of Liam, where sand was being tossed up in the wake of little footprints. It was Jasmine and Dusty, but it seemed that both of them had chosen to stay invisible, perhaps it was because we were getting nearer to our house.

We didn't slow down but kept our pace, looking all around in case one of them eventually appeared. Just as I remembered that almost every time they came around, something bad happened, a whispering voice spoke to me, like it was only inches from my ear.

"Go faster, Caleb. You'll be safer the further you get away," said Jasmine. I turned around but didn't see anything. Sweat began trickling down my face, and I could feel the cool evening air filling my lungs. I pushed Liam on, and he staggered momentarily before he too started to move more quickly.

With his longer legs, Liam was leading, but he adjusted his pace from time to time to make sure we both stayed together. Judging by the footprints and the kicked-up dust and sand, Dusty would gain ground on Liam and then slow up, just like he did for me. I wondered if he'd been a fast runner in real life or if this was a quality of the spirit world. Perhaps he floated like Jasmine did through the wind. I then almost laughed to myself as I realized I was thinking about ghosts without assuming I had gone crazy.

As we kept running, Jasmine kept whispering to me, "Faster, faster, don't stop!" Just as I felt we might be getting near home, a sudden darkness momentarily blinded both Liam and me. As our eyes became more accustomed to the heavy gloom, I realized we were still in the wash. However, there was no wind, no breeze, not a sound in the air except for the piercing sound of silence. The day felt dead and was still.

"What was that?" I asked, hoping for an explanation to the overwhelming darkness that managed to stop us dead in our tracks. When I talked, I realized my head felt like someone had smashed a board into it as it throbbed in pain. "Does your head hurt too? Like you ran into a wall or something?"

"Yeah, pretty bad. Like an instant headache."

Then I heard Jasmine's whisper, "Don't stop."

"I think we need to keep moving," I said to Liam as we forced ourselves to push forward.

Although each step felt like someone was trying to split my head open with an ax, we kept our pace. I knew we would be safer at home and kept wishing this as the pain intensified.

Now the temperature began playing tricks on us. If we ran faster, it got hotter; when we ran slower, it cooled down to almost freezing levels. Right as I was about to say something to Liam, another voice caught my attention, and I know that Liam heard it also because he stumbled.

"Hey, *boys!* Hey, *boys!* Hey, *boys!*"

It echoed through the wash from behind us, pounding into our already throbbing heads, so loud that I thought Gene was actually in my head. We ran faster and faster, only to be struck again by a wall of darkness, but this time we felt safer and didn't stop running. My headache was gone as the wind returned, along with the natural sounds of the desert carried through the darkening sky. Now we could see stars appearing over the hills and knew we were going to be home late.

"We have to hurry up, Liam."

"Yeah. It's going to be completely dark any minute, and Mom's gonna be really pissed. By the way, I'm guessing we went into the shadow zone but not completely."

"I guess, but you heard Gene, too, right?"

"Couldn't miss that. His voice was in our heads, Caleb. In our heads! Like he gets us into the shadow zone, and he can get right in our heads!"

"I know. I was there too, and I heard his voice. Weird thing is"—I paused to catch my breath—"I didn't see him."

"What does that have to do with anything?" Liam asked, panting too as we continued to run. "We know he's there and probably more powerful. He's probably trying to suck us into that place for good. Then it'll be just you and me against all the evil of that place and that lunatic."

"True, but we might have help."

"What do you mean?"

"Jasmine and Dusty. Even though they seem a little out there, I think they have our backs in this."

"I sure hope so, but we can stop running now. I see the house."

It was good to catch our breath before walking inside the house so we didn't seem too stressed from running a mile and a half through the wash. We'd just have to tell Mom we'd lost track of time and hope she didn't stop us from going out for a while.

"I think Dusty and Jasmine were trying to warn us to run faster and escape the shadow zone that time. Remember Dusty's footsteps and Jasmine's voice?" I said to Liam as we started up the driveway.

"Jasmine's voice? I never heard that! What is it with Jasmine's secrets with you?"

"What do you mean?"

"Well, she was whispering something to you at the fort. She gave you, and only you, I might add, a warning before the incident with Gene and Dale. Now you say you heard her voice when we were running, and I didn't hear anything any of those times."

"I don't know. It's not my fault."

"I know. I just worry that there's more to it. Everything right now and . . . well . . . every little thing, for that matter."

"Maybe. We've been figuring this out together so there's no need for bad feelings. We need to tell each other how we feel, including little things that happen just in case the other isn't aware of it, like Jasmine. I had no idea you couldn't hear her. Also, if we get mad or upset with one another, then the evil might be able to suck us in easier. Like Jake was saying. Remember?"

"Yeah. Yeah, I do, but what does that have to do with anything so far?"

"Think about it. Jasmine's anger and that situation today and Susan's reactions. It's trying to keep us apart and make us weaker one by one, so it's easier to take us."

"I bet it'll get Susan first," Liam said with a quirky grin.

"That's funny but messed up. You'll feel bad if something happens to her now, and I'm going to remember you said that." I couldn't help but laugh a little.

Poor Susan. She had been really scared, but all of us were scared. At least she hadn't been sick like Krystal, but then that might have been some kind of release.

"Come on. We need to get inside. I'm sure Mom's already worried."

She was worried, but luckily for us she wasn't mad. The next morning, I noticed she wasn't in the house getting ready and wasn't asleep in her bed. It was awfully quiet, and then I got a bad feeling that the shadow zone had taken her.

Chapter 26

As I ran around the house shouting for her, I finally saw her outside in the driveway talking with Betty. Shortly afterward, she came back inside, and Liam finally woke from his slumber. I followed her into the kitchen to get some cereal.

"What did Betty want? I thought maybe she was here to take us to school."

"When your brother gets out of the bathroom, I'll tell you."

I heard a slow squeak from the bathroom door opening, and I heard the exhaust fan power off. Liam came walking in, stretching his arms above his head.

"Mom has news from Betty she needs to tell us," I said to Liam, who finally finished stretching.

"Are you going to have cereal or something else?" she asked Liam.

"Cereal's fine, thanks," he replied and took his place at the table.

I looked back and forth at them several times before I caught my mom winking at Liam. Then I knew they were messing with me. "What about Betty?" I said in a frustrated tone.

"Oh yeah. Well, you two might have some longer days at school instead of those half days coming up in two weeks."

"Well, that's a bummer," Liam said over his spoon of cereal and a got a "don't talk when you're eating" look from Mom. "Why?" he added once he'd swallowed.

"Because you might not have school for a few days this week; today for sure."

Apparently, a train had derailed near the school, and it was loaded with chlorine that may have leaked after the crash. They would have to verify that the air, water, and soil were clean before we could return to school, and there was a five-mile evacuation zone. It was strange to hear that it happened exactly where a train wreck occurred in 1903.

I finished my cereal and headed into our room to get things ready for the day. Jake would most likely be home today, and if the evil was slowly beginning to keep us here, then we needed more answers. Mom told us we would have to stay within earshot of the neighbor's houses, and she was hoping to contact Susan's mom before she left for work. I knew that Krystal would be stuck at Susan's house for the day because she lived on the other side of the tracks and probably couldn't get home.

I finished packing everything we usually took, and we planned to grab the pocketknife from the cedar chest once our mom had gone to work. Just for a little more backup, we thought. If today wasn't the day that everything was going to come crashing down, it was coming soon, and every little bit helped. I heard my mother call out. She was looking for her keys again.

"Jasmine," I said to Liam, looking around our room.

"No. I think it's Dusty, playing games." We both started looking around for any other disturbances because we noticed that Jasmine and Dusty usually left some sign that they'd been around.

"Found them!" she yelled from the bathroom.

After saying our good-byes, I watched her pull out from the driveway before retrieving the pocketknife. When I shuffled through the cedar chest looking for it, I remembered how everything was placed so I could put it back with no evidence that I took it. I thought Liam could use the rusty old bone-handled knife that was buried with the other talismans. It would work against a foe like Gene but might not be useful in the shadow zone.

"Do you think the girls will be out today?" I asked Liam.

"That'd be cool. They might be trying to get Krystal home though. Let's just head down to the Three Trees and see if they show up. Then we'll head to Jake's."

I flung my backpack over my shoulder and headed outside. The sun was bright, and there was no sign of clouds like there had been the last few days. I figured it would eventually get stormy out, as usual. After feeding Max and playing with him for a few minutes, Liam came out, and we made our way to the wash.

"Did you leave a note for Mom?" I asked Liam.

"No, I thought you did."

"We'll just have to stop back by before we head up to Jake's. No big deal."

The sun was already making me sweat a little as we walked in silence and waited to see if the phantom footsteps would join us. Nearing the Three Trees, I could see T-shirts moving through the brush further down. I was glad it was just Krystal and Susan.

I made my way up the lower platform, Liam headed to his spot, and the girls joined us. We talked about our plans for the day. Krystal confirmed that she was stuck at Susan's house, and we were all happy not to be in school. They were both cool about going to see Jake, and we started making our way back to our house to leave the note.

I was still cautious about Gene and Dale, although Dale was injured, and I was almost certain that Gene had crossed back over into the shadow zone. Before we headed out, I suggested that Susan and Krystal make weapons for defense. Susan went right to work on hers, after scolding me for having the pocketknife and then deciding to use it. I was glad she was the tough girl I knew again, and that added to my confidence.

Krystal was also working on a spear, and they seemed to really enjoy this process as we walked along. I even managed to briefly forget that things were getting scarier each day, and everyone's mood was light. I was suddenly not worried about someone being sucked into the depression of the shadow zone and even wondered why I'd been thinking that might even be a possibility.

After reaching the area in the wash by our house, we decided that I should just run up while the others waited. I hurried across the road, wary of any vehicles that may be approaching, and when I reached the middle, I suddenly heard a loud rumble. I looked around for an oncoming vehicle, but there was none so I hurried over to safety of the driveway. When I looked toward the others, I saw them looking up at the sky.

I was expecting to see a plane, but instead I saw one of the largest thunderheads I'd ever seen. Judging by the way it slowly conquered the sky, I could tell it was coming our way. Again, I didn't think we were supposed to get any storms today, but this was a real big one.

Right then, the sun was still shining bright, and that meant we had enough time to make it to Jake's. Without any further delay, I sprinted up the driveway to our house and ran inside, forgetting to take my shoes off at the door. I hurried into the living room to use the pen and paper near the phone that my mother always kept handy. I couldn't find the pen. Was this another one of Dusty's tricks?

I headed for my bedroom to get a pen out of my schoolbag. The house seemed gloomy compared to the morning when my mom was still here. It smelled kind of musty or moldy. Then the temperature dropped, and a weird array of shadows swept into the room in patterns that didn't seem to correlate with the outside light of the day. The clouds weren't close enough to be causing this. I had slipped into the shadow zone.

Chapter 27

THE TEMPERATURE REMAINED COOL and shadows danced around on the walls, but it was not nearly as eerie as they did the first time we were in the shadow zone. I felt a sudden warmth, like some radiant source was pulling me toward it and was directly centered within my chest. I sensed that it meant me no harm. It was coming from my bedroom, and the door was closed. I heard a light humming coming from within, and a soft glow of light came from the crack under the door.

I reached for the door handle and slowly pushed the door open. The humming continued, followed by a faint giggling. I looked around, trying to see what I could without making myself more noticeable than necessary, Jasmine was sitting on the floor.

Realizing I had been holding my breath, I took a gulp of air as I opened the door fully. She turned her head ever so gently and looked at me, smiling, but her eyes still looked sad. She put a finger up to her lips.

"Sshhh."

She pointed to the corner behind the door, and now I saw Dusty. He was leaning face-first against the wall with his hands over his eyes, like he was playing hide-and-seek.

"We're playing," Jasmine whispered.

"What are you playing?" I asked, entering the room and closing the door behind me. The room felt warm.

"Nothing. Everything. Maybe something that's real somewhere else, but we just don't know its name yet."

"What's that mean?" I asked, looking around for signs of the game they were playing.

"It's whatever Dusty wants to play. See how he's holding his hands over his ears now?"

I looked over my shoulder as I sat down beside Jasmine and saw that Dusty was now covering his ears instead of his eyes.

"He makes it up as he goes along, and I join in as best I can. We used to play like this a long time ago, but we haven't been able to for a while." Her smile slowly drifted from her face, and I noticed the warmth was radiating from her and perhaps Dusty too.

I decided not to ask much as I felt that one wrong statement or gesture of any sort might ruin the good mood these two were in. I was conscious of the others waiting for me but also felt that it was a good chance to find out more about them.

"So what do you do now? When he does that?" I felt it was a simple question.

"We'll find out when he snaps out of whatever he's doing and motions for us to do something else!" she replied and a soft laugh escaped her as she nodded in confusion.

"Sounds interesting," I said, looking back to see if Dusty's posture had changed, perhaps signaling a different stage or level. "I guess I used to act like this with my brother when I was really young. He would play along the same way. I think that's nice you do the same."

"Well, if you haven't noticed yet, Dusty is young at heart and in mind."

"You mean he's slow for his age?"

"Yes. His brain stayed young, my daddy said, but his body would still grow, although differently."

"Do you play in my room a lot?"

"I thought you share this room."

"We do. I just thought you'd know what I meant when I said 'my' room."

"I do."

"So do you?" I asked again.

"Every now and then. We've had a lot more chances lately. I was jealous at first when I saw that you and your brother had all this. It was wrong of me to turn this place upside down on you and scare you like that, but you two weren't supposed to be home yet. It scared Dusty away so I kind of lost my temper."

"Well, you really had us freaked out. The cut I got on my chest disappeared, but it really hurt at the time."

"It would. You could even die here. If you die here, you don't go back. If you get hurt here, it goes away with time in the other world. It takes more time the more severe it is. You had a little scratch compared to some."

"A little scratch!" I said sarcastically, lifting up my shirt to reassure myself it hadn't return.

"You still feel the sting. Don't you?"

"A little, now that you mention it. Is that part of it?"

"Depends on how it wants to work with you. You and Liam. Let's just say that the evil spirit's really mad at you for something. That Gene guy is also very mad at you and is working with the evil spirit. Between the two of them looking for the two of you, well, it finally broke some of the evil spirit's grasp on us, allowing us to play a lot more. We thank you for that. Although..." She hesitated.

I looked at her, waiting for the punch line, the bad news, anything not to leave me hanging. She said nothing as she kept looking at Dusty.

"Although?" I said, slightly raising my voice. She went to shush me, and I realized I shouldn't have raised my voice. "Although what?" I whispered this time.

"I was about to say although you'll probably die here. All of you. The evil doesn't really care about those girls. What are their names? Susan and Krystal?"

"Yeah."

"Well, it really doesn't care about Susan and Krystal, but it sure wants you two. You make it angrier than anyone's seen in hundreds of years, if not longer."

I wanted to ask what we'd done for that to happen but asked the other question that had also jumped into my mind. "You said hundreds of years?"

"Yes, or longer."

"But I didn't think you've even been here that long. How would you know?"

"Well, a hundred years of being somewhere you don't want to be and never growing up makes you find things out for yourself and talk to others you run into. You're the only two people we've seen keep the passageway open this long and enter it so many times without being sucked into its grasp. There's something special about you two that has the others like me asking questions."

"Well, that's just great. Not only are we trying to get away from this thing and forget about it, but it's really out there to get us. That's what you're saying?"

"Exactly!" She clapped her hands on her thighs and stood up, quicker than I ever could without feeling light-headed.

She walked over to Dusty and very gently placed her hands on his shoulders. He turned around, looking mad at first, like I ruined his day, but then he smiled and waved like I was a hundred feet away, and he was nervous he wouldn't get my attention. I smiled and waved back.

"We have to go now and so do you," Jasmine said, guiding Dusty out of the bedroom and down the stairs.

"Why do you have to go? Why can't you come back to our world for a while?"

"We have to go because if it finds you with us it will make it worse for us. Also, those things are after you." She pointed toward the large window that stood next to the front door.

I nervously peered through the window, hoping to see what she was pointing at but didn't see anything except shadows that I took to be from the clouds. I looked back at her, and with a nod of her head, she motioned for me to look again. The shadows outside now flowed inside the house like nothing was in their way. It was just a constant wave of shadows.

The temperature started to drop again as the warmth of Jasmine and Dusty began to fade. Then something bumped against the window, leaving behind a smear of bloody slime.

"What was that?" I said in a shaking voice.

Jasmine turned and looked at me. "Whatever you're afraid of."

A small breeze flowed through the hallway, briefly washing away the musty smell that was beginning to return. Starting at their feet then slowly moving up, Jasmine and Dusty began fading away with the breeze, like fine grains of sand swirling in a dust devil. The last things I saw were Jasmine's sad, purplish-blue eyes.

Bang!

The thing smacked against the window again as it went by, and I had a bad feeling it was circling the house, trying to find the best point of entry. I needed to get out of here and fast. I headed back into the kitchen thinking that since I went into the shadow zone there I could return, but nothing happened.

As I began pacing and thinking, taking careful looks out the windows when I had a chance, a snarling squeal came from outside, followed by the sounds of something running in frustration. I briefly saw it as it ran by. It was large but not quite the size of a cow with hair that looked like it was made of porcupine quills. It had dark colors that molded into a bright brown-and-silver at the tip of its back, and when the light caught them just right, they gleamed like silvery lights. It ran on four legs, but I could tell it was capable of standing on two, probably rising to eight feet or more.

Looking out the windows at the creature as it made its passes, I noticed something else. The shadows in the trees and surrounding bushes were beginning to take on the form of creatures that I feared, like little goblins and monsters. I ran back into my room, closing the door before looking through my schoolbag for something to write with. I thought that if I went back to what I was doing when I came in, I could somehow cross back over.

The panting and squealing noises would fade for a moment and then rise again as the creature made its circles. A light tapping noise began outside and was slowly getting louder, and I imagined that the little creatures were banging on the windows. Soon, they would be climbing on the roof and trying to set fire to it in an effort to flush me out. I shook my head and told myself to stop imagining this stuff; Jasmine had said it was whatever scared me.

I rummaged in my bag, wondering if Dusty had taken all my pens and pencils, when the window smashed, and a rock about the size of a cantaloupe came hurtling into the room, barely missing my arm and rolling into the closet. It was made extra dangerous by the barbwire that wrapped around it several times.

I forced myself to clear my mind of frightening things, and the tapping noise began to fade. I slowly stood up, facing the window until it stopped completely. All I could hear was a faint panting noise.

Outside, I could see bristly quill hairs rising up just high enough for me to see, so I ducked down again, thinking it wouldn't see me if it hadn't already. Maybe it would continue its pursuits around the house, not knowing the window was broken.

I backed toward the door, keeping my eyes on the window as the tapping noise resumed and was followed by a horrible scream. Dust kicked up all around the shattered window. I could see blood and hair fading in between the dust just below the windowsill. Then, one of the little goblin creatures crashed halfway over the windowsill and hung onto the broken glass, trying to pull itself out of harm's way. A second later, the large creature ripped it down with such ferocity that its little bloodied hands could no longer hold onto the broken glass.

The tapping stopped. I think somehow the creature made its point in letting the others know that I was its prey.

The dust drifted away from a light breeze flowing through the house and back outside as if there were no barriers. The creature began whining and squealing like an excited dog that was in pain. A bloody paw came over the windowsill. It had long claws and even longer fingers that in some ways resembled a human hand that was stretched out.

The creature began rising over the windowsill, pulling its head over the edge and staring directly into my eyes. It mostly resembled a javelina, with sharp quill hairs. One ear was ripped out and pulled down on one side where it congealed to its face. Its lips were ripped back, forming an almost permanent smile of psychotic pain, and its horrible, bloodshot eyes extruded from their sockets like they would pop out.

I had seen this creature before... when it was just a normal dog.

I stared at it for a moment to see what its intentions were, hoping that somehow they wouldn't be the obvious. The other paw suddenly came over the windowsill as it squealed and kicked at the outside wall to climb through. I jerked open the door and ran toward the kitchen, putting the most distance I could between me and the creature. Then

I realized that the little shadow creatures would be outside. Even if I made it outside to a hiding spot, they would most likely be able to get me. Where could I hide from something that formed out of the shadows?

Going back to the idea of finding the pen and writing the note, I scrambled through the kitchen drawers and suddenly found the notebook my mom used for shopping lists and leaving us messages. I hurriedly scribbled a message for her, and as I looked up again I realized it was sunny outside. A distant rumble of thunder shook the house. The storm was getting closer, but I wasn't in the shadow zone anymore.

Walking down the driveway, I looked at Max to make sure he was okay. He just sat there and wagged his tail. I sure hoped he would never go into the shadow zone and become something horrible like that other dog. Of course, the other one was already mean and had it in for us, so when the evil took over its mind, it must have been easy.

Chapter 28

I COULD SEE THE THREE of them standing in the wash on the other side of the road. I had no idea how long I had been gone and expected to be questioned at length, but no one said anything. It certainly seemed like the timeframe was different in the shadow zone, and I suspected almost no time had passed.

I could tell Liam was leading the discussion before I reached the road because Susan and Krystal were both looking at him and nodding in agreement.

"Leave a note?" Liam said, hoisting his backpack on.

"Yup," I replied and started heading toward Jake's. I would tell them later what happened. We had to get going before the storm hit.

Everyone started following, and then Susan caught up with me, but it was a while before anyone started talking again. Susan seemed to be happy with her spear for now, but Liam and I had kept on improving ours. Mine had leather wraps for grips and a large blue bead on a leather string hanging loose. Liam had the black arrowhead wrapped in leather around his spear's grip. I wondered if Krystal was going to make anything for herself.

"Your spear looks good. Are you done with it?" I held out my hand, hinting that I wanted to see it. She let me see it with a little poke in my side instead. At least it was the dull side, and I grinned.

"Yeah, I'm almost done, but I want to add more stuff to it, like yours. Make it a crazy, tough fighting stick," she said before adding more forcefully, "one that can really do some damage."

"I'll bring some stuff from my house tomorrow if you want to make it look like mine."

"Maybe some leather, but that's all. I want to pick my own stuff out."

She kept twirling it around and then dropped back a little to show Liam and Krystal. I overheard her talking to Krystal about making one, but Krystal had given up and thrown hers away; she looked much less enthusiastic than she had back at the trees. I wondered if the idea of having to use it—and the memory of Dale's eye—had put her off. She just kept answering Susan's questions by saying, "Maybe."

The day was slowly growing darker as the clouds chased the sun across the sky. It had only been about twenty minutes since we left the wash by our house, and I could already smell the rain more than before. From my calculations, we still had plenty of time, but I couldn't tell how much sun would stay ahead of the clouds if the day kept going this way. Somehow, I felt that the disappearing sun had something to do with the shadow zone.

In the distance, I could hear the faint sound of what sounded like flute music as we saw Jake's house. We headed straight up the driveway, and I could see him outside. The smell of burning white sage drifted down on our approach but should have been blowing the other direction with the wind. The music was coming from his house, and now I was certain it was flute music.

"Hey, guys!" Jake yelled from his porch once he saw us coming. "And girls!"

I was hoping that it wasn't a bad time to show up, considering we'd brought Susan and Krystal and considering the lingering pause in his greeting. Well, at least it sounded that way. We walked up to his porch, and I could see that he had the sage smoking everywhere in full force.

"What's with all the sage, Jake?" Liam said as he took his backpack off and set it aside before shaking Jake's hand.

"Well, it just seemed like a good day to do it. All kinds of bad things are coming, as I'm sure you know. Just look at the weather. Huge storm coming in this early in the day."

We introduced the girls. He seemed to appraise them for a moment, and then he smiled.

"I imagine by now you've filled in these two with most of the details?" he asked, turning back to me and Liam.

Liam and I looked at each other, shrugging and nodding.

"I'm taking that as a maybe." Jake took a swig of what I could only imagine was his morning get-me-up.

"Mostly," I said.

"Mostly?" Krystal said in a slight angry tone. "Mostly?" She walked around on the porch before finding a spot to take a seat. "What do you mean, 'mostly'?"

"They probably told you as much as they felt they should to not drag you too far into this," said Jake, seeking to head off a possible argument with Krystal. "However, it's looking like you girls might be more into it than they wanted."

"Actually, I'm with Krystal on this. What do you mean by 'mostly'? I thought we were in this together. We were there with you the other day when that stuff went down. Why wouldn't we want to know it all?" Susan clenched her spear in her hands. Now I wasn't too sure if it was good to have the tough Susan back…with a spear.

"I guess you're right. You know how we've been in this shadow zone place we've been talking about, and since you haven't been in there yet, we thought we might try to keep you out if possible. There's really only a small little bit that we didn't tell you." I found a seat on the porch railing.

"Before we get started on all the holes in Liam's and Caleb's story, I would like to point out in their defense that it might be partially my fault they didn't tell you everything," Jake said as Susan and Krystal exchanged puzzled looks. "I told them how the evil was meant to be forgotten, and fewer people knowing about it would probably be better for the whole situation. It can grow off knowledge, so less is best, so to speak."

"I think it's leaked out and is reaching out further than we already thought. We were wondering if it made the train crash by the school keeping us in the desert," I said.

Jake rolled a piece of sage around in a small conch shell before returning to the conversation.

"You might be right about that, Caleb. So tell me, Liam, Caleb"— he gave us a stern look—"have you run into those two kids again? You know, the ghost kids."

"Yeah," Liam said, looking sheepishly at the girls. This was the main thing we'd held back from them, and they had no idea that while they were talking with Jasmine she was in fact a ghost or some type of spirit.

"Who?" Krystal said, quickly interrupting. "Jasmine?"

"Yeah," I answered.

"Wow! I knew something was off about her. Can she just, like, appear anywhere she wants to? I don't want to say anything that would make her angry if she's around, but how can we tell?" Krystal shivered a little, looking around. I was surprised that Susan had not said anything.

"No. In fact, she has certain boundaries," Jake said. "The evil spirit's kind of the center of its universe and is in fact a conscious entity that controls the others in its realm. It holds the power in that realm, but some try to refuse to be part of its evil and resist it. These ghosts, or trapped bodies—whatever they are, I'm not sure—constantly suffer when in the realm with the evil spirit. Others who work for the evil spirit have decided to join its forces to eventually reap the benefits. Kind of like the stories of hell and whatnot, with the demons working for the devil."

"So Jasmine's trapped there but fighting?" Susan looked pumped up, like she usually did before going after a school bully. Jasmine was her kind of girl, now that I thought about it, and nodded in agreement. "So she's on our side, then. But who's the other person you mentioned?"

"Dusty," Liam answered. "It's what we call him anyways. Seemed like a good nickname because he's dusty-looking, and we don't know his real name yet."

"I guess he's a little slow in his mind." I forgot that I was waiting for the right time to break the ice about going into the shadow zone again.

"How would you know that?" Liam asked, quickly realizing that he didn't know or hear something that I knew. "What else has she told you?"

"Not much, actually. I was waiting to tell you guys when we got up here to Jake's, so hopefully he might be able to clarify some things."

"Oh," Jake said, laughing a little. "You wanted to drag me into it, huh?"

"No, not that, just—"

"I'm just kidding you, Caleb. Go ahead."

"I don't know where to start. She was right there in our house before I slipped into the shadow zone, and she mentioned a few things like his learning difficulty. They were there in the shadow zone with me for a few minutes, her and Dusty, and then they just disappeared."

"You slipped into the shadow zone again? By yourself, again?" Liam asked.

"Yeah, when I was in the house. I was gone for probably five, ten minutes, but I don't think that much time went by in this world. Jasmine also said that the evil spirit was really mad at us. You and me, Liam."

"Why's it so mad at us?"

"I guess because we resisted it or something. We haven't tried to bargain with it for power or anything else. That's what I'm assuming anyways."

"Well, you might have bigger fish to fry this time around," Jake interrupted. "The reason I'm smudging so much with the sage today is because those two goons kept showing up last night around my perimeter. The thing is, they're flashing in and out of the shadows, slipping back and forth between this world and your shadow zone. I'd say you're right, Caleb, and they're working hand-in-hand with the evil spirit to bring you into the zone for keeps. I'm pretty sure, anyways."

"Why does Caleb keep going in more than anyone? And why haven't Susan and Krystal been in there yet? I mean they've been with us through a lot and have been around the talismans," asked Liam.

"Yes, but have they touched them yet?" Jake responded. "That would explain why the evil spirit hasn't tried to get them yet. But to answer your question of why Caleb is being pulled in more and more by himself, well, maybe it has it out for him the most. Sorry, kid, don't mean to freak you out or anything, but there's probably something about you that it really wants."

"So this evil and Gene and Dale are playing for keeps this time?" Susan asked.

"You've seen Gene and Dale?" asked Jake. The girls nodded, both seeming to go a little pale. Jake looked like he was going to ask more questions but changed his mind. "Well, the way they keep going in and out of the shadow zone last night makes me think they've made some sort of deal with the evil spirit to end this. With you gone, it might not have any resistance. I believe the next time you run into them will be the last. For them or for you kids. I would like to help more, but I'm afraid there are reasons why I can't join you in this one."

"Reasons?" I asked, now more scared than ever.

"Yes, everyone has theirs, and for me it's that I'm not too healthy anymore and have to be close by to my medicine. Let's just say that I'm better off here providing you with a safe place to come back to if need be."

"I don't like this. I don't like this one bit." Krystal rose to her feet and walked off the porch. She stood away from the porch for a moment in silence and hugged herself, maybe feeling uncomfortable that Jasmine and Dusty might be around.

"They can't get you on my property, at least not yet." Jake said, relieving some of Krystal's tension.

"Why can't we get any help on this? We're just kids, you know," she said demandingly, turning toward Jake.

"Because the fewer people who know, the better. It can grow more powerful if the wrong people know about it, and then it spreads further, making a huge mess of the area and sometimes the world. When this thing gets out, it causes epidemics and wars around the world in its desire to destroy the human race.

"If we don't keep a lid on all this, and make it stay as quiet as possible, those who have evil thoughts or bad intentions can use their mind-sets to make this evil spirit more powerful. They become vessels for it. They do this by corrupting others and doing harm to them. This leads to despair and anger in others who were once good, therefore making them easier targets. The fact that Liam and Caleb already touched the talismans and have been into the shadow zone makes them people who can't turn their back on this now. You two girls still have a chance to turn your back on it and leave them to themselves, but it will most likely come for you two after getting the boys. In my opinion, you four are better off really sticking together and having a very strong and supportive friendship. The more you want good in the world, then the stronger you'll be."

Jake said this in such a serious tone that his plea for the girls to help us could not be overlooked. Krystal turned around and walked back up on the porch, looking right at Jake.

"I just want the truth. Of course, I don't know you enough to question you—or even to trust you, perhaps—but I need something, something to make me believe that it's only a need for medicine that's holding you back from helping our friends some more."

Jake stood in silence. The only sound that came from him was his swallowing a mouthful of his drink. I felt bad for him, standing there with expressions that looked like remorse and fear mixed together. I felt there was something he didn't want to tell us. I could tell he wanted to help us, but for some reason he couldn't.

He was very afraid of something in the shadow zone.

Chapter 29

" I WAS THERE BEFORE. I won't tell you how or when, but that's how I know so much. If I go back, I'm afraid that I might not get out this time. I do have to be by my medicine and that...that's the truth, Krystal."

"Thank you. That's all I wanted to hear, and I'm sorry to upset you, but I know when someone isn't telling the whole truth. Well, at least I thought I did. Caleb has been hard for me to read, and now I see why. He's good at keeping to himself and not showing emotion. Kind of like you, Jake." Krystal smiled at Jake.

I think she smiled to show him she meant no disrespect and still wanted to be friends. He returned the smile. I was surprised about what we heard from Jake and imagined that Liam had the same reaction. He probably had a lot of helpful information, but I wondered how long he was there and what he encountered...or who. Jake still carried his half smile while he sifted around some smoldering ash in the conch shell. I could tell he was struggling with distant memories that he wanted to forget.

"The sage smells really good, Jake," said Liam, breaking the silence. "And I noticed you put the dream catchers and wind chimes back up." They were once again hanging all over the yard and on the porch.

"Well, the wind stopped a little, and wind or not, I think I need every bit of protection today." He walked to the side of the porch and looked out toward the east. "Look at that storm coming. Probably rip half of them down by the time it dies out. You can smell the rain, but it still looks dry in the distance. A lot of lightning coming too, from the looks of it. Hopefully we'll get some rain before too many strikes hit the ground and cause a fire."

His talking about the storm was clearly to change the subject. He'd been there before and escaped, keeping the truth inside him, and now it kind of made sense why Jasmine and Dusty didn't come around there. He had all that protection up because of the evil spirits and probably them as well since they could have been jealous of him getting out. That would explain why he never really left his house for that long; the shadow zone still had some control over him, and he couldn't leave this place forever.

As Jake had said, the storm was moving in quickly, and I felt like it was time we headed back, at least closer to our houses. If Krystal and Susan couldn't get back in time, they could take refuge at our house; we didn't want to be in the wash because of flash floods.

"Well, Jake, I think we should be heading out," Liam said, standing up.

"Probably a good idea. If it gets real bad, I can't even get my four-wheel drive through these washes to take you home if I had to. Also, I packed a little goody bag for you. It's got some sage, sweet grass, and a hawk feather for smudging. The other bag has some dream catchers to watch over you—one for your fort and one for above your heads when you sleep. I wasn't expecting all four of you today, so here, take these two as well." After handing me and Susan a bag each, he stood on an old wooden chair, took down two more dream catchers, and gave them to the girls. The chair reminded me of the abandoned house.

"Jake, what about the chairs at the old house?" Everyone except Liam looked confused. "The chairs at the house on the hill. There's one with the weird carvings. Does that have anything to do with this?" I added, clarifying my question.

"Don't know. I guess they could. You know, there're more people involved than just Gene. That's another important reason to keep it a secret. People like me have fought hard over the years keeping it that way. You see, the lifestyles some people live help the evil grow. I'm not talking about your everyday crazy guy or those obsessed with the darker things in life. These people... the ones I'm talking about, well, they really strive to take things to the extreme. I wouldn't be surprised if Gene has tried to make sacrifices, and those people he was suspected of doing something to were probably part of this. Whether he actually did something to them or just left them in the shadow zone is something I can't answer."

"So we should watch out for worshippers of evil and those who worship darkness?" Susan asked.

"Not entirely, no. People like that are more likely to be part of this whole group, but some of them live that way for other reasons. Excitement, depression, maybe just a phase in their life, or their interests. Those people usually don't even know what they're doing, but then there are those who do. Probably less than one percent of those people even know about this shadow zone. Telltale signs separate them from the others, and they're simple things too, such as the books they carry or a look of emptiness in their eyes.

"You remember those really strange murders in some of the big cities around the world a few years back? They were finding people stuffed under their cars with their heads missing, and those who did it carried a telltale sign of this evil spirit. Those poor people were real sacrifices, and the ones who did it knew how to cast the heads into the shadow zone while the brain was still living. Then the mind of that person is trapped in the shadow zone but has no way to escape.

"Your Jasmine and Dusty, they got legs and arms, so they can move around in the shadow zone, just like in the real world. You have to remember that even the evil spirit and the shadow zone are still bound by certain rules. It can't just make up anything to prevent you from leaving or to get you. The others who go there willingly share that power if they side with the evil spirit—they grow stronger while making it stronger at the same time."

What Jake said made sense, but I still felt that the evil spirit had all the reign in the shadow zone and only manipulated the others into thinking that they shared its power. When I was in the shadow zone, all around me I had a feeling of being consumed, like part of me was being stolen away and used against me even though I didn't side with the evil spirit.

A sudden, loud crash of thunder made us all jump, and that was our signal to leave, so we quickly said our good-byes and headed out.

"You guys make some haste now. Remember lightning can reach out several miles from the storm and get ya!" Jake yelled out over the fading rumble of thunder.

"I think maybe he's right, Liam. Maybe we should make this a little bit of a run just in case the storm moves in quicker than we think," I said securing my backpack.

The clouds were twirling down from the skies and then back up on themselves, taking on very different shapes that lasted only seconds before they twisted and took on other shapes. "Do you think we should just head home? You know, all of us?" Susan yelled as we ran down the wash.

"No. I think we should stop at the Three Trees and then go from there," Liam replied. Krystal agreed with him before I could.

"Yeah, he's right. The storm's still far-off, and from the Three

Trees we would still have enough...err...sufficient time to get home if it hit. Besides, Liam and Caleb's house is nearby." Krystal sounded a little out of breath from the run, but even at a time like that, she managed to slip in one of her more elaborate words.

I stayed quiet because something weird was happening inside me. I felt the same warmth I had when I was in my bedroom with Jasmine and Dusty. The wind was cool against my face, and I could tell the others were getting a little cold, even during the run; I felt warm, but the heat was coming from within me.

The clouds now formed a second horizon for the sun, chasing it across the sky. It wasn't even noon yet, but long shadows already appeared and disappeared, like dancing silhouettes.

The warmth in my chest stayed with me to the Three Trees, making me feel safe with a glowing sensation. Unlike the others, I began embracing the cold wind instead of shivering from it. Then I heard her.

"Sshhh."

Then I heard her saying my name, and the sound came from the tree line, seeming to float along the wind, like she was riding the breeze. I couldn't see her or any sign of her.

"What are you looking at, Caleb?" Krystal asked, drawing Liam's attention to me.

"Nothing. Just checking out the area for any signs of the goons."

I could tell Liam didn't believe me, but Krystal just shrugged. Why did Jasmine keep talking only to me? Maybe it was because I'd been into the shadow zone more than Liam, and I kept telling myself that, but really, I believed differently. Maybe it had something to do with the warm feeling?

I reached the others, who were taking a quick break on the embankment at the side of the Three Trees, but something kept drawing me to look at the tree line. I had an overwhelming feeling that someone was watching us.

A small swirl of dust emerged beside me, twirling around with some leaves before making its way to the fire pit. It must have gotten stuck in the confines of the rocks because it stayed there, eroding years of ash deposits until some of the underlying dirt was revealed. I suddenly realized it was revealing the talismans. The ash grew into a tall spire, and I began to hear crackling and sparking noises coming from the cloud of ash, like small electric shocks. Then I heard her again.

"Sshhh. Take them now," she hissed.

I hesitated before reacting as I briefly saw her face appear through the ash. It was mostly distorted, but still recognizable. Once the twirl of wind and ash went away from the fire pit, I dashed across and reached down, grabbing the talismans and pushing them quickly into my bag. As I headed toward the others, I thought they were looking at me funny.

"What?" Then I saw Liam pointing over my shoulder. I spun around, and Gene's face emerged through a new ash cloud, as furious as I had ever seen it. He was reaching through from the shadow zone.

Chapter 30

"HELLO, BOYS. I SEE you have some company." His voice echoed and sounded distorted.

I slowly backed away from the growing ash cloud and made my way to the tree, the others cautiously following me.

"What do we do?" Krystal asked.

"Don't know. I don't think he can do much since he's not all the way here yet," Liam said, making his way up into the tree with Susan and Krystal right behind him.

I was about to follow, but a huge bolt of lightning flashed across the sky, causing Gene's silhouette to disappear for a moment in the brightness. Dust-filled twirls of wind began blowing around the ground and through the trees even more powerfully than before, but none took on the forms of anything like Gene.

His ash cloud suddenly became still, and I saw a strange expression on his face right before his arms flung up high toward the sky, like he was begging. From his chest outward, he exploded, and through the ash, Jasmine came running toward me and grabbed my hand.

"Run! *Now!*" she yelled with a piercing shriek, and we took off just seconds before Dale sprung at me.

We went toward the tree and around the other side from our half-broken ladder. There was no quick way up. I peeked around the corner and saw that Dale had tripped on the fire pit in his attempt to grab me. He was getting back to his feet and looking around with his one eye. It was so bloodshot that the darkness of his pupil intensified, making him look even crazier.

Jasmine pulled my hand again, and we ran off into the tree line among the brush. We had an advantage out there because of our traps and because the tall brush provided someone of our height with cover. As we ran, I could hear the sounds of the others in the tree yelling at Dale. I heard him yell and cuss and presumed they were throwing rocks at him as he ran after us.

As we ran, the wind grew stronger. I glanced back and saw that Dale was about fifty feet from us, but not gaining. I think his depth perception from the missing eye was causing him some trouble. He was holding one hand out in front of his body, slightly waving it from side to side before advancing; perhaps he was having trouble seeing out of his one remaining eye since it did look really bad.

The warmth in my chest was strong, adding a level of comfort to the situation, but then I felt a sting of coldness hit my arm, shocking me back into reality. It was a raindrop, bringing refreshment to the dryness of the desert, but it was only one. A lone raindrop that had become separated from its billions of brother and sister raindrops to fall on me, but I was sure there would be more soon.

Circling around, looking longingly up at the sky, I noticed the warmth in my chest was going away, and the cold wind was invading. A slow shiver rose from the base of my spine and into my shoulders, making me tremble all over.

"Don't lose it, Caleb. Please don't lose it," Jasmine said, looking at me as she pulled me forward.

"Don't lose what?" I asked, initially confused.

"You know what!" she said, sounding like my mom when asking a question that I already knew the answer to.

The thing was, I did know. She was talking about that warm, weird feeling inside me. Maybe this was why the evil spirit didn't like me. Thinking about it made the feeling start fading away faster, and I could feel Jasmine's grip on my hand tighten, like she really could tell that I was losing it. I focused on what we were doing, getting away from Dale, and the warmth inside gradually returned. It was the same way of battling the evil as when I had written the note to my mom.

We reached a small rock ledge overlooking the west part of the wash that split around the Three Trees. There was no sign of Dale, but I could see the others in the tree. Liam was up in his crow's nest, waving at me. I was glad he could see me, and this let us both know we were all safe for the time being. And then Jasmine was gone, but the feeling of her clenching my hand in worry and anger remained.

I knew I had to keep moving, with or without her, and felt certain she would pop up again. Gene could, so why couldn't Jasmine? I saw no sign of Dale when I stepped slowly out of the brush and into the wash and was pretty sure I could outrun him, but I had no idea what Gene was capable of so I remained cautious. I made a quick dash across the openness of the wash. There was still no sign of anyone.

I couldn't help but wonder, and for some reason, worry, about Jasmine. Why did she go away so abruptly? Why couldn't she stay? I began to think it had something to do with me losing that warming feeling inside my chest, but it had come back.

I knew it would make it harder for Liam and the others to spot me, but I crouched low as I made my way through the brush; right then it was Dale I had to worry about. I began wondering why they didn't try to come help me. There were four of us, five if you counted Jasmine, and only one Dale...with a possible Gene.

I was growing thirsty from running and the wind drying out the air. I reached into my bag for my canteen, but I couldn't feel it; it must have fallen out when I took off running. I never had time to close my bag after placing the talismans inside, and I quickly made sure I had all three of them. That's probably why no one was messing with the others in the tree.

I became really worried thinking about what would happen if they got a hold of me with all three talismans. Would this be enough for Gene to complete whatever he was trying to? I had to think about the significance of the talismans. Maybe they could help us?

Dusty used the nail to hold down drawing papers. Okay, that didn't tell me much. Jasmine was always playing with her father's keys to the buildings and other locks around the mines. The knife? I didn't know anything about the knife, but I was aware that these things became something else when they appeared in the shadow zone.

Thinking about the talismans hadn't seemed to help, so I decided I needed to focus on getting back to the fort with the others. I circled around as quietly as I could and finally approached the farthest tree to the west. Here, the brush grew thinner, which would soon make me more vulnerable.

"Ha ha! You going to run for it, *boy*?"

The voice came from behind me, and I spun around but saw nothing as my eyes darted from left to right. The voice was raspy, and I knew it was Gene reaching through from the shadow zone and presumed he was trying to scare me into making a mistake. If I ran, I might run right into a trap, but then again, he might just be buying time for Dale to sneak up on me. I went with my gut instincts and took off running.

I was about twenty feet from the tree when I heard Krystal and Susan begin shouting. "Hurry! He's coming back!"

I finally reached the outermost tree and took a quick breather beside the base of it. This tree didn't grow quite as large as the other two and provided minimal cover. Still, it was enough to keep between me and someone else. There was no sign of Dale, so I started making my way toward the main tree. I was halfway there when I saw a dark T-shirt coming through the brush line just beyond the fort. Dale must have given up on his pursuit and decided to return to the Three Trees to possibly capture one reward.

If I could only make it to the tree without Dale getting me, I could get up to the first platform and cut the ropes, dropping the spikes. We could then defend ourselves, if needed, for some time and had plenty of water and snacks to hold up until one of our parents came looking for us. Unless it rained.

If it rained, it would block off the washes, and neither my mother nor Susan's parents would be able to make it to the fort because the wash split, creating an island around the Three Trees. I felt the evil could sense my fears because a moment later, I felt a steady flow of rain, and when it hit the loose dirt around me, it created little circles, like miniature craters in the fine dust.

I considered my options, I could run to the tree and hopefully beat Dale, but I would also have to climb up. Judging by the distance, I realized I wouldn't have enough time. Maybe a distraction would help? Perhaps then he wouldn't realize until it was too late, and I would be already climbing.

No one was looking at me, and I tried thinking of a way to get their attention. But how would I even tell them without giving away my position? I just needed them to throw some rocks, so perhaps acting like I was throwing a rock would work, but I still had to get them to look. I began to look around for a decent-sized rock to throw at Dale, hoping that maybe the others would get the hint.

Although we had cleared the area of rocks, I spotted a small black one near my foot. I kept my eyes on Dale as I squatted down for it, but after grabbing only a few handfuls of dirt, I knew I would have to take my eyes off him to grab the rock. I took one quick glance down, and it wasn't where I thought it was. I looked back at Dale to make sure he still hadn't noticed me and then turned my attention back to the rock. It was definitely gone.

I brushed away some soil, hoping to maybe uncover it, until I noticed it about five feet from me. It had to be the same rock since there were no others around because we had cleared the area. I stared at the rock, daring to completely take my eyes off Dale again. I saw it move. I blinked my eyes several times to make sure it wasn't just dust in my eyes causing an illusion.

I was sure that it was moving when it started to shred apart like a ripped plastic bag being torn apart by the wind. Every piece that ripped away began to take on a new form wherever it landed. The main black spot that I thought was a rock was now growing every time the wind ripped pieces from it. The pieces stretched the main mass along the ground and into the bushes as if they didn't want to separate but could no longer hold on.

I had seen something similar from our bedroom window a few nights back, and that night I thought it reminded me of a black trash bag. Now I knew it was the evil spirit releasing its minions from the shadow zone. This was it, and Gene was still in the shadow zone probably helping this moment happen. Jake and Jasmine were dead on with the strategy that these two forces would use.

I looked back at the tree, hoping that they had noticed me by now and saw Susan staring down at me. I motioned my arm over my head in a throwing gesture and pointed at Dale, hoping she would understand. Susan looked puzzled for a moment but then climbed toward Liam. I could tell they were talking before she climbed back down to join Krystal, who was now standing on the lower platform.

I saw Susan take the first fierce shot down at Dale, barely missing him and impacting the dirt just in front of him, causing a little puff of dust to fly up. Another puff of dust appeared to his side, making him look over his shoulder, like he didn't realize what was going on yet. That second shot must have come from Liam because Krystal hadn't moved since they started throwing.

After a few more rocks, it seemed like Dale hadn't realized what was happening and kept moving toward the tree. Krystal stepped into position, threw a full handful of the smaller rocks at Dale, and finally distracted him. I had to keep the tree between us as much as possible, and quick movements might draw his attention. I started to take a step toward the main tree before I realized I couldn't. My foot was stuck. No—it was being grabbed by something.

I looked down and saw a black, fluidlike substance wrapping around my ankle in the form of a hand. This stuff was sneaky and evil, and it was using distractions just like we were. I tried pulling away but stopped when I almost fell over.

I reached into my backpack, remembering that I had the talismans. They could be other things in the shadow zone so why not here, if this stuff came from there? I had no idea if it worked that way, but it seemed logical. I grabbed the knife, and in that moment I felt a horrible stinging sensation flowing through my body, like chilled water coursing through my veins. It immediately took away the remaining feeling of warmth in my chest that I was trying to hold on to, and my heart felt like something was crushing it as cold sweats broke out all over my body.

Ignoring the pain in my chest, I finally mustered the courage to try stabbing the blackness. I knelt down, trying my best to put my leg out of the way of each stab and realized that the blackness tried to shift away from the knife without letting go of my leg. Then I knew it would work.

Finally in a good position, I took a stab at the center of the substance, and it snaked to one side before it flared up into a wave, elevating itself off the ground and branching off like spider webs into several branches of the tree. I took another stab at a lower point where it clung to the tree, missing again. A split second before the blade would have stabbed it, the weblike parts scattered around the tree like a climbing spider. It started trying to lift my foot off the ground and threw me off balance. If I fell onto my back, I knew it was in a much stronger position to drag me into the shadow zone.

Chapter 31

FLUNG MY ARM BACKWARD and managed to grab a tree limb for support before I took another stab at the blackness. I saw Susan staring at a dark spot that was taking on the form of what seemed to be a human. It was probably something she feared, because she was looking right at it, unblinking. Thinking of how this blackness worked, I tried to keep my thoughts from any fears and to focus.

I turned my attention back to the blackness that now consumed my entire foot. I began caring about my leg less and less as I took what were fruitless stabs. It was growing stronger, and I knew my time was really short, so I took a fake stab to the right, assuming it would move left to avoid it. As the bulk of it moved that way, barely grazing the top of my shoe, I plunged the knife into it and finally pinned it to the ground.

A loud shrieking noise came from the substance, and several of the manifesting creatures around joined it. I sensed they were all looking toward me in pain and anger, and they began moving toward me as the blackness I stabbed shifted between shapes, trying to free itself. No matter what form it took, it couldn't break free, and it began to retract its weblike grip from around the tree, slowly growing smaller into a single black spot.

"Caleb!"

I got to my feet and was just about the grab the knife when I heard Liam scream. I spun around and came face to face with Dale as he made a desperate lunge at me. I didn't have a good grip and dropped the knife. I dove to one side as he crashed past me into a heap on the ground.

As he picked himself up, Dale noticed the knife lying on the ground next to what looked like a puddle of melted rubber. In a quick movement, he looked at me and then at the knife before he reached down and grabbed it, swinging back around so quickly toward me that I thought his back was going to snap. He held the knife partially in front of him like he was getting ready to make a quick jab at me when he got close enough.

He limped slowly toward me, his missing eye still bleeding, the blackish blood mingling with the thin lines of sweat that trickled down his cheeks. He was so close to me that his stench made me swallow back the rising bile in my throat. If I wasn't so scared, I probably would've puked. I knew I couldn't beat him back to the tree and was going to have to lead him around to put some distance between us. I ran for it.

About twenty feet into my run across open ground, I turned around hoping to see that I was leaving Dale in the dust. No chance. Perhaps spurred on by having the knife and coming so close to getting me, he was a lot faster than I thought, and the blade of the knife cut through the air just behind me, followed by a vicious grunt from Dale. I guess the evil didn't need us alive, or like Jake had said, you only had to stay alive long enough for them to get you into the shadow zone. That way, even if you made it back, you would die the instant you returned to this world.

I could hear Dale panting right behind me as I ran. I had ten more feet to the other tree, and then I would have to cut a sharp left and duck under the overhanging branches. I hoped this would slow him down enough for me to make it back.

I remembered my grandpa once told me how animals run when one is the prey and one is the predator. He said that the predator might miss its prey and then has to find another or go after it another day. The prey…well, it doesn't get that second chance if it doesn't outrun the predator the first time.

That gave me an extra boost, and right before I ducked under the branches, I ran faster. I dug a foot into the ground with a sliding motion and grabbed the side of the tree to help spin me around. I felt Dale's hand barely miss my shoulder as he went flying by me into the low-hanging branches, cursing and hollering. Then, as I regained my footing, a smoky cloud appeared in front of me.

"You going to run, *boy*?"

Gene's face! I was so startled that I fell backward heavily, and all my breath burst from my lungs. I gasped, desperately trying to restore my breath, and Dale's cursing only lasted for a few seconds before he turned his attention back on me. I looked to the fort, hoping that someone would help me. Liam was already climbing down with his spear.

Dale slowly walked toward me; he knew I wasn't capable of running. I shifted my gaze from him and looked up into the branches for something to defend myself with. Gene's shadowy face lurked above me, swirling through the branches like a snake weaving its way through the brush. Dale reached up into the tree and snapped off a huge branch as he kept his stare fixated on me.

I was slowly catching my breath, and the cool air returned to my lungs, but I was still panting from all the exertion and stress. I could now hear Liam yelling but couldn't understand him because the wind drowned his voice out. I could see Gene's nasty little smirk looking down at me because Dale was about to deliver his prey. Dale never once blinked that teary, bloodshot eye.

"You for my brother," he snarled, meaning he wanted to trade me for Robert.

"Won't work, Dale! He's already gone. He died here...or there, but something wasn't right with him."

"No!" he shouted and aggressively closed in on me.

"Yes, Dale. Gene lies to you!" I yelled back at him, pointing at the shadowy figure among the branches. Dale looked up into the tree and then back at me with a confused look on his face.

"See, that's it. You people always done thought you were smarter than me, and Gene's been there. You're trying to make me look away so you can go and run again. It won't work. This time I'm bringing Gene your head and taking you back to the house to sit in the chair, so he can bring you over easier. Then he'll give my brother back. I hope he ain't scared."

I realized Dale wasn't emotionally or mentally capable of understanding what he was doing. There was no bargaining without any solid proof, and for some reason his confused look made me believe that he couldn't see Gene.

I shuffled backward until I was up against the trunk of the tree. I had nowhere else to go, and Dale was fashioning himself a club out of the branch he broke free. Then he stopped and looked just to the side of me.

The warmth in my chest came back, and a hand rested gently on my shoulder, followed by one of my new favorite sounds.

"Sshhh. Catch your breath and close your eyes."

I had to trust her. Right before my eyes closed, I saw the knife lying among some broken branches; Dale must have dropped it when he hit the tree. Then darkness replaced the image of the knife as my eyes closed.

I didn't hear anything except the wind pounding in my eardrums and my heart beating. But it wasn't beating chaotically; it was calm, rhythmic beats that came when the warmth returned.

Sounds poured back just seconds later, and I could hear Dale panting a few feet away. Somehow, I felt that Dale knew Jasmine before this encounter. I imagined them staring at each other, each waiting for the other to make the first move while her purple-blue eyes burned like flames of hatred toward him. Then she whispered to me so only I could hear.

"I'm going to show my true self to him, Caleb. The form they left me in almost a hundred years ago. It worked before."

I heard Dale's footsteps begin cracking over the broken twigs, but Jasmine's hand remained on my shoulder; I knew she wasn't going to leave me.

"Keep your eyes closed. No matter what, don't open them until it's over," she said, squeezing my shoulder.

I heard Dale's footsteps begin to quicken, and then he gasped.

"No! What's wrong with you?" Dale yelled.

I heard a scuffling noise and the sound of branches breaking and then footsteps running away. Jasmine stopped squeezing my shoulder.

"You can open them now. He's gone," she said in a gentle and soothing voice.

She was crying but not weeping. Several tears rolled down her face as she looked at me and then turned away, cupping her face. I wasn't sure what to do. Perhaps she just needed to have someone see her do this to make her feel better, so we stood there in silence.

I looked to see how close Liam had gotten and realized he was no longer running, just walking and cautiously looking out into the desert. Concerned with Jasmine, I signaled him to give me a minute. He nodded and stood watch about halfway to us.

I looked back at Jasmine, and she was no longer crying, but her cheeks still reflected the wetness of spent tears.

"I showed him what they tried to make of me in the shadow zone. The way they sent me back all those years ago to scare everyone. Do you understand, Caleb?"

I did understand. Those people who abducted her all those years ago found the skinned body of the girl. She used it to scare Dale away but didn't want me to see her like that. For all I know it could be her true form, and the Jasmine I saw in modern dress was just a disguise. Whatever the situation was, she couldn't escape from it as long as she was trapped in the shadow zone.

"I think I understand." I said softly and sympathetically.

"You do, and you don't. The door's open now, and more's coming. Not tomorrow, not tonight, not today. Right now."

I reached down and grabbed the knife only to feel the warmth begin disappearing. I quickly dropped it into my backpack, remembering not to touch it again if possible.

"See, Caleb. They work different with the shadow zone. They're stronger, and that's why Gene wants them so bad, but you have to get *his* talisman. He's the one holding the door open because, right now, the evil spirit isn't powerful enough. At least, that's what the others are saying. Some of them are using this opportunity to sneak out, but unfortunately that might give the evil spirit more strength because these people have opposed it for many years. These are good ones that are getting away."

I sensed what she was saying was true, because not all of the shadow creatures were taking on forms and moving toward us. Some were trying to slither away, unnoticed. Still, I needed to get to higher ground. It was better than nothing.

"Jasmine, are you staying this time?" I hoped she would stay since I felt so much better and more confident with her around.

"I can't stay. Not yet anyways. There are too many things looking for me on the other side, and I have to find Dusty. By the way, I also call him Dusty now. He seemed to take a liking to his nickname you gave him. His real name's Jasper. I can't leave him alone for too long. Get to your friends, and remember, you must try to get the other piece from Gene. It should close the door."

Just like before, the wind slowly dissolved her figure, and she was gone, but this time she had left me with some advice. We had to get Gene's talisman. Easier said than done; we didn't even know what his was.

I made my way toward the tree, meeting up with Liam where he stood guard.

"You okay, Caleb?"

"Yeah, I guess."

"So what happened with Dale? One minute he was going after you, but then he ran off like something scared him to death."

"Jasmine did something, but she told me not to look, and you wouldn't have seen because she was behind the tree. I'll tell you about it later. She told me what we have to do to end all this."

"Really! And what's that?"

"It was a lot to take in, but we have to get another talisman from Gene. Do that, and it will close the door. He's the one holding it open. I don't know what it is or if he has just one, but Jasmine insisted we do it."

"Sounds easier said than done," he said. "And what's up with all these things forming out of nothing all over the place?" The black stuff was only in small pieces, but it was constantly changing its shape, as if trying to work out what it wanted to be.

"It's like we've talked about before, our fears make these things. Stuff we imagine. I've seen them in the shadow zone, and they formed a lot quicker there. They might be slower here because they don't have the power like they do in that place."

"Okay, I guess, but what was going on in the tree above you?"

"It was Gene, but only his face. I think he's somewhere between this world and the shadow zone and was waiting for Dale to send us over, but Jasmine ruined his plan when she scared Dale away."

"So come on, tell me. Why did Dale take off running?"

"She showed him what she looked like a hundred years ago. Remember the story Jake told us about the skinned girl? It was her. I guess it's really horrible so she made me close my eyes. To tell you the truth, I don't think I would've wanted to see it."

"Must be horrible for sure," Liam replied with a shudder.

"Let's just get to the tree. I think we can keep this to ourselves for now."

"So we don't tell them?"

"I really don't think Jasmine would want Krystal and Susan knowing for some reason. Would you?"

Liam just shook his head and went over to our main tree. The wind was still blowing fiercely, and the rain began falling in intermittent showers. We reached the tree, and Liam yelled up for one of the girls to grab his spear so he could climb up easier.

We carefully looked around for any close threats before giving up our weapons, and then I threw my spear and backpack up to Krystal. When she caught the bag, the top came open and the talismans fell out. She quickly grabbed them and placed them back into the backpack before they could roll off the platform. As she did so, a cold driving rain hit my face.

The creatures that were slowly forming around us were now getting more active, and this got me going up into the tree a little faster. Liam and Susan were busy securing one of our tarps over the platform. Krystal set the backpack down to help wrestle the tarp into place.

"Liam, is everything up?" I yelled over the loud, flapping tarp. It was whipping all over the tree and getting caught on branches.

"Yeah. I'm good," he hollered back, barely able to see them under the tarp because of the constant flapping.

I cut the spikes loose and let them swing down; they looked like they would work pretty well against a human, but I wasn't sure about the shadow creatures that were moving faster and growing stronger. I just hoped that the dog creature wouldn't come back, because tree or no tree, it would get us.

Needing to give me something to keep my mind occupied, I went to help the others secure the tarp. Underneath the green plastic, I could hear them trying to give each other instructions, and I was just about to dive under it myself when it pulled loose and fell over the top of them. That's when I realized that something was wrong. I saw four heads moving around under the tarp.

"Keep pulling it away, *boys!*"

Everyone stopped and went silent just before another strong gust of wind blew the tarp back up, revealing Gene between me and the three of them. Krystal screamed, and Susan tried taking a quick swing at Gene before the wind lost its power, dropping the tarp back on top of them.

"Get out! Jump if you have to!" Liam yelled.

I started untying another of the ropes that already secured the tarp, hoping that it would fly loose and allow them to see what was going on, but before I got it loose, Susan grabbed my hand.

"I'll help you," she whispered as she began pulling on the tarp to relieve the tension on the rope in one of the corners. Now she made it a bit easier, but I still worked frantically trying to untie it. Suddenly a clicking noise began coming from under the tarp and then all around; it had to be Gene trying to scare them.

I felt something crawling on my hand followed by a sharp pain—a kissing bug, and then there was another on my arm. As I slapped at them, the tarp flapped up again, allowing Liam to get out. As I finally let go of the rope, I could see Susan and Liam were fighting the same battle with the bugs, but Krystal was still under the tarp with Gene; we had to get her out.

A strong gust of wind came through, finally ripping the tarp loose and entangling it in some branches further away. Gene was gone. And so was Krystal.

Chapter 32

"WHERE'S KRYSTAL?" SUSAN YELLED.

"I don't know. Gene must have taken her!" I yelled back. Liam was looking around at the creatures that were still forming and moving closer to the tree.

"We have to do something quick. I don't think your spear trap is going to do much once these things start coming!" Liam yelled over the wind, throwing a rock at one of the creatures.

The rock hit and injured the creature, which twirled and toppled over itself from the impact. This was a good sign. At least we could hurt them or at a least hold them off. The creature shrieked and then retaliated by launching a handful of sticks and dirt toward the tree.

"We have to get Krystal back. We have to get her now before that horrible man does something to her." Susan said, looking desperately anxious, like she was ready to go down and start fighting the creatures with her bare hands. "What if he took her over to the shadow zone? You think he did? How do we get there?"

We didn't know what he planned on doing. I was sure he took her to the shadow zone, but I had no idea how to cross over since I'd never intentionally done it. That didn't stop them looking at me as if I knew how.

"I don't know how," I said after a brief hesitation.

"Jake probably knows, but he won't mess with it. Those shadow creatures came from somewhere, didn't they? So what's to say we can't use the same route?" Susan said, sounding rational again.

"She might be right, Caleb. The only thing I can think of is the house on the hill. They obviously used that place for something."

Then I remembered Jasmine saying the talismans were something else when they were in the shadow zone. If the door was open between the two worlds, then they might already have some of that power.

I kneeled down on the platform and dumped the contents from my backpack. Liam reached down, grabbed the pictures, and shoved them in his pocket. Susan knelt beside me to look at the talismans and hopefully find an answer. The problem was we didn't know what the question was.

"You think Gene's holding the door open, right?" Susan asked.

"Yeah, that's what Jasmine said," I answered, realization dawning.

"Well, wouldn't you use a key in a door?" She held up the key.

Liam quickly tried to stop her. "No don't touch it." But it was too late. They would now be looking for her as well. We sat for a minute before Susan finally remembered what Jake had said, realizing that the simple thing she just did had condemned her.

"The shadows," Liam said. "Is it that simple?"

One of the creatures was now close to six feet tall. Its lower jaw sunk down, broader than the rest of its face, and two tusklike teeth protruded outward. Its arms and legs were growing muscles, turning into the ogre creature from the game Battle Masters. This must have been one of Liam's fears or possibly my own. That meant the others would probably keep taking on the legions of trolls and goblins and other creatures from the books we read.

I had to concentrate on crossing over. The key would work with a skeleton key lock, but who was to say that simply placing it in a shadowed area wouldn't do the trick? Just like the creatures emerging from the shadows, we would have to try to go through that way.

"Quick. We have to find an area with shadows!" I said to the two of them, and they looked at me like they already knew what I was thinking.

Liam was already looking around. "There's nothing up here, only along the ground and behind the trees. We can't go down there with those things. Look at that ogre son of a—"

I cut him off. "It's the only way to get over there. Think about the rock, Liam. It hurt that one, and we have our spears. We can fight them off until we find some decent-sized shadows. There were all kinds of shadows by the tree where Jasmine saved me from Dale. We can make it."

"What if it won't work, Caleb? What if we leave this tree with no way back up, and it doesn't work?" Susan said, still grabbing the other talismans and placing them in the backpack to get ready to leave.

I didn't have an answer. Neither did Liam. The way I figured, if this didn't work, then we could at least try running.

"We have to try, Susan," I said, and she nodded. It was strange that I was kind of becoming a leader when I was the youngest. "We have to jump down from here and roll to avoid an injury. Then we'll need to hurry to the tree before one of those things grabs us."

"Okay, that's exactly what I was thinking," she said sarcastically; perhaps I wasn't the boss after all.

"Good. I'm glad we're all on the same page," Liam said with a smile.

"You guys are idiots. You know that, right? Maybe a little crazy!"

"Right, but we're the idiots that are trying to rescue Krystal!" I said, losing the smile, "And I hope we're the good kind of idiots, the ones that live and get to tell the tale!"

Liam yelled, "Let's go!" and jumped out of the tree, landing with a slight roll to absorb the impact. I tossed the backpack and spears to him, and he stood guard as Susan jumped down next. I followed her, totally botching my jump by overextending my roll and eating the dirt a few feet past them. I scurried around on my hands and knees and then got up to get my spear from Liam before grabbing my backpack and running toward the tree. Susan readied her spear and followed behind me, with Liam right behind her.

The creatures noticed our departure and slowly changed their direction of creeping. The large ogre creature was now growing hair and didn't show any signs of its original shadowy form. It seemed to be the most aware, and instead of shrieking like the others, it startled us with a horrendous, deafening roar. This didn't scare me. I just decided to run quicker because I wanted to.

I looked back, noticing Susan was some distance back, so I slowed down. The tree was approaching quickly, and I needed her to retrieve the key from my backpack.

"Susan!"

"What?"

"When we get to the tree, you need to grab the key."

"Okay, but we're losing Liam!"

I looked toward Liam, who was standing his ground just a short distance out. Maybe he thought he could buy us some time because every so often he would turn and launch a rock at one of the creatures. This seemed to hinder their development and movement because they would pause and look at the injured creature before continuing. Susan came sliding in right behind me when I reached the tree. She already had her hand in the backpack and was digging around for the key. Seconds later, she was handing it to me.

Liam stopped about ten feet from us. "Hurry up with whatever you're going to do! They're starting to do something."

I desperately poked at the shadows in the tree, hoping that something would appear or happen soon. As irrational as this seemed, I could think of no other way into the shadow zone.

The creatures now seemed to be communicating with one another, turning and looking at each other as they made small noises resembling chatter. I poked around with the key, feeling more and more anxious with every second. Then Susan bumped into me from behind.

"Caleb, behind us!"

Still wiggling the key around as if I was trying to get it to connect with a lock, I spun around. Some of the shadow creatures were slithering between us. They moved under our feet and toward the tree like a snake, and Susan shifted her feet to avoid being touched. They kept moving until they formed into a solid mass of darkness. It started twirling around the tree trunk, stretching several feet high and wide and becoming distorted in shape. It seemed to shape itself according to the natural features and contours of the tree by flowing around twists in the trunk and old broken limbs.

"Here!" a voice echoed from the distorted mass of darkness.

I turned back around in the direction of the voice, and the swirl revealed a small knot in the tree. I looked carefully, trying to figure out why this knot was revealed and then realized that a crack in the center of the knot had taken the shape of a keyhole.

"Susan, look."

She faced the tree and saw it. "Use it!"

"But what if it doesn't do what we want it to? What if it takes us somewhere else?"

Liam finally came to join us next to the tree. "Somewhere else would be good," he said and pointed in the direction we'd come from.

The ogreish creature was beginning to rally the others and stepping in short movements toward us. The other creatures would look at it and then toward us, like they understood what they must do. Making a decision, but hoping I wouldn't regret it, I stuck the key in the hole and turned it. It clicked just as a regular door would. It couldn't be that simple, but it was.

The tree began glowing with an eerie light between the cracks of the aged bark. The light wasn't blinding, but more of a translucent glow that filtered out somewhere between the light of sunset and sunrise, but holding onto the colors of darkness. Greens, blues, and purples flashed down the tree as the bark began separating and breaking down, revealing a core of darkness.

"What's it doing, Caleb?" Susan asked.

I didn't want to take my eyes of the beautiful display, but I gave Susan a confused look regardless. The creatures were still moving toward us and quickening their pace.

I brushed my hand against the glowing, flickering lights and heard thunder in the void of darkness before me. Then I noticed lightning and quickly retracted my hand, thinking I might get shocked. I thought I knew what we had to do.

"Both of you get close."

"Caleb!" Liam said frantically. "We need to do something or get running. Now!"

The creatures were right on top of us. Without thinking, I stood up and grabbed Liam and Susan, and then the three of us fell backward into the void.

Chapter 33

I T WAS SOOTHING, ALMOST comfortable. I was floating but unafraid in the darkness of storm clouds that suddenly surrounded us. Susan and Liam looked scared but also consumed by the awe of this place. Although I was falling, I was in control and not worried about impact.

"Caleb, what did you do?" Susan asked.

"I panicked when I saw how close those things were and pulled us through. I think it's the shadow zone, but it seems less hazy than usual, like someone controlling a storm."

Liam shifted his body to a standing position, but it felt like we were still in midair. "Maybe it's like this when we enter willingly. Maybe we... or you... have some control this time."

I shifted around to face Liam, and Susan did the same once she broke her gaze from the ridiculous arrays of lightning moving around in the clouded surroundings. The air smelled clean and crisp, like a fresh storm. I liked it, and I think they did too.

A break in the clouds below us revealed what appeared to be mountain peaks rising in the distance. After it cleared a little more, I realized it was the mountains by our house in the real world. I didn't recognize the more jagged and barren mountains in the other direction. Then I heard a cry in the distance. It was Krystal.

They were down on the ground, about a quarter mile from us,

and I could see Gene dragging her as he held onto one of her arms. She was putting up a good fight. As we continued to drop, I saw that Gene was heading for some structures in the distance and realized it was the camps. He had a reason to go there, and it was probably part of his plan so he could cross back over again from the shadow zone. After all, Jasmine said the evil spirit would likely go after him once it was all settled.

"Looks like Gene's taking her to the camps," I said, wondering how we might speed up our descent, but I didn't want to get down too quickly.

"Yeah, I see them too," Liam said.

The look of anger once again consumed Susan as she stared at Gene and Krystal. She clenched her fists until her knuckles whitened.

"Me too. I think Liam's right. I think you have some control here. I feel safer when I am closer to you, and you've been here more than any of us. But why did I come through? I thought it was after you two."

"You touched the talisman, Susan. Liam tried to stop you, but it was too late. Krystal did the same thing, and that's how easily it gets you." Susan looked away and said nothing, but still stayed by my side.

With the gracefulness of angels touching down, we safely landed clear of any cacti. The land was strange; it seemed to be the same as our world, but different. Besides the constant bombardment of lightning, the sky was dark with clouds, but the ground glowed like it was illuminated by moonlight from below.

The plants and trees were scattered, except in certain areas where they grew in dense clusters. The ground was almost barren from anything except for loose dirt and sand, with almost no rocks or grass to be seen. The hills rolled from one to the other, the same as in our world, but the mountains in the distance were different.

Creatures flew across the sky, and considering the darkness of the land, I thought perhaps they were ravens or owls, but then I realized they weren't even birds. Looking down, I also noticed what looked like small animal tracks in the dirt. They were about an inch in diameter.

"Insects," Liam said.

"What?" Susan asked.

He pointed at various distinctive spots on the ground where the tracks were. "Insect tracks."

"What do you mean, insect tracks? I don't get what you're trying to say," Susan said with an agitated tone.

"Tracks after something walks through the dust. In this case, it's tracks from insects."

"No, no. They're way too big." Her agitation now turned into nervousness.

"Well, we're not in Kansas anymore," Liam said. Susan looked even more nervous as I let out a chuckle because I saw that expression coming.

I was trying to block out the horrible thoughts of bugs the size of rabbits walking or flying around, especially if they were bad insects, like spiders, scorpions, or centipedes. Of course, this would probably be the case in our situation. If we didn't want something because it scared us, that's what we got.

"Help!" came a distant cry.

Susan clenched her spear tighter and looked at us. "It's Krystal. Come on, guys, we've got to get moving."

Picking up our pace, we tried to close the distance between them because we needed to get Krystal before Gene made her a permanent feature in the shadow zone... and before the evil spirit found out we were there, if it didn't know already. I could hear hollering and shrieks behind us and could only imagine that it was more shadow creatures. It sounded relatively far-off, and I hoped that we could make it to Krystal first.

We crested one of the hills and saw a wash below, only it wasn't like the wash in our world. This was a stream flowing steadily with water. We would have to remember that things were different in the shadow zone; a dry wash in our world was a rushing stream in the shadow zone. It didn't look deep, so after figuring out a good crossing point, we used our spears to check the depth. We interlocked our arms together and made our way slowly across. It was only about a foot deep but was flowing fast enough to knock a person down.

We walked up the embankment on the other side, noticing that we were further into the hills and closer to the camps than I thought. Standing on top of the ridge was making me feel exposed, especially with the glow that came from the ground. I crouched down and heard the distant noises getting louder. I motioned for Susan and Liam to keep still.

"We have to keep moving and get Krystal before they get too far away," said Susan, clearly growing anxious.

"I know, but we can't lower our guard and leave ourselves exposed. Right?" I hoped Liam would back me up.

"He's right. We don't know what's out there or if Gene's leading us into a trap. Also, we have no idea what this evil spirit is capable of."

Susan said nothing, but I could tell she begrudgingly agreed. Eventually we moved off down the ravine, crouching as best we could without hindering our stability. About halfway down, Susan suddenly stopped and jumped back.

"What was that?" she said, pointing to a distant bush that stood alone.

I looked where she was pointing but couldn't see anything. "What was what?"

"It moved!" she hissed.

It resembled a tree or bush in our world when it becomes infected with mistletoe. It did look strange and I believed her, but it didn't move while we watched.

"You sure it wasn't just the wind, Susan? Did you see anything, Caleb?" Liam asked, less convinced than I was.

"I swear it just moved, and I thought I saw eyes. I saw them blink," Susan answered back.

I still couldn't see anything and wanted to keep moving. "Come on, let's go. We only have this ravine, and then it's a straight shot to the camps." I hoped I hadn't made the wrong decision.

I took the lead and began making my way down, rounding the bush but keeping my distance. Still, nothing moved, but just when I took my eyes off it, I heard something fall. Looking back at the bush, I could see that one of the clumps had fallen off and was now making a clicking, crackling noise. Then it slowly started moving and pulsating, like it was breathing, with a slight wheezing sound as it began to grow.

We froze on the spot, unsure what to do, as a fluidlike substance began trickling out from underneath it. The wheezing turned into sounds of pain as what looked like an oozing sack grew larger, stretching out like something was trying to free itself from within.

A slight breeze blew through the ravine, carrying the stench of sour milk and feces from the sack, and we all gagged, almost puking as a hideous head emerged through a murky membrane, like something from a horror film. It shifted around, sniffing the air before growing silent. I clasped my hand over my mouth and nose, trying to block out the smell, hoping my gagging wouldn't draw attention to me.

The creature continued emerging and eventually took on the shape of something that looked half human and half bear, but with no fur. It shook uncontrollably as the eerie light glowed through the creature's translucent pinkish-red skin, revealing its organs and weird bone structure. It arched its head back and forth, trying to look around, and I desperately hoped that it could not see very well, but its eyes were disproportionally large, with a shiny silver layer that absorbed the faint light of this world. Lightning flashed across the sky, making it appear like the creature was blinking.

Half of its body was still connected to the sack, and the exposed half clawed at the loose dirt, attempting to free itself. It eventually managed to break free from the sack and took several staggering steps back toward the bush; its feet were large, with two massive claws that touched the ground at separate times. I was glad to see it walking away from us and that it didn't seem too concerned about us so we silently crept away across the ravine and up the other side.

I managed to climb to the top, remaining silent until my foot slipped, sending a rock rolling down the side of the ravine and into the sandy area below. As I regained my balance, I looked toward the creature but found that it had disappeared. Only some small tracks remained in the sandy soil, and a small, rope-like object extended from the bush to the side of the ravine below. None of us could see it because of the angle of the ledge—at least that's where I assumed the creature was.

"Where did it go?" Susan looked over the ledge, leaning a little too far for my comfort.

Suddenly, there were thumps on the sandy soil resembling a beating heart, and the rope-like object shifted and began dragging from one side of the ravine; it must have been attached to the creature, like the umbilical cord of a human baby. Now the creature appeared again, still pinkish-red but maturing rapidly as hair grew on its body.

It appeared to be playing with the rock I'd dislodged, looking confused, sniffing it and then the air before licking the rock like it wondered if it was edible. The creature then began whining with frustration and irritability just before it looked straight at me. Its cold, bright eyes reflected like silver plates in the dim light, putting a terrible shudder down my spine. Then it wrapped its long, clawlike fingers around the rock and hurled it at the three of us. It flew right past us, barely missing Susan's head, but it still managed to do some damage.

Susan lost her balance and went sliding feet first down into the ravine until her momentum shifted her into a roll for the last twenty feet. Eventually, she lay there at the bottom, and we made our way down as quickly as possible. We had no idea if she'd been knocked out or not, but it certainly seemed that the creature's intentions were to harm us. We had to hurry.

We reached the bottom, relieved to find out Susan was already getting to her feet. She looked okay except for a few minor scratches on her arms and face.

Liam grabbed one of her arms. "You okay? Nothing feels broken, does it?"

"I don't think so. Just a little shook up, that's all."

The creature paced back and forth, looking at us unsure of its next move until it suddenly came running toward us, unleashing a high-pitched shriek before jumping into the air in violent fury, kicking sand across the ravine as it left the ground. Just as we were braced for its impact with our spears, the creature jerked to a sudden halt in midattack, and the angered shrieking turned to cries of pain.

We stepped back a little while, helping Susan, and watched the creature writhe on the ground in pain. Its guts were lying in the dirt, spread out across the last few feet of its attack and still attached to the cord that connected it to the bush. I then realized that the umbilical-like cord must have reached its limit in midair and ripped the creature's guts out. The disemboweled creature was shaking and quivering as it slowly died, and I somehow pitied it, wondering if this was one of the lost bodies or souls in this dreadful place.

I took my spear and stabbed it through where I thought the heart would be. It jerked several times and then laid still. I had never really killed anything before that, apart from kissing bugs. The bush began shaking again, withdrawing the remaining cord into itself, and I hoped it would fall still again. Instead, it started rattling and clicking very quickly before another sack fell off, and then another and another.

Liam was already halfway up the ravine with Susan when I heard him yell down to me that it was time to go. As I ran up the hillside as quickly as possible, I wondered what would become of these creatures once they did detach and reach their maturity; I just hoped I wouldn't be around. As I caught up with Liam and Susan, I could tell Susan had hurt one of her legs. As we crested the top of the ravine again, the shrieks and cries that were in the distance were getting louder.

"Susan, Liam, do you hear that? They're getting closer. I think they know we're here."

"We need to hurry," Susan said weakly. "I'm already tired of being here and dealing with all this stuff. I just want to grab Krystal, break Gene's nose, and get the hell out of here!"

"She's right, Caleb. We need to get Krystal and get out of here. If we even know how to."

I reached into my pocket and pulled out the key. "We use the key again."

"What if it doesn't work that way? Have you thought about that, Caleb?" Susan didn't sound weak anymore when she said this but angry at me.

She was right. I hadn't fully thought about the situation. I was just trying to get Krystal back and close the door. I didn't consider how we'd get home to our world.

Chapter 34

WE HEADED ACROSS THE rocky ridge toward the camps. The location was the same but in many ways different. The cat's claw bushes growing from the rock outcroppings seemed to grab at me with more thorns than usual. I assumed that just about everything here was trying to drag a person down.

We decided to take a break behind a large rock to give Susan's leg a rest and figure out what to do next; soon we'd be at the camps and weren't sure what to expect. We hadn't seen any more signs of Gene or Krystal and weren't sure if they were even there at all.

"What do we do when we get to those buildings?" Susan was not used to calling the area "the camps," like Liam and I did.

"I think we should make our way to the nearest one and see if we can figure it out. Everything might change by the time we get there," Liam said, and I agreed with him. Every time we moved around in this place, something changed or we had a new idea or it felt like we should have approached it differently.

"Worst that can happen is we run into Gene and have to deal with him. At least we can find some cover from those creatures getting closer in the distance.

"Wouldn't it be an obvious place for us to hide, Caleb, if those things are after us?" Susan asked.

I looked across to the camps, not seeing much of anything until I focused in on something in a window of the building that looked like a church. I waited a minute to see if it would move again, and it did.

"Look, you two, in the second floor window of the little church. I saw something move. I think they're in there!"

Susan and Liam turned to look at the window. I tried pointing out to them the best I could. It was weird how the remaining white paint on the buildings reflected brilliantly from the lightning flashing across the sky. I think this helped me notice the object move in the first place.

Susan suddenly got excited. "I saw it move!"

Liam motioned to hush her. "Me too, but we can probably be heard from here and need to be quiet," he whispered.

We all saw it, and it couldn't be mistaken. It was Krystal's strawberry-blonde hair moving around.

"It's a trap." I said. "He wants us to see her and come running. We need our own distraction. One of us needs to go straight up the path while the others go around the side."

Susan and Liam both just stared at me. It was clear they both thought that I'd be the one on my own since it was my idea. Then Susan started rubbing her ankle.

"I can't move quickly and think I might have sprained my ankle in the fall. So, I guess if you go down the middle, Caleb, Liam and I will come in from the side, trying to stay out of sight."

"Okay," I replied, suddenly unsure of my plan, but I couldn't back down. "You two should head out first to get a head start, since my path's easier. And I think we need to get moving because one of those sounds in the distance is familiar, and I'd rather not see that thing again."

"What thing?" Susan asked.

"This thing, this...creature I ran into in the shadow zone once before."

Its shrieks marked the air as it let out a foul cry in the distance, letting me know that it was the beast I feared. We would have no chance in the open with that thing and needed some kind of shelter.

"Well," Liam said, hesitating, "be safe, bro, and we'll have your back."

I just nodded. I watched Susan and Liam move out ahead of me; soon I couldn't see them and hoped it was the same for Gene. I waited for another minute and then headed out.

The air grew stale and sour as I got closer to the camps, like the same smell in the house on the hill. The wind began blowing harder, and swells of dust began forming in the gaps between the buildings; I strained to see through the dust for any possible signs of Gene or a trap.

The eerie light and the continuous flashes of lightning illuminated the camps, and in a moment of brightness, I thought I saw some sort of movement ahead. I froze, not sure what it was, and realized I was completely exposed to a possible attack. I looked for a means of cover and tried to not look away from the object ahead any longer than needed.

The object appeared to be moving between the buildings, so I continued forward, trying to be quiet and move steadily. I noticed the object seemed to stay away from one of the buildings. That would be my immediate target because this would also bring me nearer to the path Liam and Susan were taking. I just hoped it wouldn't put us too close together.

I was about two hundred feet from the building and was confident that I would make it there unseen. I was wrong. The object stopped moving between the buildings and turned toward me. I could feel its eyes on me, like it was preparing to do something. I tried to look around nonchalantly for Liam and Susan, but there was no sign of them. I turned my attention back toward the distant silhouette. Was it Gene, and if so, why wasn't he moving?

I shifted my walk so that I moved closer to the building as I approached the camps, hoping to hide from my motionless observer. I did this thinking that there might be a chance it hadn't noticed me through all the dust, but I knew I was kidding myself.

I reached the edge of the building, leaned against the wall, and waited to see what the figure was doing. I could only assume it was Gene, but somehow the presence felt different. It had absolutely no fear of me. I peeked around the corner, and the figure was still standing motionless in the open. I ducked back and decided to make my way toward the other side of the building and try to get a glimpse from there.

As I hugged the wall, I slid my hand along the stone and felt something sticky and slimy on the wall. I quickly pulled my hand away, and there was sticky residue left on my palm. I saw a wet spot on an old doorframe; it was the color of blood and clear mucus. It looked like a knot in the wood until it blinked. It was an eyeball, and it began looking around.

I walked a little closer, hesitant and yet curious, and then I recognized it. I couldn't mistake the eye I looked into right before I thought I was going to be bludgeoned to death. It was Dale's. I put the pieces together; Gene was somehow using this eye to find us.

I dropped to the ground, trying to escape its gaze, but it followed me like it had no boundaries. I grabbed a handful of the powdery dirt and threw it in the eye. It quickly blinked and quivered as I heard a scream from the other side of the building. The eye closed, slowly dissolving back into the wood and forming a regular knot. Then came another yell.

"Hey, *boy!*"

I looked back toward the figure between the buildings, realizing it was making its way around to the side of the building where I stood. A gust of wind swept through just quickly enough to pull back the hat from my pursuer, revealing Gene with his yellowish, bloodshot eyes staring through some type of glasses in my direction. I turned and ran toward the other corner, tripping on some rotted wood that had fallen off the building, but managed to regain my footing fairly quickly and keep moving.

Reaching the other side, I looked back to check that Gene wasn't behind me, and a flash of lightning revealed a shadow approaching the corner. I breathed a sigh of relief as I saw Susan and Liam sneaking inside the building that Krystal was in. The plan had worked, but I still had to keep Gene distracted until they freed Krystal. But where could I go from there?

There was the pit and the other buildings, but neither one offered much cover. Without any more thought, I ran with no set destination. Out of the corner of my eye, I saw him running toward me, moving so swiftly that the duster jacket he wore flapped above him, giving him the appearance of flying.

I made a hard right toward another building that I assumed was the old mining office where they discovered the paperwork. If I could make it there, I could weave in between the broken structures and possibly buy myself some time. When I got to the door, it was locked. Gene was quickly closing in.

I could finally see that he had some sort of goggles under the brim of his hat, probably to block out the horrible dust. The lightning flashed harder across the sky, followed by the roar of thunder echoing with a weird distortion like it was inside a tunnel. I kicked at the door, but it didn't open. I was trapped.

Chapter 35

GENE WAS NO LONGER running but walking in long, confident strides toward me. Shaking like a leaf, I tried to prepare myself for the fight, raising my spear to jab at his middle when he got near. But he didn't hesitate one bit as he kept moving forward. Then the warm feeling came with a comforting voice.

"Sshhh."

I looked around but didn't see her. The wind whipped around even harder now, stinging my eyes and making me close them to regain my vision. When I opened them, Gene was even closer, but he was slowing down. The wind swirled furiously, pushing and pulling him off balance, and he tried to fight it, angrily swinging his fists into the air. I couldn't imagine how he thought this might resolve his situation as he was pushed back, legs locked and digging into the dirt as the wind tore at him. Then in the dust surrounding Gene, I could see Jasmine.

Through the noise of the wind and Gene's agitated grunts, I heard her tell me to run.

I didn't need to be told twice and took off fast toward the building where the others were. I only hoped that they had already freed Krystal, and as I approached the stairs, I exhaled a huge sigh of relief as I saw the three of them making their way down the stairs. Krystal, thankfully, looked unhurt. In turn, they looked very surprised to see me.

"Come on! I think Jasmine can only hold him so long!" I yelled up to them.

The building moaned and creaked in the intense wind that Jasmine was stirring up, and as we made our way outside it, looked like Gene was gone, along with the wind.

"I think we should head toward where the Three Trees would be in our world and see if the key works again in the same place!" Liam shouted.

"Sounds good, except for that!" I replied, pointing at the hordes of creatures making their way toward us. They would cut us off from reaching the Three Trees; judging by the dust cloud in their wake, I assumed there was a lot of them.

As they got closer, I could make out some of the creature's details, and these were very different from the black things that had attacked us before and much more frightening. Some wore pieces of garment and armor, carrying medieval weaponry that they waved in the air with fury. There was no way we'd try for the Three Trees, and, in panic, we started arguing about our options.

"No, no, no. None of those ideas will work *boys*... and *girls*."

By the time we could react, Gene already had his arm wrapped around Krystal's neck, using her as a human shield to prevent us from getting to him as he stepped back a few paces.

"I can only do so much here, but now those things are here to kill all of us, you idiots! I had plans, and you wouldn't believe the things I could have done with *it* backing me up. The world was mine, and it still will be! *The world... will... be..... mine!*" He finished off this rant with a psychotic laugh that made me tremble even more.

"Let her go!" Susan took a step closer, but this only made Gene tighten his grip, making Krystal gasp for air.

Liam pulled Susan back. "Stop! He's going to hurt her."

A tear came down Susan's face, but she wasn't sad. She was angry. "*So what do we do, then?*" she spat, almost as manically as Gene

In an instant, everything went still around us, and in the silence came a blinding flash of light. We all flew backward, and Gene lost his grip on Krystal. She stood up and ran toward us, but Gene was too quick. He reached out, grabbing her arm as she kicked and squirmed, but it was no use. He was too fast and strong here.

"I guess I'll have to settle with just one of you to barter with the spirit," he sneered, holding onto Krystal's arm with a viselike grip. Then a sudden gust of wind whipped off Gene's hat, exposing the goggles up on his forehead. There was something about how old they looked...

"His talisman!" I screamed, pointing at the goggles.

"What?" Susan and Liam cried.

"The goggles! They're his talisman! We need to get them, or he'll use them to disappear with Krystal. Don't you two get it?"

"Clever boy! Yes, I put these on, imagine somewhere else, and poof. I'm gone," he said as he began to lower the goggles over his eyes. "See ya. Have fun with those things."

His body began to disappear, and Krystal would soon follow.

"Well, have fun imagining this!" Liam shouted as he jumped toward Gene.

I hadn't realized it, but Liam had grabbed the knife talisman out of my backpack and was now thrusting it down toward Gene's arm. Then something incredible happened. The knife began glowing like molten metal that should've burned Liam's hands, but it didn't. The blade began extending long and full as the handle grew outward, forming a full grip. Now Liam was holding an ancient Roman-looking sword.

With a strength I could never have imagined Liam had, it came crashing down, severing Gene's arm just below his elbow. He was shocked at first, and as the severed limb fell to the ground, he let out a blood-curdling scream. His other arm lost its grip on Krystal. As I reached to grab her around her waist, Susan leaped for the goggles, but Gene wouldn't let go. He continued to fade away, but very slowly, and Susan looked at him, clenching her fist.

"I told everyone I'd do this!" she yelled. With all the strength she could muster, she slammed her fist into his nose, flattening it as blood burst out from both nostrils and split across the top. He let out another scream, but still he didn't let go of the goggles as she tried to pull them off him.

I knew we had to get them and reached in my pocket to pull out the small Statue of Liberty knife and unfolded the blade. As his body continued to disappear, the goggles themselves were still very clear, and I pulled at the strap before I sliced the blade through it. Susan and I fell backward with a crash, still holding onto the goggles.

Badly winded, I felt hands moving around me and could only imagine that the creatures were already there to seize us, but it wasn't. It was just Liam and Krystal helping us up. I looked toward Gene and held out the pocketknife, ready to stab at him if he approached, but he was gone. At least most of him was gone. His arm lay on the ground with the hand clenching tightly around something.

Liam stepped toward it and then got down on one knee to take a closer look.

"Huh. It stinks," he said, laughing as he pried open the fingers on the hand. It no longer moved, blinked, or winked, but I knew it was Dale's eyeball. It was crushed from the nerves tensing in Gene's severed arm.

"Well, I wonder if Dale's still looking for that!" said Susan, gaining a smirk from all of us.

"Horrible thing," I said. "Gene was using that to look for us. Like he could see what it saw."

Krystal and Susan looked at me like I was crazy and then simply shrugged it off. They had to remember for a second where we were. Brushing off dirt from my clothes, I looked into the distance.

The dust cloud was growing larger, and the horrible noises were growing louder. We didn't have much time left. Krystal began walking in the opposite direction. "We have to move and now."

Liam started to follow her. "She's right. We can't stay here. We need to keep moving until we figure this out."

Chapter 36

D ESPITE WANTING TO GO back to the Three Trees, the only way
to get away from all the creatures was to head higher up into the
mountains. As we made sure we had all the talismans, Susan wondered
about our parents and, presuming we got back to our world, how long
we would have been gone. The best I could do was to suggest that
when in the other world, time in our own stood still; Liam suggested
that was still the least of our problems. I agreed, but said nothing.

When we got further up, I heard the sounds of boards snapping
and shrieks and cries and looked down toward the camps. A small
group of the shadow creatures had arrived and began ravaging through
the area. They were probably searching for us; they didn't know we
had left. That was good news. I couldn't see any sign of the big dog
creature, and that was a little more good news, but I guess it wouldn't
be long before it showed up.

"My leg's hurting pretty bad, you guys." Susan knelt down to rub
her swollen ankle.

"We're going to have to try carrying her. We can't stop," I said,
catching my breath. We had never been that far up the mountains
before, and I hadn't realized how steep they were. If we could only
make it to the first peak, we could get some idea of where to go or
what to do.

I grabbed one of Susan's arms, and Krystal got under the other to help relieve some of the weight from her ankle. We began to move again, but Liam just stood where he was, looking at the sword. It was no longer glowing, but he was looking at it, and I could tell that he was thinking about possibly fighting the creatures off.

"Come on, Liam!" I shouted, forgetting the creatures were at the camps. I instantly regretted shouting. I looked to see if they had noticed, but once again, luck seemed to be on our side as they continued rampaging through the camps. I apologized for yelling, and we all agreed we needed to keep our noise down.

"What do you think they're doing down there? Do you think they're looking for us or are just plain crazy for destruction?" Susan winced and stood on just one leg. I could sense her pain and wished we could do more for her; then I had an idea and got everyone to stop again.

I pulled off my shirt and got Liam to cut off the long sleeves with the sword. Then we fashioned them, by splitting them along the seams, into a makeshift bandage. Susan smiled gratefully as Krystal played nurse, and I put my shirt back on. Liam gave me a look that suggested he had no idea what our mom would say.

Hoping we had a good head start, we were almost to the first peak with maybe a hundred feet left to go. As we started getting closer to the summit, I felt the warmth returning to me, and I felt powerful again and comforted.

"Jasmine's up there!" I said and began to move faster up the slope, feeling like I was practically carrying Susan by myself.

"How do you know?" asked Liam.

I simply told him that didn't matter.

We got over the last little bit of rocks and moved toward her while she waited at the top of the peak for us. I was expecting a smiling welcome, but when we reached her, she didn't say a word as she looked down at the evil hoard devastating the camps. Then I heard the particular howling noise I was dreading to hear; the dog creature was there now. Because it seemed to be more responsive and quicker than the other creatures, I knew it wouldn't be long before it realized we were no longer there.

"Jasmine," I said, still happy see her, "what should we do?"

"Sshhh. Don't talk so loud," she replied, still unable to take her eyes off the camps. It finally occurred to me that she was watching her old home being ripped to shreds.

As I was talking to Jasmine, the others sat down to get their breath and allow Susan to rest her ankle. Down in the camps, the creatures went from building to building, randomly smashing whatever they could. Maybe our scent was still there, confusing them. I looked at Jasmine and noticed she was staring at me. Her eyes looked sad, and I thought she would cry, but she didn't.

"The big guy's very mad at you four," she said, pointing at the mountains in the distance. "You know a little of how this place works, and he sure don't like it."

"He?"

"Well, it usually sounds like a man's voice when it speaks so we call it 'he.'"

The clouds above the mountains were spinning quicker than before, centering directly over the highest peak. The lightning seemed to focus on striking this peak, sending trails of electrical charges down the mountain as if it would come to life like something from a Frankenstein movie. Now, tears began trickling down Jasmine's face.

"It will be here soon. I mean he will be here soon. I wouldn't be so worried about them, those horrible things down there, but you need to get out of here. You have to find a spot, like the one you came through. That's how it works for people who aren't stuck here, like me. Use the same talisman; otherwise it takes you to different places or changes things around. The only way to return and keep the door closed is to go back the way you came."

"So we have to go back to the same tree?"

"Huh, no, stupid!" she said laughing a little, shaking the tears away and then smiling to show she was only teasing. "You just have to use the same talisman. Remember, it doesn't work everywhere, but there are places all around, and you just have to find them. Use the goggles, but whatever you do, don't imagine your world with the goggles on or you might slip through. Alone."

That was going to be hard to do so I didn't leave the others stranded. I also wished I could take Jasmine and Dusty back with me.

"Think of me when you wear them," she said, reaching out to hold my hand, squeezing it so tight I thought I would lose all feeling. But after a moment she relaxed. "Don't be afraid. You have to get back and close the door. We'll hold him off as long as we can, and once you get through, separate the talismans and hide them and don't tell anyone you don't have to tell."

I put the goggles on as best as I could. As I looked around, I noticed that things were different. They were like binoculars, and I could focus in so much further than with the naked eye. Things close by were not blurred, but those far away were magnified maybe a hundred times or more. I immediately looked toward where the lightning was striking and could see a shadowy figure standing at the top of the other peak of the strange mountains. I could tell from where I stood that it was staring at us.

I turned and looked back at Jasmine. She looked the same with the goggles on, but she had a glow surrounding her. Then I noticed Dusty standing to our side. I quickly removed the goggles, and he was gone; I guessed he didn't want to be seen right then. I put the goggles back on, and there he was again, smiling up at me.

Jasmine pulled at my hand. "Come on, walk with me."

We headed along the ridgeline, moving further toward the main peak, and the walk was easier than I thought it would be with the goggles on. The warmth in my chest and the feeling of confidence overwhelmed me into thinking everything was going to be easy and okay. I could see different shades of glowing colors coming from underneath rocks and around the base of cacti and shrubs all around me—blues, yellows, oranges, and so many different greens. Some colors mixed together, glowing like fiery Christmas lights, which added to the illusion that I was out of harm's way.

"Look for a cold feeling. Look for the blackness beyond blackness," Jasmine said.

Dusty was slowly trailing behind, and the others were still further back. I knew they couldn't see Dusty and wondered if they even saw what was going on with me and Jasmine. After all, they seemed to miss so much when Jasmine was around.

Uphill, just ahead of me, the peak seemed to be changing. I could see something strange, like a wall of broken glass with all the pieces moving around. Each piece seemed transparent, but together they formed a blackness that seemed to go on forever. I realized, trying to shake off the chilling feeling that even eroded the warmth in my chest that this was the cold feeling I was looking for.

There was no real color, only shades of distortion that created an overwhelming sensation of emptiness; this was the blackness she was talking about.

"You see it, don't you?" Jasmine said as we stopped walking.

"Yes."

"Doesn't give you a good feeling to look at it, does it?"

"No, not at all," I said, turning to see that the others were following me now. Despite her ankle being strapped, Susan was still limping, and Krystal and Liam were doing their best to keep her moving.

"This is where you'll find the keyhole for the talisman," Jasmine said and turned away.

"Wait!" I said, grabbing her arm. "You're coming with us, you and Dusty."

"We can't. This is our place, and we can't go back, not now. There are too many of us here fighting this thing to keep it in this realm. We're trapped now, just as trapped as we were a hundred years ago. We can't break free without finding what we lost, our pieces. Don't you get it? We all used to have something that the evil wanted. Some of us still do. For those who lost theirs, the evil has them now and won't give them back until our spirits die, adding to its power.

"It happens to everyone who comes in. People like Gene provide people who don't want to go back because they know they'll die once they get back. That's why they cut off the heads of their victims before sending them through. Those people, those poor, poor souls, they have nothing to fight for because there's nothing to return to. They simply join with the evil, adding to its creations of mangled creatures and whatever other nightmares that he wants to make with their spirits."

I had no idea how to respond to this, since we were in no position to fight this evil; it appeared that no one was. I could only look at her and let her sadness carry over into me, slowly losing that warm feeling inside and the glow of invincibility.

"Dusty and I have to look after each other here, Caleb. And we've also got her."

She pointed behind me and past the others who were still making their way toward us. Walking behind Susan and the others now was a beautiful woman in a blue dress, with long blonde hair blowing in the wind of the oncoming storm that never ceased. She also glowed, even brighter than Jasmine.

"She was your flash of safety earlier. She already knew you guys were coming here, somehow, and she broke Gene's grip on Krystal."

I took the goggles off and on, only to see her disappear and reappear. "Who is she?"

Jasmine put one arm on my shoulder and leaned close to my ear whispering. "Her name's Sonya. She used to live in the other world, not long ago."

I watched as she moved closer, trying to see if I recognized her. She didn't look familiar, but for some reason Jasmine was hinting that I should know her.

"She's married to a person you recently got close to in the other world. She's Jake's wife." With that, Jasmine took her hand off my shoulder and walked toward the others. Dusty followed, leaving me alone with the blackness.

It was a lot to take in. I couldn't imagine what pain Jake must have been in or the fear he had of this place, knowing that he lost his wife here. But how? I sought to force such thoughts from my mind and began looking through the brush for the keyhole.

I brushed off some dust, exposing a flat stone in the ground with some carvings on it that reminded me of religious or family crests I once saw in a book. I took the goggles off to see through the dust, hoping to locate the keyhole. I found it and blew hard on the rock, realizing I had no moisture left in my mouth.

The keyhole was clear, and I shuffled around to get the key talisman out of my pocket. Once the others arrived, we could cross over when I opened the door. I had to think of a way to come back for Jasmine, Dusty, and Sonya and any others that we could before rendering the door useless.

As I stood up to tell the others what I had found, I felt a soft touch on my chest. I could tell by the feeling that it was someone's hand. Jasmine was talking with Susan and Krystal, and Liam was staring off into the distance, sword in hand. I put the goggles back on and saw Sonya standing in front of me.

She didn't say anything, only smiled. I wondered for a moment if she was incapable of talking for some reason like Dusty, but then I remembered he had disabilities that crossed over in both worlds. She pulled the wolf tooth necklace out of my shirt and held it.

"My Jake gave this to you?"

"Yes. He believed it would protect us."

"It did. It let me know you were here and where." She kept her smile and tucked the necklace back into my shirt. "Now tell him something for me."

"Yes, anything," I replied, wishing desperately that I could do more.

She lost her smile, and I could tell she knew I was upset we couldn't take them back.

"Tell him I love him, and it won't be long. Tell him obscurity is rising, and the door is broken."

"What's that supposed to mean?"

She said nothing more, and I decided not to ask again.

I just nodded my head and left it at that. I watched her go, not sure if I should say anything because it might ruin something. I finally said a simple thank you, but she just kept walking.

I could see the others looking at me in confusion, and I forgot that I was the only one who could see her with the goggles. I quickly took them off because I was thinking of telling Jake about her when we got to the other world and feared this might make me cross over.

Chapter 37

THE STORM CLOUDS AND lightning swirled around the peaks of the mountains behind us in a violent fury that showered down blue flames from the sky. I believed the evil spirit was getting ready to attack us at any minute, feeling like it was right behind me, watching, or somehow sensing my every move. One way or another, I knew we had to get going.

Through the goggles, I saw Sonya join Jasmine and Dusty, taking their hands in hers. The ominous light around them began to grow brighter once they were together. They were preparing for something because the warmth in my chest returned, and my heart began beating rapidly. I realized that I was somehow connected to them in a way I couldn't explain.

"Caleb, did you find it? Jasmine said you found it!" Krystal said excitedly as she joined me by the rock. I already had the key in place and just had to turn it.

Susan and Liam slowly made their way to join us, and we all gazed down at the key, perhaps unsure which of us should turn it. Maybe we were all just staling because we felt guilty leaving the others behind, but I was sure that was something I was more concerned about. I looked at the three of them behind me before returning my gaze to the key after I removed the goggles.

"I guess we just hold on to each other, and it works the same as last time."

Just then, I heard a voice, and as my head shot up I knew the others had too. It was soothing voice, yet still menacing.

"Caleb, Caleb, Caleb. Why would you want to leave when you can have all the power that Gene threw away? He was old, and I didn't want him from the beginning, but he brought you here, and that was what I wanted. I want you and your friends to stay, Susan and Krystal, but most of all, you and your brother. You two could be *kings*! *No* boundaries! *No* fear! Just power!

"Don't worry. I will let you go home from time to time to check in on...your mother. I can make sure she never has to work hard for anything again. Yes...yes, don't you realize you can control those things from this world? We have more control and power than you could imagine to influence and motivate people in the other world. Think about it. No harm will ever come to her; she would be happy knowing that you were happy."

The eerie voice sent shivers down my spine, and I felt the warmth start to subside. That's how I knew it was wrong. I knew it was lying to me. I looked at the others and started humming, trying to block the voice out of my head. As I resisted, the warmth in my chest turned into pain, and I found myself crouching over, pressing my arms into my chest.

I could tell it was still talking to them too, but Susan made me nervous. She stopped rubbing her swollen ankle, and the bruising went away as she smiled almost deviously toward the stormy peak.

"Think, Caleb. I can make this pain go away, and you can have all that warmth back," the voice said, and it took the pain away. "No pain ever, just freedom to do whatever you want. You know I took care of Gene. He's older than you think. You could live that long too. Longer. Think about what we could accomplish together. The riches you could have that you will never have in the real world. Think about the people you will lose without me, that you can protect when you are by my side."

"No, it's *wrong*!" I screamed, snapping Liam and Krystal out of their trance, but Susan remained lost in the evil spirit's broken promises. Slowly, Krystal and Liam turned back toward the peak, lost in the trance again.

"If they want to go with me, Caleb, will you deny them that? One is already over here with me. Go ahead put on the goggles and see for yourself," said the spirit in a triumphant tone.

I scrambled to put the goggles over my eyes, but didn't strap on them in case I needed to remove them quickly. I could see the shadowy figure with glowing eyes through the distant blue flames and beside it was Susan, holding her hand out toward me as if welcoming me to join them. I ripped the goggles away to see Susan standing just a few feet away. He was capturing her spirit, her essence. Her soul was drifting away.

"*No!*" I yelled, as loud and long as I could, and this time all three of them looked at me.

"We have to go now. Don't you see what it's doing?"

Krystal came to stand close to me. "He's right. I could feel myself...being pulled and I...I so wanted go."

"Susan! *Let's go!*" Liam yelled, right in her ear before he tugged hard on her arm to try to shake her out of her trance.

She shook her head, and we could all see that she was troubled making a decision. Then she turned to Liam with a reluctant look. "Okay. But it sounds so good..." she said, almost as if she knew she shouldn't have said that to us filling our minds with doubts.

"It's evil and lying and...you saw what it did to Gene. You don't want to turn out that way." I held my hand out to her, but all the time I was grimacing with pain that kept hitting me in waves.

She took my hand, and I turned the key. It made a rumbling noise, and the ground began shaking like an earthquake. I could see the creatures were racing toward us, but the shaking earth slowed their ascent...except for one. It kept its pace as it sprinted toward us in a fury. It was the dog creature.

Eventually, the rock shifted aside, and a fluidlike blackness was revealed. It was cold but welcoming because it felt real and from our own world. I looked back toward the opening we had to go through, and standing there just a few feet away from the doorway was the figure I'd seen on the distant mountain.

The evil spirit still retained a shadowy appearance, without any solid form, but then it started to change into a man. He had short blondish hair with fair features that made him still look young but old enough to have experienced life. His eyes were pitch-black and no longer glowing as they stared at the others and then directly at me. In one fluid movement, he reached out and grabbed my arm, lifting it out of the void. His touch was so cold that it burned as he began dragging me up into the air.

Chapter 38

S USAN GRABBED MY OTHER arm and began tugging me in the opposite direction, and then I felt Liam and Krystal coming to help. As they slowed down his pull, the evil spirit's mouth began opening, revealing the same twirling blue lights from the peaks deep within him. The gapping mouth distorted his whole face. With horrible breaking and stretching noises, the bottom jaw snapped loose from the upper part of his head and then divided at the chin, much like a snake does to consume its prey.

I was still moving toward him when I felt more hands on my shoulders pulling me down. I glanced over my shoulder to see Sonya and Jasmine on one side and Dusty on the other. All six of them pulled me down until we hit the ground. Then a swell of light burst out from behind me as Jasmine, Dusty, and Sonya passed through me and collided with the evil spirit. It attempted to move away, but they were too quick, and a cry of anger and pain came when they collided, sending him rolling and tumbling backward.

Jasmine reappeared momentarily to look at us and smile. She told us to go and then merged with Sonya and Dusty again. With another burst of light, they all slammed into the evil spirit, again sending him flying down the ravine and smashing into the horrible doglike creature that was almost upon us. Before something else could happen, I reached back, grabbing the others, and dragged them into the void.

Waves of light passed in the opposite direction as they did when we entered the shadow zone. The feeling of falling upward almost made me sick as we watched the camps fading away and clouds consumed our view.

Just before we lost sight of land, I heard Krystal yell, "I know those mountains!"

Lightning flashed around us from every direction, and the fury of thunder followed. It was a miracle that none of us were struck, and I was nervous about touching the others, fearing that all of us would suffer a shock if only one was hit. Then I crashed into something.

I felt around at my head and noticed the others were doing the same; it was dirt and I was facedown on the ground. I lifted my head and felt a huge surge of relief as I saw the Three Trees in the distance. The storm was still around us, but it was a normal storm.

I quickly got to my feet, ready for anything as I looked to make sure the others were all there and were okay. Liam was already walking around while Krystal and Susan inspected Susan's sprained ankle.

Remembering the door and thinking I should close it, I ran to the tree to find that the door and the key were both gone. The keyhole, however, remained. I looked around for the key but couldn't find it until something poked me through my pocket. I reached in, feeling around, and then pulled out the key.

I was already wondering how to properly use the goggles, but I knew I had to focus on getting other things resolved right now. There were several issues, like Sonya's message to Jake concerning obscurity and why Jake hadn't told us about her.

I put the key back in my pocket and walked toward the others, who all still looked wary. Liam's sword had disappeared somewhere, but he still held onto his spear, ready to attack. I almost forgot that Gene probably returned here and would be even more vengeful.

"Is everyone okay?" Liam looked at me like I was the one he cared the most for. I assured him I was okay by nodding my head.

"My ankle's all messed up again," Susan answered. "And my side hurts an awful lot."

"My arm feels like I pulled it or something," Krystal said, looking up from Susan's ankle. "Probably from Gene jerking me around. Oh, and by the way, what was with that burst of light?"

I tried to hide it but couldn't. "What burst of light?"

"You know exactly what I'm talking about, Caleb. You somehow know more than the rest of us, and Jasmine has her little secrets with you."

A full answer seemed to violate my trust with Jasmine. So I tried to change the subject. "I think we need to go talk with Jake. That will clear up some things, and besides, I think he might have more answers for us." I wanted to see everyone's reaction when I revealed that I saw Sonya to Jake. Only then would I determine how I moved forward with this.

"Okay, but what if it storms on our way? It's all wash, Caleb." Liam said.

"We need this to end today. So I can finally sleep again at night. Don't you agree?" I asked, scanning their faces. I thought I would get a quicker reaction from the group, but they remained silent.

"My ankle's pretty messed up, Caleb. But I think you're right." Susan finally said, as she rubbed at her ankle. Krystal and Liam simply nodded in agreement.

On the way to Jake's, the mood was somewhat more elevated than I thought it would be. Rain began falling but nothing to make us worry, and I welcomed the cool breeze on my face and the cool rain trickling down my arms and neck. It was nice having a gentle breeze compared to the crazy multidirectional wind in the shadow zone.

"How's your ankle?" Liam asked Susan.

"Not too bad. Could do without the walking. My parents are gonna be pissed about it." Susan laughed a little after she said it, and I understood what she meant; a twisted ankle seemed nothing compared to what could have happened to us.

We reached Jake's driveway, and I could already see him. He didn't seem to have a care in the world as he sat in his rocking chair, smoking a pipe.

"You four look like you've been through a little bit of hell and back. Yeah?"

"Yeah," Susan said, limping her way to the swing chair. The bandage made from the sleeves of my fairly new shirt looked like bits of old rag.

The rest of us found seats around the porch and began sharing our journey with Jake. We filled in the parts where the others might have missed something, never arguing once on what happened in the shadow zone.

"So you four had a trip and made it back. Gene's missing an arm and no longer has the goggles and will probably start aging. Dale's missing and eye and is probably halfway to Mexico by now with the authorities hot on his trail..."

I cut Jake off. "What do you mean, the authorities?"

"I heard somewhere down the road a neighbor reported a guy running and screaming through the desert with his face all bloody. They called the sheriff, and I think Dale knows it. He'll make a run for it, like him and Robert used to do back in the day."

"I don't really understand the aging thing." Liam said.

"The shadow zone makes you feel young and full of energy and appreciated so that it doesn't have to find replacements that often.

Sure, it leaks out and infects some people or weak animals from time to time, but it's uncommon to see it on Gene's level. He was already given this gift by the spirit in the shadow zone to help him stay young." Jake smiled like it was something to be proud of.

Krystal jumped into the conversation, but her question was clearly more aimed at me. "And the flash of light?"

"The flash of light?" Jake asked back, looking a little more on edge.

"Yeah, Caleb, tell him about the light now, the one that knocked the evil spirit and Gene away from us," said Susan. Everyone was looking at me, and they wanted answers.

"How close did you get to the evil spirit, Caleb?" Jake interrupted.

"It grabbed my arm and lifted me up."

Jake's pipe fell from his lips and down his shirt, and he brushed frantically at the glowing bits of tobacco to stop them from burning his shirt. "You mean it touched you…skin on skin?" He was shaking a little now.

"Yeah and for a while. Then came the light and presence."

Susan looked up at me with an irritated look. "What presence?"

"Well, there were three. Jasmine, her brother Dusty…"

"But I never saw them!" complained Liam. Krystal nodded her head in agreement.

"I think you need to spill the beans," Jake said as he got up to pour himself a drink.

I could tell that the others needed to hear everything to get their closure just as much as I did. I also wondered why Jake was so upset that the evil spirit touched me.

"Well, yeah. Okay…there was a third presence…" I started hesitantly.

Jake stopped pouring his drink to pay attention. "A third presence?"

"Yeah, a third, Jake." I waited for him to sit. "This one had a message for one of us...well, for you, actually."

"I knew something else was going on!" Krystal yelled at me. "Who does it want now?"

"Nothing like that, Krystal." I looked at Jake. His hand was trembling, and he was in danger of spilling his drink.

"Well, Jake...she said, 'Tell him I love him, and it won't be long. Tell him the obscurity is rising and the door is broken.'"

"My...my wife...my Sonya?" Tears began to puddle in Jake's eyes.

"Yes," I replied quietly.

Chapter 39

THE OTHERS WERE ALL shocked and frozen to their seats as Jake tried to take in what had happened. I felt bad because, somehow. I felt like I placed some new burden on this poor man who had lost his wife to the shadow zone.

"She's still there?" Jake said, pulling himself together and trying to brush the tears away. Krystal got up to comfort him, placing an arm on his shoulder. "I thought she was lost to it already."

"No," I answered. "She's a fighter there. Jasmine works with the wind, and Dusty has some tricks, but Sonya...she works with a majestic flash of light that just disrupts everything. When we were coming back through the door, she got together with Jasmine and Dusty, and the three of them attacked the spirit to rescue us."

"I lost her so long ago. We were too close to an open door. We took a journey to another area to do so. We found the door and closed it, but some crazy ranchers came after us. I think they thought we were doing something illegal. Or they could have been this other group of people in those parts who are looking for something else. We got in the truck and hightailed it out of there, and the next thing I know, she's no longer in the car. She vanished. All I saw when I realized she was gone was a flash of light in the dark sky that completely exposed the whole Superstition Mountain range."

"I knew I recognized those mountains," Krystal said. "I used to pass by them going to the lakes with my parents. I could see them in the distance, but not as close as they were in the shadow zone."

"You saw them in the shadow zone?" Jake asked.

"Yeah, just a few miles from our mountains right here." Liam pointed at our mountains.

Then Jake continued. "People gathered all around the area for the next few weeks, swearing up and down that UFOs were flying around that night. I could have told them what it was, but that would break all the rules of hiding this evil spirit."

With that comment from Jake, more things from this world began making sense. The significance of our world and the shadow zone coexisting so close together was becoming more of a reality.

"We already drove several miles, fast. I would have noticed the door opening or the window being rolled down at those speeds. She tried to stop more than she could handle. I brought her into this mess and left her there to be consumed by the evil spirit." Jake's voice trailed off, and I feared he might start losing it, so I kept the conversation moving.

"You were pretty concerned with it touching me."

"What?" Jake asked, like he had barely heard.

"The evil spirit. It touched me. You seemed concerned."

"Yeah, why did you freak out so bad?" Liam asked.

"Once you see the evil, you're marked. Like touching the talismans. If you can tell people about it, then it really wants to be friends. It wants to be exposed to the world. It wants to be discovered, so people search for it. Don't you get how it works yet?" Jake took another drink and stoked his pipe. "It touched you…well…I'm afraid it really wants you."

"But why? What did Caleb do to make it want him so bad? The spirit touched him. He didn't touch it," Krystal asked in my defense.

"Caleb knows what it feels like. He'll recognize it in this world just as easy in the next."

"You mean Caleb can sense evil now?"

"Yes, but not all evils. There are evils in this world created by mankind, decisions that people make on their own without any influence from the evil spirit. It seems you have all made good decisions so far and need to stay on that path."

As Jake said this, he kept his eyes on Susan, like he knew how close she had come to moving over to the shadow zone.

"Obscurity is rising," Jake said, breaking the new silence.

"Yeah, and the door is broken." I answered back.

"That's no good, no good at all. Sure, you might have closed the door today but, if it's broken..."

Krystal stepped back from Jake. "What? What if it's broken? Can that stuff come through again?"

"Heck, you can cross over with your talismans, so why can't it? The good thing is, there're only so many talismans. That limits what and how everything can crossover. Most of the talismans are still hidden or lost. Some say there's some in those Superstition Mountains, but these are just rumors among an even smaller group of people. However, if they're right, and the talismans are discovered, then it could be chaos. And if the door's broken anyways, then there's no telling when the evil spirit will find a way through."

We all thought about this until a bright flash of lightning lit up the sky, immediately followed by a ground-shaking boom of thunder that seemed to snap us all out of our mood.

"Looks like a good storm coming. You four have nothing to worry about tonight or any time soon, as far as I can tell. This storm, however, is going to be your biggest concern, and if you don't want to get in trouble, you'd better get home. I got a lot of thinking to do. Hearing about Sonya gave me a whole new perspective. Perhaps sitting here on my butt isn't the way to end this. Remember to stick together, and watch out for one another."

With that, we gathered our stuff and made our way off the porch.

Liam looked at Jake, sitting there alone with his drink almost gone. "You sure you're going to be okay, Jake?"

"I'll be fine. In fact, I'm better than I've been for some time. Weird, huh?" Jake said with a small grin.

"We'll be okay too, Liam," I said, putting an arm around his shoulder.

"I know. However, Susan needs help walking right now, so why don't you let her put an arm over your shoulder for a while?"

"We have to promise not to tell anyone about this. Not until we're sure what's going to happen. Like Jake said, if it gets discovered, it becomes more powerful. Agreed?" I held out my hand like people do in the movies when a group of friends swears on something.

"What are you doing, you nerd?" said Krystal as she slapped my hand away. "You know we will. I still can't believe all this happened, and to us ... four kids. That's stuff you hear about in books and movies or to people who mess around with demonic worship or Ouija boards and stuff. Not us. Why, do you think?"

"I guess because we were here ... or there ... at the right or wrong time," Liam answered her, and I agreed.

"We all good, Susan?" Krystal asked her.

"Yeah ... I guess so."

"You guess so?" Krystal said, a little sterner this time. I found it interesting to see Krystal acting like the older kid in this situation.

"I mean, yes. Yes, I'll keep it a secret. Sorry. I'm just taking it all in, still." Her voice was shaking, and I suddenly realized that her brusque and slightly aggressive manner was perhaps her way of trying to mask her sensitivity and perhaps even a lack of confidence.

When we got to Susan's, the rain was coming down harder, so Liam and I decided to not stick around any longer then needed. Susan's mom came rushing toward us when she saw us in the driveway, and she helped Susan. After a few quick questions, she took Susan inside and told Krystal to come with her. We parted ways, but not before I caught a glimpse of Susan's dad inside the doorway, toying with something in his hands and wrapping it around his one fist.

The door closed, and I tried to focus my attention on getting home, but as we started running, I realized that something was wrong with the whole situation. Something didn't feel right about leaving Krystal and Susan. The storm picked up and was now starting to drench us as we passed the Three Trees. It seemed that every time the thunder roared across the sky, the rain came down a little harder.

I could tell it was late when we reached home, although I didn't know the actual time. I was glad to see that my mother wasn't home, so I could put the knife away. Max began barking at us and spinning around in excitement. We both walked toward him to pet him and talk to him a little bit, asking the typical questions that a dog can't answer but for some reason humans ask anyway.

"Hey, can you feed Max for me while I put the knife away?"

"Sure. But I want to hurry in tonight and put on a movie to help me forget the day."

"I hear that."

The house was quiet but normal. Our mother would be home shortly, and the rain was coming down hard, so we hoped that she would get home safely. We both paced around the house, feeling restless, when in fact we were probably overtired to the point of mental exhaustion.

It wasn't long after putting on a movie that we heard her key in the front door. Our mother came rushing in to avoid getting any wetter than she already was.

"Oh my gosh, you guys. It's really storming out there. I'm lucky

I got home when I did, or I would have been stranded," she said putting her purse down and taking off her muddy shoes.

"What are you two up to? Did you have a good day?"

"Yeah, we had a good day. We're just watching a movie now," Liam replied.

"How was your day, Mom?" I yelled out from the bedroom.

"Okay. Busy up until the end, when people could tell the rain was coming. They know better than to be driving around here when it rains."

I went to go see if my mom needed help with anything, and Liam followed, perhaps thinking the same thing. She was putting stuff away from the day and already preparing for dinner.

"I was thinking we could have soup and sandwiches tonight since it's cold and rainy," she suggested.

"Sounds good to me. Do you need any help getting anything out of the car?" Liam asked.

"No. No, I'm good. I got everything. I do want you two to take a shower in case the power goes out again. I can't believe this lightning for an autumn storm. Also, I heard they got the railroad tracks cleared up, so I'm sorry to say you'll have school tomorrow."

Why did she have to frown when she said that? She knew we didn't like going, but she still looked sarcastic. After our showers we sat on the couch in the living room and ate, watching movies while it poured outside. Later, I lay in bed and could tell that Liam wasn't asleep yet either. I had to bug him about something I was thinking about.

"Hey, Liam, do you think anything else might help us out in all this? Like animals?"

"Why would they?"

"I don't know, but I think we're...you know...What if we're not out of it, like Jake thinks?"

"Maybe you're right, but for now, even as much as we might hate it, we can't talk about it. We probably just saved the world but can't tell anyone. We have to go to school and put up with other kids' crap."

He was right. He couldn't have said it any more bluntly. I could see how the evil spirit would try to get to me. Little temptations here and there to make us talk. That's what it wanted. Miraculously, that night I slept.

Chapter 40

THE NEXT DAY, EVERYTHING was in chaos at school with evacuation drills and seminars on safety. After our lunch break, I headed toward the recess area and kept a lookout for any of the others. I finally found all three of them standing next to a tree in the shade. Susan had her back to the tree and was crying. Krystal and Liam were blocking the view from others by boxing her in.

"What's wrong?" I asked when I got closer to them and knew no one else could hear.

Krystal and Liam looked at me but didn't speak. They looked back at Susan, who was now rolling back her shirtsleeve to show me the welts and bruises on her arm.

The image of her father standing in the doorway burst into my head. I didn't have to ask what happened, but I did. "Why?"

Krystal answered for her. "When we got home too close to the storm, her dad was pretty mad and noticed her ankle. That made him go...err...well, he went kind of nuts. He's probably going away this time."

I knew something had felt wrong when we left yesterday. Thinking of her dad looking out at us through the doorway angered me. I wished I could go back and make it right, somehow.

"You guys couldn't have done anything about it," Susan finally

253

said, fighting back her tears. "Everything came crashing down yesterday. I could've been a queen, and it was taken away. My dad was taken away. Who knows? I might be taken away."

She walked away with Krystal, and Liam looked at me. "We have to make sure she doesn't say anything."

"What makes you think she will? Besides, who will believe her?"

"It's not that. Did you hear what she said? She said she could have been a queen. What did the evil spirit promise you? I bet it was great. It was great for me. I bet it promised to make Susan a queen. Maybe she feels like we took that away from her, especially after her dad went crazy. Krystal says he's been like this a while, but last night, he even did it in front of her. She called her parents, and they called the cops. Susan's world crumbled yesterday, so the evil spirit's promises probably seem like everything to her now."

He was right. Just seconds after Liam finished speaking, Krystal came running back.

"She wanted me to tell you she's sorry, and she'll be alright. She was just venting a little. She knows it's not our fault, and we're friends. So don't worry, guys."

That was the last I saw of them that day. The rest of the school day went well. No one messed with us, and we stayed with each other the rest of the day, going to the assemblies and all the safety stuff after the train problems.

My mom was home early from work that day and told us she could pick us up from now on because of a schedule change at work. It would be less stressful, and we would have more time to spend with her.

That night, while feeding Max, I looked at the clouds breaking up in the night sky. There was a sharp coldness on the air and the ground. There would probably be frost in the morning. This was strange weather for that time of year, but I loved the rain and welcomed it. I watched patches of stars begin to shine through the breaking clouds and was lost in a tranquil moment—until Max jumped on me. I patted him on the head and dumped his food in his bowl, watching him sniff around for any special treats I might have mixed in with it.

I walked back to the shed to put Max's food containers away and became lost in the clouds again. The breeze was blowing gently but carried the dampness off the ground from the previous rains, making it extra cool. I felt a little happiness come back as I walked. I was happy that things were a little better for my family. My mom seemed to be feeling better because of the change at work, and my brother and I had gone through a full day of school without being bullied.

But part of me still worried. I worried for Susan and her family. I worried for Jake and his troubles. I worried about the door being broken and whatever Sonya meant when she said, "Obscurity is rising." For some reason, the main thing I worried about in all of this was Jasmine. I wanted to get her back to this world, along with the others.

The sun finally set, so I hurried to get inside. Making my way from the shed toward the house, the cold breeze blew stronger and then turned into a full wind. I looked up to see if another storm was coming in. The sky was still clearing from clouds and revealing more stars. Suddenly the breeze wasn't cold anymore. I wasn't cold at all. I smiled as I made my way toward the house, excited to feel that comforting feeling again. My chest slowly warmed, and I felt like a charge of electricity was moving through me. Then the breeze stopped, and I heard something.

"Sshhh."

It came from behind me. I slowly turned around, more excited than ever. The last of the fading sunlight revealed nothing in the driveway or the surrounding desert. I looked back and forth but only saw Max looking off into the distance with me. Strange—usually he'd be eating already. I took a few steps out into the growing darkness, squinting my eyes and trying to adjust to the lack of light, but I still couldn't see anything.

After a few moments, I gave up. Maybe seeing her was too much at this time, and her powers were too weak. Maybe not enough of the talismans were in play. I thought of the pouch with the four talismans we stuffed in Max's doghouse. Maybe I could use them to see her. I scratched that idea as quickly as I thought of it. It would be dangerous, and I couldn't do that.

At least not yet.